House of Lies

Lyndsy Spence

First published by Endeavour Press Ltd in 2017.

For Ashley

'They call it heartache because missing someone is an actual physical pain, in your blood and bones' – Lucia Berlin, *Welcome Home*

.

'It's very difficult to keep the line between the past and the present' –
Edith Bouvier Beale

.

1920

Set the scene, that's what the policeman told her to do. 'It was an accident.' Marina's mouth moved slowly, disengaged from her brain. She could not think straight, or control the words that she spoke. Her body was rigid, she pressed her damp palms onto her bony thighs, the fabric of her dress ruched a little at her knees. 'My mother...,' She could not finished the sentence. She closed her eyes and took a deep breath.

Flashes of memory came back, he had opened his arms to block her view, and then placed his hands on her narrow shoulders. She felt the ground wobble beneath her feet, and the colour drain from her pale complexion. He walked her to the living room, still in this strange position as though he were exercising some sort of mind and body control. There, he pushed her onto the sofa and had told her not to move. They felt one another tremble.

'There has been a nasty accident,' George whispered into the telephone, his voice muffled and concealed down the hallway, steps away from the scene of the crime. He had rehearsed it in his mind, and was about to say it out loud, when his mother, Sybil, answered the phone, but his words were stuck.

'That's how you can tell a madman from a sane man,' Marina said, years later. Their words struggle to form, they get stuck on the roof of the mouth. Sane men speak so eloquently. Or perhaps, with a degree of hindsight, she might have said it was the opposite.

His heart thumped, threatening to explode in his chest. He took short, shallow breaths. The voice of his mother rang in his ears, her words were urgent. 'What did you do? Dear Lord, what did you do?'

'I killed Evangelina Belfry,' he said, looking over his shoulder as he did so.

'My God.'

*

The killing of Evangelina Belfry was the result of a misjudged confession, and a clumsy attempt at authority. How could he ever be a real man if he could not sleep with a whore without falling in love with

3

her? How could he swagger around as the man of the house, receiving unscrupulous favours in lieu of rent, if he told her this?

'So sweet,' Evangelina had said in a voice which sounded like a hiss. She was not snakelike, but rather dark and intriguing, a witch.

'I do. I do…love you,' he pleaded with her. He was desperate for her to believe him. All at once it occurred to him that she was the one in charge; the older woman, and he a mere boy, appearing younger than his twenty-one years.

'So sweet,' she said once more, before turning away.

The way she had said it, the monotony of the words, told him she had said it before. Perhaps to another man. She was skilled at cutting people down. She placed a gentle hand on the bannister and he touched it. She looked up at him and smiled, her painted mouth a red gash. It made him feel pathetic, like a fool. She must have thought about what he had said because she let out a ridiculous laugh and appeared to shake her head a little. That's when he grabbed her by the shoulders. He'd only wanted to frighten her. He wasn't sure about that, exactly. He'd seen his father use brute force on his mother, which always seemed to stifle her bravado. But as he did so, he tripped on the carpet and fell forward, into Evangelina.

She let out a shrill noise, not a scream but a small sound of unexpected excitement as she fell backwards. Her fingertips grazed his sleeve as she tried to prevent herself from falling. It was too late. She bounded down the staircase, her body hitting it with such a thud it turned over and her neck snapped. George heard the snapping. She'd only hit the floor seconds before Marina came in; she was still warm.

Marina remained seated, the policemen paced back and forth. 'Ah,' one said as George entered the room. 'You look as though you've seen a ghost.' The other policeman offered him a stern look, but Marina thought it a witty remark, an unintentional play on words. 'So sorry.'

Her eyes followed George around the room. She did not cry, or appear hysterical at all. Instead she was calm, as though she were dead herself. The policemen would tell George this was shock.

They asked George to tell them what had happened. He thought about telling them the truth, that he'd had an arrangement with Evangelina Belfry which had been instigated by his father, Walter Greenwood, whose estate he had inherited. Of course, he did not mean Evangelina was part of the Will and Testament, but it was his house and how else could she afford the rent? He was naïve, and assumed their going to bed together whenever he called was a sign that she loved him. She was simply adhering to a routine; it beat standing in a shop all day until she keeled over, or worse: her legs spoiled by bulging veins climbing up her calves, like wisteria.

'I am her landlord,' he said. 'The front door was open. I... I.' His slight stutter came back, causing him mild panic and embarrassment. His mother said it was the result of having measles in his teens, and he recalled the doctor saying there could be dire side-effects. But he could not make sense of it. He took a deep breath which trembled, as though his breathing was also flawed. The policemen coaxed him to continue, he felt unworthy of their kindness. 'I... I ca-came in.'

'Yes, and?'

'And-d-d-d she wa-wa-was,' his words vibrated through his pursed lips.

Marina listened to his voice and in the pit of her heart she felt sorry for him. She could see the less kind policeman, and how he wanted to say 'spit it out', or finish the sentence for him. In a way she was drawn to pathos, though she herself was not a sympathetic person.

'You came in and she was lying at the foot of the stairs. Is that correct?'

George nodded.

'Speak up.'

'Yes!'

He didn't mean to shout. He glanced in Marina's direction and wondered if she would say that she had let herself in.

'Do you know this gentleman?' the policeman asked Marina.

She nodded. There was a heavy pause before she spoke, as though she enjoyed keeping them in suspense. 'Yes,' she said in her quiet voice. It was the first time George had really heard her speak. She often mumbled a pleasantry when she let him into the house, often passing him as she left.

'Yes. He is our landlord.'

George smiled at Marina, catching her eye. She turned away, but was not cross at him. He felt confident, and relieved.

The policemen left the room to do their investigations. He knew a coroner's report would be drawn up and they'd see that Evangelina had indeed fallen down the stairs. They'd say she was drunk.

'Don't worry.' He took Marina's hand in his. She turned and looked at him, her mouth was slightly open but she did not speak. 'I... I'm going to take care of you.'

That was how Sybil found them when she rushed through the door. She looked at Marina as though she weren't a person at all, as though she were made of stucco. She vaguely knew of this girl, and that she was somewhat younger than George. How unlike Evangelina she was; she had her beauty and dark hair but she was bigger, with her father's blue eyes. She admired her composure, even though she knew it was inspired by trauma.

'Thank God Maguire hadn't taken the car into town. It's his day off, you know. Thank God you rang when you did,' she said to George, as if she were berating him for some minor inconvenience.

George got up and ran out of the room. He threw up on the pavement outside. Sybil thought it an unnecessary thing to do. She sighed and wrung her hands, looking at Marina and smiling, or at least attempting to. She looked like a grinning skeleton, brittle and blonde, and her boniness made her appear older than her years. At first glance Marina assumed she was in her early forties, the same age as her own mother. The undertaker had come to take Evangelina away, and Sybil hovered in the doorway while Marina remained on the sofa.

'I'm sorry for your loss, my dear,' Sybil said after she had let the men in. 'But you're not to worry.'

Marina looked up at her, and her lips quivered as she fought back tears. She sniffed and turned away, looking out the window at her mother's tiny corpse wrapped in a body bag.

'Perhaps she would have died anyway,' Sybil mused. 'The flu might have taken her. It's so rife in town.'

*

George ran down the street. He ran and ran, his footsteps thumping in his ears and the air catching in his throat. He almost crashed into two women walking in his direction. He stopped, gasping for breath.

'George,' said the familiar voice. It was his sister, Louisa, with her companion, Joan. They had run away together earlier in the year, nobody spoke about it or tried to understand. 'George,' she said once more. She was concerned and told Joan to go on without her. She knew they despised one another, but she lingered by her side.

He looked at his sister standing before him, a mirage of ivory muslin. 'Louisa,' he said. 'Oh God, Louisa.' He tried to walk to her but his footing was off. He staggered as he steadied himself, the pavement was spinning beneath his feet.

'Are you all right, George?' she curiously asked as she walked to him. Joan stepped back, watching from a close distance.

'Oh, God,' he said once more. She took his hands in hers and looked him in the eye. 'It's s-s-such a mess,' he finally said.

'What is?'

He broke down crying and fell into her arms, she was shaken by his reaction.

'Come with me.' She hooked her arm under his to support his body. 'We'll sit down over here.' She guided him to a bench in a small communal park in the middle of the street.

They sat on the bench, he kept his hand in hers. She smoothed down his hair and asked what was wrong. 'Now take your time,' she told him, recalling that his stutter was prominent when he was nervous and that his speech therapist had told him to breathe through it. He felt like a small child.

'I... I... I killed a woman,' he said.

The words alarmed her, but she did not feel threatened or unsafe. She knew her brother better than to imagine he was a murderer.

'I p-p-p-pushed her. I pushed her d-d-down the stairs.'

'Who was it?'

'Evangelina Belfry,' he burst into tears.

'When did this happen?'

'Today,' he said as he buried his head in his hands. 'Mother's at the house, and Ma-Ma-Marina too. And the police were there and I lied to them. What if they find out? I'll go to p-p-p-prison.'

'You pushed her?' she asked.

'I didn't mean to. She was g-g-goading me, Louisa. Laughing at me. I wanted to s-s-scare her, to reprimand her.'

Her back stiffened at those words. She recalled the scenes of her father hitting her mother, always in the drawing room. Always when he thought the children had gone upstairs with their nanny. She hated men.

7

'It went too far.' He looked up at his sister. 'She f-f-fell backwards. She's d-d-dead, Louisa.'

'What will you do?'

He took a deep breath, his eyes were filled with dread, and he jumped to his feet and looked down the street, at the house. 'I've got t-t-to go.' He began to walk away.

'George,' she stood up and called after him. 'George, wait.' He stopped. She looked into his eyes and said, 'If you need an alibi say you were with me and Joan. Isn't that right, Joan?'

Joan's green eyes narrowed and she turned her head, he could see she had an under bite.

'We were at the Tropical Ravine all afternoon. You hear? The Tropical Ravine. There's an exhibition on, but that's not important.'

'I've already said I'm the one who f-f-found her.'

'That's okay. Just say you were with your sister and her... friend, all afternoon. Do you hear?'

George nodded and repeated the alibi into himself. He ran off towards the house.

Joan gave him a snide look as he passed her. 'Aren't you going to ask where she's been?' she shouted. 'Aren't you going to ask where we live?'

*

He found Marina where he had left her, sitting on the edge of the sofa. She did not look at him, or acknowledge his presence as he entered the room. Sybil hovered by the window, her hand resting on the sill, looking out at the silent street. He took Marina's hand, she looked straight through him.

'Don't worry,' he whispered, hoping Sybil could not hear him. She felt his breath against her cheek, but she did not pull away.

Sybil left the room and stood at the foot of the stairs, looking up to the landing. George crept up behind her. 'Wh-wh-what should I do?' he cried on his mother's shoulder. She noted his stutter, he had not stuttered in such a long time.

Sybil drew away and, without emotion, she said, 'You must help the girl.' She shook him by the shoulders to steady his growing hysteria. 'Listen to me. You must help the girl.'

*

8

'People are sort of thrown together, aren't they?' Marina later asked George.

He said it was down to fate.

She thought him a fool.

1938-1939

Chapter One

The early morning mist rose from the stretch of lawn, creeping forth and engulfing High Greenwood, a two-hundred-year-old country house. It slipped through the cracks in the window frames and slid down the chimney, fanning the burning embers of the coal as it turned to ash. Marina's sleeping body was rudely disturbed from her slumber; the bedclothes scarcely warmed her, and her exposed flesh and the ends of her hair were awakened by the chill. Footsteps outside the door creaked back and forth, pausing before pushing it open.

'Time we set off. I'll go start the engine,' said George.

She turned onto her side, keeping her back to him until he left. When she was certain the coast was clear, she got out of bed and began to dress. Although she could have slept for another three hours at least, she told herself today would be a good day. Everything would return to normal.

The fire in Daphne's bedroom smouldered until the final pieces of coal dropped through the grate. She responded with a lively 'I'm up!' when Marina, her mother, knocked on the wall separating their bedrooms. There was no gentle nudge on the shoulder, or a brisk opening of the curtains to bring Daphne from her sleep. She knew the drill. The illustrated calendar on her wall told her it was Monday 5 September 1938, and the clock on the cabinet next to her bed told her she had exactly ten minutes to get ready. She prided herself on efficiency. Jumping from her bed, she went to the basin a few feet away and splashed cold water on her face.

'Hurry up and get in the car,' Marina said as she passed the door.

Daphne hopped around, putting on her underwear (the regulation navy knickers and scratchy wool petticoat), pulling up her socks and buttoning the white blouse that could have done with an ironing. The shapeless pinafore went on over her head and she slipped on her shoes before she left the room. She ran back to grab her well-thumbed copy of *Rebecca*, a present from her father after their visit to the newly-opened children's zoo – he knew she would delight in sharing her first name with its celebrated author. 'But you share your name with the king,' she told him, as though he was somehow superior because of this.

Fumes from the car's engine piped out of the exhaust, lingering heavily in the morning air. They caught in Daphne's throat. She coughed on the back of her hand and dived into the car.

'Where's your suitcase?' Marina turned around in the passenger seat. 'Fix your pinafore,' she said before looking away.

'In the boot,' Daphne smoothed the navy pleats across her knees.

They set off down the long and winding driveway, passing the rose bushes succumbing to black-spot and various forms of neglect. Lighting a cigarette, Marina inhaled deeply and glanced out the window as the mirage of green zipped past. She inhaled once more, and leaning forward she pulled open the small ashtray as George's hand negotiated the gear stick. Careful not to spill ash on him, she kept her eyes on the burning cigarette, ensuring every last drop was deposited in the ashtray.

'Not long now,' George called to Daphne, who had nodded off in the back.

Greeted by silence he peered up to the windscreen mirror. Seeing that Daphne was sleeping, he briefly glanced at Marina and smiled. She kept her eyes forward. He noticed that she wore an unusual coloured blouse, a dusky pink; unflattering against her pale, sallow coloured skin, tucked into a herringbone skirt. In that split second he had observed more than she knew: the flatness of the tiny buttons running down the centre of the blouse as it sat against her concave stomach and the crease of the skirt, giving the illusion of fat which did not exist, and the way the fair hairs on her arms stood on end as the chilly breeze cut through the gaps of their rickety car. She wore a thin, gold wristwatch and a finely strung pearl bracelet below the watch strap. It was too big, and it hung over her wrist-bone, touching her hand. Along the edge of her palm he spied traces of black ink too stubborn for soap and water.

'Look out!' Marina said, bringing George back to the present. It was the first she had spoken to him. Her voice was soft, even sweet, and it masked a hardness, a meanness. Sometimes he pretended she was gentle, because of her voice.

Instinctively he swerved, narrowly avoiding a milk-truck carrying crates of empty glass bottles. 'Close call,' he commented, hoping to ease the tension.

She remained mute. Her lips were squeezed together in a tight, irritated expression. George looked at her once more, attempting an apologetic smile. Raising her eyebrows, she parted her lips and let out a small, disapproving sigh. He caught a glimpse of her teeth, the front ones had a small gap, which obscured her beauty and made her seem, in a way, approachable.

Had Marina taken a moment to study George she would have noticed his bony legs and slack posture; he'd been losing a lot of weight as of late, and a greyish hue had taken over his usual pink complexion. Brown circles hovered below his eyes, framing his sunken eye-sockets, emphasizing the hazel iris. She could hear a faint stutter when he appeared worked up or unsure of himself, but it was not as bad as it had once been. Thank God, she thought. It embarrassed her how he tripped over his words and she would have to appear understanding, or pretend it was not happening. It pained her more than she could say.

Perhaps a caring wife might have asked how he was getting on at work. She vaguely knew of his job at a bank in town, which he went off to every day. The money was decent, but it was not enough to sustain High Greenwood – the estate he had inherited along with his father's title. A baronet, Sir George was his legal name and he was listed in Burke's Peerage, but that scarcely mattered to Marina, for she had warned him in one of her acid moments that a baronet was the equivalent of a dustman when comparing the hierarchy of the aristocracy.

'Real gentlemen don't work,' Sybil used to chastise him in her voice which sounded like the rumbling of an avalanche. The estate, what there was of it, haemorrhaged money. There was no farmland to lease or cottages to sell off, the house itself absorbed every penny. Perhaps they could keep hens and sell eggs, but he knew Marina would never go in for feathers and fowl. Thank goodness she could write her books, he was apt to think when all seemed hopeless. Thank goodness she had something to bring in an income, should his vanish.

Under ordinary circumstances Daphne would have been withdrawn from boarding school and taught at home by a governess or, as a last resort, sent to a day school nearby. The well-meaning family doctor, Doctor Glendinning, never hesitated to remind Marina and George that the school was vital to her health. Or, perhaps having said it so many times to George, she believed the white lie was originated by the doctor.

13

It was a boarding school for asthmatics, on the outskirts of the countryside where the chalk cliffs sloped down to the sea. The sea air was said to be good for the lungs, not the salty air, but the vigour of the permanent chill that swept through the wide, opened windows of the girls' dormitory. It was a maverick idea, invented by a charitable woman whose son had died from an asthma attack. She came to the school every so often and was seated in the centre of the assembly hall, like a prophet, while a girl from each form read a sonnet or a testimonial to the school's health properties.

Unlike the other girls, Daphne never had an asthma attack; her asthma was not very bad or troublesome, but Marina was adamant she must go. Under a cloud of gloom she had enrolled in the school at the age of eleven, ushered through the heavy wooden doors as the tears stung her eyes. Marina puffed on a cigarette to the disapproving glance of the headmistress. Daphne coughed from the smoke and not her asthma.

'There are many things that can trigger asthma,' said the headmistress, an efficient woman named Miss Gwendoline Fag. 'An unhappy home-life. A childhood trauma.'

'The doctor said it's because she was early, if you catch my drift.'

'Yes, indeed. Undeveloped lungs in infancy, I see.'

'Good,' Marina snapped. She cast a withering look at Miss Fag for daring to undermine her.

Being an only child, Daphne struggled to adapt to the dormitory where twelve single beds were arranged, six on either side, with a small cabinet separating each bed. The windows were permanently opened. Baths were far and few between because it was said to be bad to have water on the back, so close to the lungs. Hair was rarely washed in winter. The best thing about it all was the lack of milk and other dairy products, for Daphne loathed them, and the headmistress warned that a glass of milk would cause a nasty cough. Sleeping, at first, was difficult because she was not used to the chorus of dry coughs as the girls tried to nod off; some made choking sounds in their sleep, and others went red in the face, wheezing and barking and trying in vain to rid themselves of the ticklish feeling that sat between the chest cavity.

Here she was, still alive and back for another term. The car crept along the driveway lined with willow trees, approaching the tall, Gothic building. George waited in the car with the engine running and Marina ushered Daphne inside.

'Ready for another term?' Miss Fag welcomed her with a gentle smile.

'Yes, I suppose so,' Daphne replied.

'She's all yours,' Marina said as she gave her a slight push.

There was no parting kiss, no friendly hug goodbye. Marina loathed bodily contact. She hated everything to do with bodies; their mechanisms were disgusting, the various things the body could do was, in her own words, humiliating. She'd often reminded Daphne of the indignity she had to suffer to bring her into the world and how, even though almost thirteen years had passed, she could not look the family doctor in the eye. 'Why?' Daphne asked, and was told to mind her own business. Only a disgusting girl would ask such a provocative question.

*

After the ritual of unpacking and pushing their suitcases under the bed, Miss Fag entered the room. 'I want you to meet somebody very special,' she told the girls. 'She's come all the way from India.'

A frenzy of whispers and muted voices rang out.

'Celia,' she called out.

In walked a short girl wearing a pinafore that seemed much too long for her frame. It dangled past her knees, reaching her calves, and her cardigan sleeves were rolled up. She stood next to Miss Fag, holding a suitcase, her wide eyes scanning the room full of strangers. What struck Daphne was how pale this new girl was in comparison to the rest of them, who were tanned from the holidays. Her own arms were bronzed and a patch of tan swept across her wide forehead where the baby hairs along her brown hairline had been lightened by the sun.

'Girls, this is Celia Hartley,' Miss Fag repeated.

'Good morning, Celia,' they all sang.

'Hello,' she answered in a small, shrill voice. 'Miss Fag,' she turned to the headmistress with an air of self-control which caused the girls to fall silent. 'Miss Fag, I don't seem to have a bed.'

'Oh, my,' Miss Fag raised a hand to her silver hair.

'She can bunk with me,' Daphne stepped forward.

'For the time being, at least.' Celia walked to Daphne's bed and threw her suitcase on top of it. She had already marked her territory.

*

Marina and George drove back to High Greenwood in silence. Now they had disposed of Daphne, Marina was glad they could revert to their silent intolerance of one another. Or what she perceived to be an ill-feeing between the two. When he braked unexpectedly or took a corner too sharply she would sigh and roll her eyes. He was reluctant to ask what infuriated her, and she was determined not to be the first to utter a cross word.

'You look nice,' he said without looking at her. She acknowledged him with a quick smile, her lips felt tight from the lipstick, and so it was the equivalent of a polite nod.

When they arrived at the house, he stopped the car and she got out. 'Will you,' she began, holding onto the door, unsure of what to say. 'Will you be home for dinner? It's just... I have to let Cook know.' She looked up at the overcast sky, waiting for his response.

'I don't know. Perhaps. I'll telephone if my plans change.'

'Righto,' she pushed the door shut.

He sounded the horn as he drove off. She stood on the driveway, knowing he was watching her through the mirror.

Chapter Two

Marina heard the front door closing and a rustling sound as George removed his overcoat. She walked to the hallway, self-conscious of the clicking noise her shoes made. She hated the black and white tiled floor, it sometimes gave her vertigo.

'Oh,' she said without emotion. 'You're back.' When he did not answer and made for the staircase, she followed him. 'Where were you?' Again, he did not respond and continued to climb the stairs. Ignoring her was easier than telling a lie.

He went to his bedroom and she went to hers. It was after his mother's death that George began to act peculiar. When Sybil died he moved into her bedroom without an explanation as to why, and slept on the bed that her corpse had lain on. He had his own bedroom before her demise, and Marina did not question why he was drawn to that room. She thought it morbid.

George waited until Marina was in her bedroom before he went to the library to use the telephone. He sat down at his desk, it looked deceptively neat and compact but the drawer pulled out to reveal a secret writing top and several tiny compartments, with a shelf tucked above. He skimmed his hand along the shelf and retrieved a moleskin book, his fingertips disturbed the dust. Opening the book, he scanned the numerous listings for Greenwood, stopping at a Miss L Greenwood, and instinctively he knew he had located the right person. 'Hello,' he whispered under his breath. 'Hello, it's George.' As he plucked up the courage to reach for the phone, the door opened.

'There you are,' Marina said without looking him in the eye.

She had a way of looking at him, but looking past him, as though she were focusing on the top of his head or at something far away. If his eyes were to meet hers, she would often look away, but continue to speak. Her appearance was ragged, she had thrown on her clothes in a hurry. From his lowly position at the desk, his eyes looked directly at her midriff and he noticed she had missed a button and he could see her navel.

'What are you doing?'

'Nothing,' he coughed. 'I was... I was looking up the number for my tailor in town.'

'Right.' They were silent and she blinked to emphasise her lack of interest. 'Well I hope you haven't gone daft, you never wear that waistcoat you insisted on ordering.'

He was not in the mood for a fight and he dismissed her remark. 'Was something the matter?'

'Yes, the boiler's on the blink again.'

He sighed. It had been banging and clattering all morning but he ignored it and had bathed in cold water without complaining.

'I was about to have my bath. It's all very inconvenient.' She turned and walked out of the room before he could respond.

The moment was lost. He tore out the page and closed the phone-book.

*

Celia was an only child, this she revealed to Daphne a day after they had met. 'You might as well stay with me,' Daphne told her in a bossy sort of way. She herself had been the new girl two years before, and since nobody had joined the school after her, it had remained that way until Celia's arrival. 'They all have their own friends,' she pointed to the older girls who congregated on the grass, next to the pond.

'Oh look,' Celia announced. 'A lido, do you swim?'

'Miss Fag says we're not allowed to.'

'Shame. I used to swim all the time in India.'

'Where?' Daphne asked in an accusing tone. The only vision of India she had was formed from Kipling's stories.

'At Ceylon, where we'd go on holidays. It has a sea coast.'

'Does it have palm trees?'

'Yes, it even has sand.'

After their lessons in the morning they were free to rest or take short walks on the grounds. The curriculum was not too demanding and the girls were constantly referred to as 'in delicate health'. The state of their health called for a gentle introduction to arithmetic, general history and religious education. They were ordered to repent in childhood, for silly misdemeanours like stealing sweets and talking back to their parents, to Miss Fag. With their life expectancy uncertain, though Daphne never felt close to death, Miss Fag was not taking any chances. There would be no sinners on her watch.

George had tried to teach Daphne arithmetic and Marina had taught her to read and write, long before she went to the school. It was the only occasion in which she spent one-on-one time with her mother. She was left to her own devices with history, and her historical facts were gleaned from the dusty old books at High Greenwood. Celia hated reading, except for the *Beano*, but she loved drawing and was very good at it. She drew insects with great precision, as though she had studied them under a microscope.

'In India,' Celia began, 'the blackbird used to wake me up every morning. We had snakes, too. Poisonous ones.'

'We have grass snakes,' Daphne interrupted.

'And dangerous dogs,' Celia talked over her. 'One day, a dog escaped from the village and bit the little boy who lived next door to me.'

'What happened?'

'He died.'

Celia must have noticed the horrified expression on Daphne's face, for she added, 'Not from the bite, silly, though it did have rabies. The stupid nurse gave him porridge made with *their* water. Typhoid got him in the end.'

Another dangerous topic dominated the chatter. All anyone could talk about was the threat of war. Hitler's name was scarcely out of the newspapers, and the politicians, whom Miss Fag called 'inties', often discussed him and the foreign sanctions against Germany on the wireless.

'My dad said there isn't going to be any war,' Celia piped up in history class after they learned of the Munich Agreement and looked at a newspaper photograph of the King and Queen standing with Neville Chamberlain on the balcony of Buckingham Palace.

'Stand up!' the history teacher bellowed. 'I won't have girls talking out of turn in my class.'

Defiantly, Celia rose to her feet and turned her back on the teacher to look her classmates in the eye. 'My father fought in the last war and he said that would be the war to end all wars. Why do you think he's still in India? Because he knows there will *never* be a war.'

'Is he an Indian?' a girl asked.

'Certainly not,' Celia replied.

Daphne looked up at Celia, who stood with such confidence, and she took in her physical appearance: short, quite plump when she removed the thick, woollen cardigan, ash coloured hair and green eyes. Her nose turned up and she had small, thin lips. She was quite pretty, like a doll. In comparison, Daphne felt like a great big lump of granite. She was tall and thin with brown hair and greyish-blue eyes – the same as Marina's – and her nose was straight without an upturn in its profile. Now that her suntan had faded she was ghostly white, the paleness emphasised by her dark eyebrows and eyelashes.

'I know what you are,' the same girl announced. 'You're a feringhee.'

'A what?' Daphne tried to ask over the din of the girls laughing. 'What's that?'

'Shut up,' Celia hissed at her.

'Feringhee, feringhee,' the girls chanted. 'Celia's a feringhee.'

The teacher whipped the desk with a ruler, calling for order in the classroom. 'That's enough!' she roared, and then she looked at Celia with a smug glint in her eye. *That's put you in your place*, it seemed to say.

*

Marina sat at her dressing table, going through the pages of her manuscript and fixing the corrections. It was not an occupation she enjoyed, but the routine was familiar in a comforting way. The new book followed the same formula as her previous ones: a woman whose virtue was at stake, an impoverished aristocrat, a seaside setting. She tried to liven things up by using a Russian count who had fled the Bolsheviks, only to realise it had been a mistake. She knew nothing about Russia, and it was too late to start again but she hoped by calling the gents names like Sergio and Vladimir that nobody would notice.

From the long window she could see George at the small burial ground across the lawn. She curiously watched as he kneeled at the stone cross marking his mother's grave and began to pull weeds from the gypsophila he had planted in the grass surrounding it. It was an appropriate plant for Sybil: dainty but tough, a deception. His father's grave, a stone block with an urn placed on top, was adjacent to his mother's. He visited Sybil's grave every day, and in summer he'd go out after dinner to bid her goodnight. Marina thought it an unhealthy obsession; she could not abide anything as ritualistic as standing at a tomb, talking to a decaying corpse. The coffin in the ground, so dark and compact; so much like a womb, she thought. Life and death, why did everything have to revolve around a sort of incarceration?

Marina was glad Sybil was dead; she had made her life hell during the five years in which she had been married to George. Often, she spoke of divorce and the different factors which might lead to this shameful path. One particular topic had been Marina's laziness in producing an heir. Sybil said not to worry, that it should happen one day, and George fretted and implored her to see Doctor Glendinning. Sybil was firm that she should not see him. 'He's not a specialist,' she had said. So Marina was packed off to the hospital in town where they poked and prodded her and declared her fit and fertile. Although they had given her a clean bill of health, Sybil hinted that problems were on the horizon. She did not specifically blame Marina for this shortcoming, but she did not openly say it wasn't her fault. 'It's always the woman's burden,' she unhelpfully added.

Marina set her pen on top of the pages and moved to the wardrobe and selected an outfit. It was almost lunchtime and she was still in her dressing gown. As she dressed in her writing uniform of a cardigan and skirt, she decided she would ask George about the war and whether or not he thought there would be one. This might explain his visits to town, and why he seemed cagey whenever she asked where he had been.

When George returned from the garden Marina heard his heavy footsteps walking past her bedroom door, stepping on the creaking floorboard within her earshot. She wondered if he did it deliberately to interrupt her work. No, he wanted his presence to be known. She sprung to her feet and rushed from the room.

'George,' she called after him. And, pushing his bedroom door open, she followed him into his room.

'What is it?' he asked as he pulled off his jumper and slipped on a jacket.

'I was thinking... we might have a spot of lunch together, if you're up to it?'

Without thinking, George looked at his watch and at Marina. His eyes glistened and he asked in a hopeful voice, 'Really. Have luncheon? Just you and I?'

'Who else?' her voice was less kind.

Lunch was interrupted before it began. She wasn't hungry and made no effort to eat her soup. George did not want to seem impolite so he held onto the spoon and swooshed it around in the bowl without eating it. He asked her if she felt sick, if something was the matter. She sighed and raised her voice, a soft shrill like a hard whisper, and told him nothing was wrong. 'Why *must* anything be wrong?'

It was a relief when the telephone rang and Gladys popped her head around the door to say it was for Marina. 'Urgent,' she said before leaving. As much as it inconvenienced Marina to speak on the phone (she hated it), she felt an air of superiority in receiving an *urgent* call.

'Hello, who is it?' she asked as she lit a cigarette.

'Mother, it's me. Daphne.' The voice caused her heart to sink. 'May I come home for the weekend?'

Marina sighed. She glanced in the direction of George sitting at the table, eating his soup in her absence. 'You know that I'm awfully busy...,'

When Marina returned to the table, George asked her who it was. 'Oh,' she said as she dipped her finger into the soup. 'This is cold,' she pushed the bowl away. George wanted to remind her that she wasn't going to eat it but remained silent as to avoid a petty argument. 'It was Daphne,' she looked down at the tablecloth.

'Is anything the matter?'

'No, nothing's wrong.'

'Are you going to eat that?'

She slid the bowl to him. 'Be my guest.'

That's not what he meant but he smiled and accepted the soup. 'You're awfully distant these days, darling.' It had taken him a great amount of courage to say that to her.

'Am I?' was all she said.

*

The girls invented a story that a bout of 'flu was sweeping through the school and to be on the safe side they were to leave for the weekend while the others recuperated.

'Your mother will never believe us,' Celia said as they travelled down to High Greenwood on the train.

When they conversed they tended to shout over one another until the loudest voice dominated the chat. The ticket inspector told them to be quiet but Celia told him to bugger off, it was a free country. The passengers around them tutted and shook their heads. 'What a disgusting girl,' one of them said.

'She won't care,' Daphne said, mindful to keep her voice down.

The reason behind Daphne dragging Celia down to High Greenwood was based on pure vanity. She'd never had a friend before and she longed to show off her bedroom with the tall windows overlooking the small woodland at the back of the house where a freshwater stream trickled through the grounds. She boasted that Marina was breathtakingly beautiful and that George could speak French.

'Catch me while I faint,' Celia said in an exaggerated voice.

The mood at High Greenwood was flat. George sat in the drawing room, hiding behind his newspaper, hoping Marina would fail to notice how jumpy he was. She watched him, her eyes fixed on the paper that created a barricade between them. After his charade of reading, and turning the pages to make it look realistic, he lowered the paper and looked at her. 'When I get back,' he said as he folded it in half and set it to one side, 'we have to talk.'

'Yes,' she nodded. For a moment he kept his gaze on her, and rather than rebuffing him, she kept her eyes on him, too. 'Soon, I hope.'

He was off again. Marina knew he had a dubious past, though he never talked about it. She knew he hated his father and that there was a strange and complicated history that tied him to her, long before she had met him. He said it had something to do with being at the mercy of one's parents, and how they shared that common thread. 'Was my mother a whore?' she once asked George, who seemed shocked by the question.

'I...,' he began, lost for words. 'I shouldn't think so. Why?'

'Just something your mother said.'

'I shouldn't pay too much attention to mummy. She's becoming quite senile.'

'What's your definition of a whore?' she asked him.

'Do stop it, Marina,' he scolded her. 'Stop saying that word. I hate it when you're vulgar.'

*

The taxi pulled up carrying Daphne and Celia. It was drizzling outside, and Marina stood in the doorway wearing a thick cardigan with its sleeves pushed up to her elbows. Celia looked in her direction: Marina appeared to her as a girl. As she moved closer, Celia could see the faint creases in her forehead, above her thin eyebrows, and the spidery lines below her crystallised eyes. 'Is *that* really your mother?' she whispered.

'Yes,' Daphne glowed with pride. 'Told you she was a picture.'

'You must be Celia,' Marina said as she went to pay the taxi driver who had ferried them from the station.

'Hello, Lady Greenwood,' Celia chimed. 'How good of you to invite me here.'

Marina gave Celia a quizzical smile, and was taken aback by Daphne who dared to kiss her on the cheek.

Marina hid her fury well. She felt put out by their arrival. Now she would have to put on a front, be a gracious hostess, and refrain from staying in her nightgown until lunchtime.

The girls changed out of their school uniforms and into their ordinary clothes. Celia's things were nicer than Daphne's; they looked brand new and were livened up with pretty bows and dainty buttons. She wore jewellery, and Daphne spied three fine gold bangles on her wrist which jangled when she moved her arm. They were a gift from Uncle Christopher, she said, but she did not elaborate except to say he wasn't her real uncle but her father's friend. Daphne felt slightly envious, for nobody cared if she looked nice or not.

'Is this milk boiled?' Celia asked as they drank tea with Marina.

'Why do you ask?' Marina replied without answering the question.

Celia pushed the jug to one side without using the milk. 'You see, in India we had to boil our milk. But most of the time my mother just gave me my own bottle. We couldn't take that chance.'

Holding the cup of tea to her lips, Marina stopped before taking a sip, and said, 'Well you're not in India any more. And the milk is not boiled, it is clean.'

Marina said she had a headache and got up from the table. 'Time of the month?' Celia asked and was ignored, though Gladys gave her a sideways look and the remark went over Daphne's head.

As Marina walked along the landing she turned and went to George's bedroom door. It was locked. She wiggled the door handle up and down, hoping it was stuck, and when it did not open she swore under her breath and went to her own bedroom. Too irritated to do any work, she lay across the bed, fully dressed, and enjoyed the soft breeze from the opened window as it blew through the room. For a brief second, the thought of Daphne as a baby appeared in her mind and the frustration she felt towards her. She could not stand people needing her so ferociously.

The girls ate dinner without Marina, who had a tray sent up to her bedroom. She was a picky eater and did not like food in general, merely seeing it as fuel, and she stuck to a bland diet, usually made up of a baked potato or a plate of vegetables. 'Your mother's so bohemian,' Celia observed as the housekeeper carried the plate past the girls. Celia was accustomed to a small staff in India and found their reduced living conditions grim. Marina and George employed a housekeeper, Gladys, who was more of a daily worker and Jack-of-all-trades, and a cook (whom they simply called 'Cook'), who had been with the family for ages because George did not have the heart to pay her off. She slept in a small room, off the kitchen, and worked for a pittance as it were.

'What's your father like?' Celia asked as she shovelled forkfuls of food into her mouth.

'What do you mean?'

'Is he nice?'

'Oh yes, very,' Daphne told her. 'He's very nice to me, but I don't get to see him too often. He's always in town, working.'

'Who do you love more? Your mother or your father?'

Daphne hadn't thought about it. She shrugged, too ashamed to give it any thought or to answer such a question. 'What about you?'

'Oh my mother, without a doubt. Though sometimes she's a silly old bitch.'

'And your father, what about him?'

'I hate him,' Celia said.

*

They met in a teashop in the centre of town. It was lucky that she had agreed to show up, George felt elated that he had managed to track her down on the very day he had free. He was going to suggest reserving a table at a restaurant just as the lunch hour finished. It would be quiet, they would have time to talk before the tables were reset for dinner. But no. She said a teashop was best, it was close to her flat and she could easily drop in between lessons.

'Sorry to keep you waiting,' she said. 'Is this table all right for you?' She looked over her shoulder at the empty table behind her. 'We could always sit next to the window, if you prefer?'

'No, this is quite all right,' George replied. The window seat was too risky, somebody might see them together. He watched her as she took off her coat. How odd that she had barely aged a day since their last encounter on the driveway at High Greenwood. Her dark blonde hair was a shade duller, it was pulled back off her face, buried beneath a hat which she wore far back on her head. 'Would you like some tea?'

'Coffee, but make it quick. I've got to leave in five minutes,' she said as she sat down. 'Mind if I smoke?' She removed a silver cigarette case from her handbag.

'What a jolly hat. Is it new?'

'A mystery needs a hat,' she said.

He pulled out his own packet of cigarettes. He hoped the gesture would make her see that he was on her side. 'I'm sure my phoning you was a shock. I was going to write, but letters are so easily discarded.'

'Not a shock, per se. It was a surprise to hear your voice. Your speech...,' she realised how condescending she sounded and quickly added, 'You appear so confident.'

'I'm glad you think so.'

'Goodness,' smoke escaped from her mouth as she spoke. 'Is it hot in here?'

He was glad when the waitress brought the pot of tea and cup of coffee. She hovered on the spot, setting down the cups, the sugar, a jug of milk between them, and the napkins. When she left, George leaned forward, ignoring his tea as she stirred her coffee. He reached over to take her hand but she pulled away and put it on her lap.

'The thing is,' he looked over his shoulder and lowered his voice, 'the thing is, I'm finding money a bit tight. I might have to sell the house. Afraid it's all become a bit too much to handle, it's falling down around me. I can't afford the repairs; the new boiler almost bankrupted me.'

'So why did you ring me up? Why did you bring me here?' The nonchalance of her voice, her devil-may-care attitude, rattled him. She could see right through him. 'Unless there was something else?' She kept her gaze on him. 'Because I don't see what High Greenwood has to do with me. I've scarcely given the place a thought.' She made it a point to look at her watch, which he knew was an act. 'Afraid I've got to go. I'm expecting a pupil at one. Saturday afternoon is always the worst.'

He reached out and grabbed her hand. 'Please,' he pleaded with her. 'Please, may I c-c-come to your flat?'

There it was, the old George, a bundle of nerves. She stared at him, openly scrutinising him as he sat opposite her. 'Well,' she paused as she looked past him, out the window, at the people on the street. 'I suppose so.'

He took a deep breath to steady his composure. 'Thank you.'

'Do you know where it is?'

'Morrow Place?' I'll find it.'

How odd to see Louisa again, his youngest sister. He almost wished he hadn't bothered to find her, to look her up in the phone-book and, by chance, dial the number. How he wished she had slammed the phone down or refused to see him.

The sight of her standing outside the teashop, buttoning up her coat and putting on her gloves filled him with an air of nostalgia. How he had loved her when she was a girl; she had always been his favourite sister. The way she stood there, directly in his line of vision, without a care in the world. Then again, why should she care? To her knowledge she had done nothing wrong. It was George who had behaved so badly. You killed a woman, the words rolled off her tongue too easily. She looked up at the autumnal sky and walked into the crowd, down the street and across the road, slipping out of sight as she turned a corner.

The day went slowly, the anticipation of waiting for four o'clock to come round stalled the afternoon until it faded out. At three o'clock he felt the urge to get up, to leave the empty office where he had been passing the time and go round to her flat at Morrow Place. Ghastly area. When it was time to get the bus he waited with the other Saturday shoppers as the number seven stopped, headed to Morrow Place. He turned around and walked away. He had lost his nerve.

He could not face returning to High Greenwood. He felt drained, seeing Louisa and talking to her in person took every last morsel of energy he had. It was as though he had been saving it up for her sake. His club membership had been paid up until the end of the year and he returned there to sleep. Marina was under the impression he had cancelled it and, in a way, he felt guilty for having deceived her. Still, he reasoned, what she did not know could not hurt her.

*

As the night wore on, Marina could hear a whimpering sound coming from the room next door. She sat up, switched on her lamp and listened. The familiar nocturnal sounds: the squeaking of bats, hooting of owls, and the occasional squeal of a woodland creature could not distract her from this desperation.

'What is it?' Daphne pressed her hand against Celia's shoulder. 'Did you have a bad dream?'

'I'm so...,' her chest racked back and forth. 'I'm so... terribly homesick,' she sobbed.

'Do you miss school? Is that what it is?'

'I want my mother.'

'She's so far away,' Daphne said without thinking. 'I'm sure you could write to her.'

Marina pushed the door open and turned on the light. The glare hurt Daphne's tired eyes and she strained to see her mother standing in the doorway. 'Is everything all right in here?'

'Yes, Celia's a bit upset.'

'What is it, Celia?' Marina walked to the bed.

Celia looked at Daphne, prompting her to speak for her. 'She misses her mother.'

'Oh, poor thing,' Marina pulled a handkerchief out of her dressing gown pocket and passed it along. Celia dried her eyes and blew her nose. 'Your mother, is she dead?'

'Dead?' Celia sniffed. 'No, she's in India.'

'Would you like a drink of water?'

Celia took a few short breaths to steady her breathing, and nodded.

'Go fetch Celia a glass of water,' Marina ordered Daphne.

Daphne put on her slippers and left the room. She resented being ordered about, and she knew her mother would never cater to her like this. Marina's favourite way of handling a crisis was to tell the person not to involve her. She cared little for life's trivialities and she certainly never responded to Daphne's tears. It was easy to be charitable towards those you weren't responsible for.

When Daphne returned she found a composed Celia talking to Marina about India. Frankly, Daphne was sick of listening to tales of India; she had heard enough about the place to feel as though she, too, had lived there. If it wasn't memories of the sweet ayah, it was horror stories about lepers' corpses spilling out of the roadside ditches. She didn't believe it, and she assumed Celia had invented the story.

'Your mother's so wonderful and kind,' Celia whispered as they settled into bed.

A feeling of pride swelled in Daphne's heart. She knew it was a lie, but she was glad Celia had been impressed. It certainly made a change from being put down all the time.

Afterwards she said, 'You're not to mention this again. If you do, I shall burn down this house.'

'Mention what?'

'My crying. If you do, I'll say it's a lie. Do you hear me?'

'Don't worry,' she assured Celia. 'Your secret is safe with me.'

Chapter Three

When George returned to High Greenwood he was highly charged, his words were erratic and he darted from one subject to the next. What was more troubling to Marina was that he seemed pleased to see her and was enthusiastic about being in her company. 'I've missed you,' he announced before lunging forward to kiss her. He aimed for her lips but she turned at the precise second it had been delivered and it hovered clumsily between her chin and the edge of her mouth.

'How was the drive?'

'The train, you mean?' he called from the drinks cabinet. She rolled her eyes, she hated to be corrected.

'Medicinal,' he held up a glass of brandy before gulping it down. 'Fine. The train was a little crowded.'

'Don't you hate that?'

'A baby screamed for the duration.'

She got up and stood in front of the fire. 'So, the trip. Was it a success?'

George stared at Marina with a bemused curiosity. Although relations were often tepid, verging on a sort of semi-estrangement between the two, her physical attractiveness still appealed to him. She was beautiful in an aloof way: her pale silvery blue eyes seemed fixed in a permanent, cold stare, and her small, pert lips were devoid of lipstick. He hated lipstick and felt she did not suit it – it seemed to intensify the colour of her eyes in an unattractive way – but he lacked the nerve to tell her so. Her dyed blonde hair, usually worn in a slight wave, was tied back with a ribbon. She kneeled down and picked up a log from the small stack on the hearth. She inspected it for signs of bugs, as she was apt to do, and seeing that none lived on the log, she threw it on top of the smouldering ashes. Watching her take the poker and push the log back before she placed another one on top, he took in the sight of her slender frame. The sharpness of her shoulders jutting through her cardigan, buttoned all the way up. The neat waist emphasized by the tight waistband of her slacks and the gap between her thighs, giving her an almost bow-legged gait. When had she started wearing trousers? he wondered. The thought troubled him; it reminded him of his first cousin, Pamela Manners, an actress who wore trousers and men's jumpers, whom he had had a fling with when they were young.

'What's all this? Why the list of questions?' He watched her expression change from a forced sincerity to fury.

'If you're going to be churlish I shall leave,' she snapped.

'No. Stay. I was only teasing.' He refilled the glass with brandy. 'Nice slacks.'

'You too,' she said.

*

Daphne and Celia lay on the bed, the thin mattress weighed down by the two bodies. They scribbled in their diaries; Daphne had very little to say except she had been having headaches and was relieved when the optician tested her eyes and said she did not need spectacles. Specs, she thought, would make her all the more unattractive to Marina. Celia liked to write her entry inside brackets, the entire thing. Daphne asked why and was told, matter of factly, that the brackets resembled a cupped hand over the mouth, as though one were whispering a secret.

It was a strict part of the curriculum, the writing and not the whispering, since Miss Fag had given them diaries as a Christmas present. A macabre thought lay behind this unremarkable gesture. They were told of their mortality and the real threat of death that shadowed them, and how important it was to keep a diary. Daphne assumed it was a way of keeping a legacy, not that Marina would have read it. She imagined her mother would have tossed it into the fire like she did with their Christmas cards in the New Year.

Nobody had died in the two years that Daphne had been at the school, though Miss Fag warned of past pupils returning home only to succumb to an asthma attack, and she spoke of poor Mary Nightingale, a sickly girl who died before Daphne had enrolled in the school, and she wondered if it was Mary's bed that she had inherited. As she had never had an asthma attack she assumed she was untouchable, and should one sneak up on her, she would not have a clue what it was. So, she thought, it was best to die in ignorance than in fear.

'Have you ever had an asthma attack?' she asked Celia.

'Oh yes,' she announced. 'I used to have them all the time in India but I seem to have grown out of them.'

'What are they like?'

31

'Oh you know...,' Celia bent over to tie her shoelaces. That was another thing Daphne coveted from her friend. She, too, longed for lace-up shoes and not the silly ones she had to wear with a leather strap and button. 'You sort of go blue in the face. And you die. Well, that's what the Indian doctor told mummy. He said I'd died for a moment because my lungs collapsed.'

'How did you come alive again?'

'I don't know, except mummy says it was the Holy Spirit watching over me.' With a glint in her eye, she peered up at Daphne as she laced the other shoe. 'And that is how I manage to get exactly what I want.'

'What do you mean?'

'I simply hold my breath and mummy panics. She *always* gives in when I do that. Silly old bag.'

Daphne knew if she tried a stunt like that Marina would let her die, and she'd probably order the housekeeper to dig a hole in the garden and bury her among the moulting cabbages.

'Celia,' said Miss Fag as she loomed in the doorway. 'Celia, your mother is here.'

'My mother?'

'Yes. Gather yourself up and join me in the office.'

'She's not going to take you home?' Daphne grabbed onto Celia's arm. 'She's not taking you back to India, is she?'

'I don't know.'

A wave of anxiety washed over Daphne. She felt panicked, sick to her stomach, afraid.

'If I don't come back, I suppose she is,' Celia added for dramatic effect.

Celia's mother had crossed the ocean on a steamship which seemed to take an eternity to reach its final destination. 'Mummy!' she ran to her mother.

'Oh my darling girl,' Mrs Hartley held on to Celia, who was her exact height.

Miss Fag discouraged hugs and kisses, and she looked on, agitated by the cross-contamination happening before her eyes. 'Steady on, Celia, you don't want to tire yourself out.'

'Won't you show me around your school?' Mrs Hartley took her by the hand. 'I'd so love to see it.'

'Yes, a brief tour should do, Celia,' Miss Fag gestured to the door. 'But not the dorms, not while the girls are resting.'

*

Marina longed for the day when George would cease to find her attractive. She despised physical contact with all manner of human-beings and she thought sex was pointless when one lacked the biological urge to reproduce. But she realised that Sybil was right: men were weak. Although she did not love George, she was fond of him in a way a person becomes used to something, and she begrudged those times when he began to look at her differently for she knew what would surely follow. It did not happen often, and she was not shy in rejecting him, but to save a bitter scene she obliged him this time.

Marina knew he was hoping to have a son before it was too late. She knew otherwise, and sometimes she only slept with him to see if she could become pregnant again. There was no success on that front, probably because of the Volpar Gels which she'd started to use after Daphne was born. Secretly, of course. George didn't know, and Gladys was a good sport to buy them from the chemist for her. She told herself if it did happen again she would get rid of it. It had become a game to her. When she was pregnant with Daphne, all those years ago, she recalled the odd feeling of being aware that something was inside her, a while before the quickening confirmed it, and she imagined a pebble floating about and how she would squirm and wriggle around, hoping to dislodge it. She had had a dream just before the birth: the sheet was sticky, she recalled feeling it and, so certain it was blood, she said to herself: 'I've lost the baby. I've lost the baby.' She woke up with a relieved grin on her face, thinking it had slithered out of her during the night. It was wishful thinking: the sheet was dry, there was no blood, and the baby was safely tucked inside her.

The same questions haunted her. Where had he been? What was he up to? She patiently waited for the right moment to ask him. Lulled into a relaxed state, all his previous tension seemed to evaporate. He thought her more compliant than before, she did not turn her head when he kissed her. She must love him.

'What were you in town for?' she asked in a gentle voice, hoping to engage his trust. She felt like Mata Hari, giving him sex in exchange for his secrets.

'Hmm?' he mumbled, miles away.

'What were you in town for?' She was tempted to use a firmer tone, instead she placed a gentle hand on his chest and felt it going up and down, rapidly, and then petering out to a steady rhythm.

'Oh, nothing much.' He took her hand in his. 'Just stuff to do with the bank and this blasted client we've taken on from America.' Strobes of sunlight filtered through the heavy curtains that were drawn across the window. With his eyes accustomed to the semi-darkness, he used the threads of light to study the palm of her hand, tracing the lifeline with his index finger. 'You know Cook would have a field day with your hand.'

'I beg your pardon?'

'She taught me some palmistry, years ago. Yes, this is the life line, see? Yours is good and strong. And this is the heart line, it is jagged.' He kissed her hand. 'But I suppose you think it's all stuff and nonsense.'

'The American chap, is he rich?' She slipped her hand from his grip.

'Mmm, very.'

'He must be worth the effort, then.' Looking up at the ceiling, her eyes met with the faint yellowing patches of damp forming on the ivory coloured plaster. She hadn't noticed it before, perhaps the darkness made it seem so. 'Do you think there will be a war?'

'Perhaps. But let's not be gloomy.' His voice was firmer than before and he put his arm across her as to not appear brusque and pulled her close to him. She wanted to say 'don't touch me' and wriggle away but she realised he would take offence, and so she put up with it.

The noise of Gladys bounding down the landing reached her ears, they remained silent until Marina felt compelled to speak. 'Sounds like a baby elephant.' There was a clattering sound. 'She's sweeping the stairs,' Marina said, irritated.

George yawned, groaning as he stretched. As he did so, she sat up and this gesture created the invisible boundary that she longed for. The wooden headboard pressed against her spine. She wanted to get up and leave but she felt trapped. The thought of passing Gladys in the landing filled her with shame; she knew she did not have to explain herself but she felt self-conscience all the same.

All was quiet, and George appeared to be sleeping. Marina pulled the covers to one side and sat on the edge of the bed. She quickly dressed, and stood up as she buttoned the trousers which had prompted the bemusement from George.

'Afternoon,' Gladys's voice startled her. She had just closed the door of the linen cupboard.

Marina flushed crimson as she closed the bedroom door. She patted her hair and offered a slight smile. 'Good afternoon,' she managed to say. 'Please don't disturb Sir George, he's... he's not well.'

Gladys nodded, holding an armful of bedding. 'Just as well you said. I was about to go in there and change the bedding.'

Marina walked on, horrified by the thought and relieved by her timing. She wished she did not have such hang-ups.

*

'Mummy, this is Daphne Greenwood,' Celia pointed to Daphne as she stepped forward, extending her hand.

'What a lovely girl,' Mrs Hartley smiled.

Daphne returned the smile. She was intrigued by Mrs Hartley's voice, a sort of shrill English accent punctuated by a twanging lilt, like pennies dropping into a tin box.

Tea was laid out in the visitor's room, which smelled of mahogany furniture and potted hyacinths. The three of them sat on the burgundy velvet chairs at the round table, so small their hands touched as though they were doing a séance.

Mrs Hartley was older than Daphne had imagined; she had pale, pinkish coloured skin which looked waxy, it had a sheen across her full cheeks and sloping forehead. She wore dark red lipstick which clashed badly with her complexion and green eyes. Her hair was the same colour as Celia's, though darker and with yellowing strands. Mrs Hartley told the girls about her long journey from the foot of the North Cachar Hills to Guwahati railway station, and how the train had snaked along the tracks for two days before it reached Bombay, where she caught the boat. She did not tell Celia of the hostility that was in the air, or how English people were leaving in droves. And she did not tell her that her husband had sent her over to look for a house because he was selling the tea plantation – their home. 'We're not short of money, or anything like that,' she had told the estate agent when he asked why.

'Mummy's fifty-five,' Celia interrupted.

Fifty-five, Daphne thought. Already she had imagined a background for Mrs Hartley; perhaps she had been married before, a war widow. She wanted to ask 'who was your first husband?' but realised the question was much too grown-up and would sound precocious coming from a child.

'Celia, what have I told you?'

'That a lady never talks about her age,' Celia droned.

Fifty-five seemed ancient to Daphne, and she could only imagine how old Mrs Hartley must have been when Celia was a baby. 'My mother is thirty-seven,' she said.

'So young,' Mrs Hartley answered between sips of tea.

'Tell Daphne what it's like in India. Tell her about the Bengal tiger.'

Mrs Hartley gave a small, deep sigh and rolled her eyes. She grinned as she spoke to Daphne, trying to stifle a laugh. 'Celia's a most imaginative child; we don't live in Bengal and there is no tiger.'

'No, but you know there are tigers, mummy.'

'Yes, in the jungle,' Mrs Hartley reminded Celia.

'It must have been a dreadful shock when that little boy died,' Daphne added.

'What little boy?'

'Celia told me that your neighbour was bitten by a dog and he died.'

'Good heavens, no.'

Celia turned bright red, as though she might explode. 'I said he died of typhoid and I didn't say he was my neighbour, I said my neighbour knew of a little boy. You're always getting things wrong!'

'Now, Miss,' Mrs Hartley warned her, 'you mind your manners.'

The subject was quickly changed to that of Mr Hartley, whom Daphne learned was still in India overseeing his tea plantation.

'Pitā's awfully sorry he couldn't get away,' she told Celia, who turned away from her mother and stared out the window. Pitā, Daphne was told by Mrs Hartley, was Hindi for father.

'Daphne's father's a lord,' Celia snapped, hoping to wound her mother.

'Is he? How splendid.'

'He's not a lord, he's a baronet.' She felt embarrassed for Mrs Hartley. 'But he works in a bank,' she said, hoping to make her feel better. 'When did you move to India, Mrs Hartley?'

Celia leaned back in the chair, she folded her arms across her rotund chest and rolled her eyes to display her displeasure.

Relating her experiences of India, Mrs Hartley told Daphne how she had been born there, how her father was in the army and her mother had died when she was young. 'When I was a little girl I had to care for my other brothers and sisters,' she confided. Daphne felt sorry for her; there was something about her manner that evoked pity.

'Oh mother, *please*!' Celia roared.

The ease in which Celia spoke badly to her mother alarmed Daphne, she felt nervous and on edge. She never would have talked to Marina in that voice, nor would she have been overly familiar, either. Marina scared her, and she felt she was a poor choice of a child for her, surely that was the reason she never bothered with her.

Mrs Hartley had five days to spare before she sailed back to India to tie up loose ends, repeating the same tiresome journey. This time she wondered if the tea plantation would still be there, if their wooden house with the second-floor veranda would still be standing. Would the militants from the nearby village follow through with their threat to burn the house and everyone in it? Was her husband dead?

'Are you staying at an hotel?' Daphne asked, bringing Mrs Hartley from her daydream.

'Yes, a lovely place in town.'

'Can we go there for tea?' Celia asked.

Mrs Hartley smiled. There was no hotel, only a house. She did not tell Celia that she had found their new home and that she would never see India again.

'What are you thinking?' Celia poked her mother's arm, making a nuisance of herself.

'It's a secret,' she smiled once more.

*

'What's on your mind?' Marina asked George as they sipped their coffee and listened to Ambrose on the wireless.

'Nothing,' he smiled.

Maria was convinced George was having an affair. Although it did not bother her, she had no other explanation for his lengthy disappearances. Early in their marriage, he had had an affair with a certain Venetia Spry, a friend of the family whom he had known all his life. They were similar in age, in fact Venetia was six months older than George, and Marina found this madly intimidating. Sybil knew all about it. Like a sphinx, she knew everything. She encouraged it. Marina, by her own admission, was *frigid* – Sybil's choice of word, but she did not quibble. 'And, after all, George is a man,' she justified her son's infidelity. She had told Marina everything, it was her way of offering her daughter-in-law an incentive to step into the wifely role that was expected of her. She spoke of her own husband, Walter, and how he had kept a mistress for years and years – a long-standing arrangement, really. Instead of *bothering* her, as Sybil referred to it, he went to the mistress, but occasionally he would approach her 'for it'. 'But,' Sybil was quick to add, 'not at the same time; he wasn't depraved, or anything.'

Marina gauged Sybil was fond of intervals, or intermissions – their entire lives happened in phases. Now that she had Marina's attention, or pity, Sybil confided how fickle men were and sex ('that thing', as she called it) was nature's way of giving wives the upper-hand. She told her that one must never refuse, and that it was somehow acceptable for one's husband to force them to do it, even if they didn't want to. She had given birth to four children, which included two girls born in the same year; one at the beginning, one at the end – 'the twins', as everyone had called them. *The same year*, she stressed to Marina, as though she had done something marvellous like discovering radium or climbing Everest. It was an achievement most women in her position could only dream of. Marina thought of her as a pedigree dog, producing litter after litter of expensive puppies, and she stifled a giggle when she imagined Walter patting his wife on the head and saying, 'Good doggy.'

Not even the companionship of marriage could interest Marina, and everything else was inconvenient and against the grain of what she wanted to do. George had rescued her when she was frightened and alone, having found herself motherless and, before that, working as an occasional typist when money was tight. There was the nasty business of her mother's death, the grisly probing of what had happened in the past and present, and the humility when her mother-in-law referred to the marriage as George 'saving the day'.

The following morning, Marina awoke in a bad mood. She was agitated and felt a headache coming on, the curse was imminent. The echo of George's voice in the hallway met her ears. She stopped typing and listened, she could hear another man's voice, it was gruffer. They were climbing the staircase, and she heard their footsteps pausing about halfway up. She got up and walked to the landing.

'What's all this?' she asked as she took in the sight of George and the man standing before a vast oil painting of George's ancestor on horseback, a hero of Waterloo. Mr Roper was a short man who wore a felt hat and an ill-fitting suit. She recalled George saying he was a 'nice sort of chap'. No, she thought: he looks like a wife-beater and child molester.

'Oh darling, this is Mr Roper, the insurance man.' Marina's frosty silence compelled George to continue. 'He's come to take note of the inventory in case of a fire, or some other unpleasant event.'

'You're not the chap they normally send,' she said. She preferred the man who usually visited the house, he was much older and wore a porcelain mask. George said he had been in the Great War and that half of his face had been blown off. He was a war hero, and therefore trustworthy. Marina felt sorry for him and often felt a pang in her heart when he stood in profile view and she could see the hollowness through the small gap in the mask which hooked behind his ear like spectacles.

Mr Roper looked at Marina with his dark, beady eyes. He was disgusted and amused that a woman dare address him and tell him his job, and his place.

'Anyhow, I didn't think we were due a visit so soon.'

'Ah, yes. Formality, darling. Afraid they needed an update.'

'But why?' For some reason she would not let the subject go. 'Surely nothing has changed.'

'Like I said, formality.'

'You don't need to take an inventory of the bedrooms do you, Mr Roper? It's just I'm frightfully busy working on my novel.'

'Not unless she's got any valuables,' he spoke to George and not her.

*

The girls said goodbye to Mrs Hartley, who had stopped at the school on her way to the station. She kissed Celia on the forehead and smoothed down her hair. Daphne noticed that she whispered something into Celia's ear and Celia nodded, squeezing her lips together. 'You promise?' she asked Celia as she walked away; at least that was what Daphne thought she overheard. Celia did not respond. Mrs Hartley got into a taxi and

39

rolled down the window. She was without her gloves, and Daphne spied a crescent moon-shaped scar between her index finger and thumb.

'Your hand,' Daphne blurted out without meaning to.

Mrs Hartley smiled, avoiding eye contact with Celia who kicked the gravel beneath her shoe. It was a bite mark, a scar from Celia's pointed teeth. They stood in silence, with Daphne thinking Mrs Hartley would explain the scar, and Celia hoping she would not. Then, she blew a kiss at Celia as the car drove away.

'What did your mother say to you?' Daphne asked.

'Nothing,' her voice was cool. A moment later she flippantly said, 'She asked me to write to Pitā – my dad.'

Daphne thought of Marina and George, and as she opened her mouth to speak she sneezed.

'Come on.' She walked ahead of Daphne, as though in charge. 'Let's go inside. It's freezing out here.'

*

'What did Mr Roper want?' Marina asked George over dinner. She made an effort to come down and join him at the table even though she felt ill.

'You look dreadful,' George said without thinking. 'What I mean is, you're quite p-p-pale.'

Marina gave a weak smile. 'I suppose I'm working too hard. That is, I ought to be doing the work, not just thinking about it... *dwelling* on it.' Gladys brought her a headache pill fizzing in a glass of water, which she gulped down and winced from its chalky taste. She took a deep breath and rubbed her temples, asking him if he would mind if she retired early.

He was glad to see her go; he had avoided her question about Roper and he was unsure what he might say if she asked again.

It was a small relief when, the following day, Marina said she had a migraine and stayed in bed. He had been trying to reach Louisa all morning, to no avail. There was nothing in particular that he wanted her for, only to tell her that Roper had come to value some paintings and bric-a-brac. Keeping her abreast of things might gain her trust, making him seem honest and reliable.

I'm not the man you think I am, he longed to tell Louisa. To make her see that he did not mean to cheat and to lie.

He wanted to tell Marina the very same thing. To make her see that he had cheated and lied.

Chapter Four

Miss Fag telephoned Marina with the news that Daphne had taken ill. It was quite serious, she warned, and to ensure a swift recovery Daphne should be moved to a sanatorium. 'But why?' Marina protested. She held the phone to her ear, listening to Miss Fag's panicked voice, as she scribbled on the invoice the grocer had sent. The diagnosis was influenza and, as a result, Daphne was at risk of developing pneumonia – often the outcome of such seasonal ailments for people with her condition. The sanatorium's bill weighed heavily on her mind. In the meantime, Miss Fag assured Marina that Daphne had been moved to the isolation of their sick room, but for the sake of the other girls, she should be removed from the school. 'Yes, yes, yes,' Marina was barely listening to her. She kept her eyes on the invoice, and with her blunt pencil she engraved a question mark beside the hefty total of the grocer's bill. She could not remember ordering three tins of sardines and shoe polish. 'I'll send the car for her,' Marina said. 'She can stay here until she's better.'

'But the sanatorium...,' Miss Fag tried to argue.

'Is so dreadfully expensive. She'll be perfectly fine at home, I'll keep the windows open.'

As George ferried Daphne home in the car he felt an overwhelming sense of pity for the girl. She was limp, pale-faced and wheezing for breath. The death rattle, Marina resisted from making a joke. 'Should I telephone Glendinning?' he asked Marina as he assisted Daphne into the house.

Marina shot him a stern look. 'Gladys will take her upstairs. Go on darling, follow Gladys.' The housekeeper obeyed the orders and placed a protective hand on Daphne's back. 'I've placed a bell in her room,' Marina said as though it were the most charitable thing anyone had ever done. 'God knows why... I am frightfully busy with work.'

'Of course you are,' George said with an ounce of disgust in his voice. He detested this air of superiority and thought women earning their own living was most unattractive.

She rolled her eyes as she read the invoice. 'Who ordered the sardines and the shoe polish?'

'I did,' George replied in a low, whispery voice as he made for the staircase.

*

George opened the door and carried a tray to Daphne's bedside. She was sitting up in bed, reading a book, and coughing and sneezing. After a few congested groans, she blew her nose on a linen handkerchief that had seen better days.

'Fresh hanky?'

'Yes, please.'

He pulled a white handkerchief from his trouser pocket and handed it to her. Without a hint of squeamishness he took the damp handkerchief and threw it in her laundry bag that hung on the post at the foot of her bed. This seemed nothing more than a common cold or seasonal 'flu, a term that was so often used to over-dramatise a bad strain of the sniffles. Colds were the norm for him; the germs lingered in the carriages of the train that whisked him from the railway station into town. He could sympathise with the aches and pains and the heavy feeling in one's head, but he could not see how Daphne differed from any other healthy person with a cold. Just why she went to that school, he did not know. His mind turned to Sybil and how she often said that children were like goldfish: they either grow to the size of their environment or they become unruly.

'I'm going to take the day off work and look after you,' he assured her. His thoughts drifted to Marina and her intolerance of anyone who needed her. 'Don't ring the bell, darling. We don't wish to disturb mummy, now, do we?'

'No,' she croaked.

'Good girl,' he said as he took the empty glass from her. He would have to bring a jug of water to leave on her bedside cabinet, he would do this just as soon as he returned the tray to the kitchen. Other thoughts came to him, perhaps there were some Beechams powders in the pantry; he'd have to ask Cook. It was no good asking Marina, aside from the occasional sleeping pill, she had an almost pagan attitude to health and self-healing.

*

George was highly animated as they sat in the drawing room. He spoke of the Kindertransport. 'That's German for children's transport,' he helpfully added, much to Marina's annoyance. She loathed being told anything. What was it? she asked, not that she cared. He explained how Jewish children were being rescued from Germany and placed in British homes. 'Foster homes, orphanages, schools and farms, mainly.'

'You'll be getting ideas for High Greenwood,' she snapped.

Yes, perhaps he would.

Daphne sat in the corner of the drawing room reading one of Marina's magazines, and turning the page she stumbled upon the horoscopes. Turning the cover over she noticed the magazine was a week out of date. She wouldn't dare read her horoscope, thinking it was bad luck if it had expired by as little as a day.

Believing in the ancient law of astrology, Daphne often read Marina's horoscope in Miss Fag's newspaper before she returned home for a sporadic visit, as she felt it gave her a head's up on her mother's mood. And, being a Pisces, she braced herself for Marina's dual personality which swung from plain intolerance to passive aggression. George, she knew, was a Cancer. While writing out their charts copied from a book on astrology she had found in the library, Daphne pieced together a small, slightly hare-brained essay on their compatibility.

'Father with his claws trying to catch you. And you the slippery fish, swimming away,' Daphne said.

George smiled and raised his eyebrows from behind the newspaper. 'What type of fish is your mother?'

'A goldfish,' Daphne replied. She wanted to say an electric eel, but she knew Marina would not appreciate the slithering, snake-like imagery.

'Who'd ever heard of such a thing?' Marina said. The corners of her mouth twitched as she resisted a smile.

Chapter Five

A letter arrived from Daphne, written on the pale blue stationary which George had given her for Christmas. *'May I come home at the weekend. P.S. Can Celia come too?'* she wrote in her upward scrawl. Marina crumpled the letter and threw it to one side.

'Who's that from?' George asked as he drank his morning tea and read the newspaper.

'Oh, the child,' she absently replied. 'Oh lovely,' her tone became chipper as she read the royalty cheque that was tucked in the other envelope. She put it in her dressing gown pocket and anticipated a secret outing to buy clothes. They got into a petty argument when she realised he was reading the theatrical reviews. 'You're too late,' she said.

'What for?'

'Pamela Manners. She's gone to New York with her latest play. Something about a female traveller who is taken captive by a tribe of cannibals. I believe the costumes are very revealing in certain parts. Or so I'm told.'

'I'm sure I don't know what you mean.'

It was a pointless thing to say, and he was certain she had only said it to irritate him. Pamela Manners: his first cousin, childhood companion during the summer holidays, first love and so forth. He hadn't seen her in years and had no intention of doing so. She was a prig as a girl, and now as a famous actress, he was certain she would be intolerable.

'The last I heard she was off her head on morphia, the same goes for that brother of hers. *Gerald.*'

'Don't you?' she pressed him.

'Don't I what?'

'Know what I mean.'

'I knew her as a child. We didn't see one another from one summer to the next, what with her being thousands of miles away in South Africa,' he became defensive, rising to her goading.

'Unrequited love and all that.' She meant it as a tease but he took offence. And yes, as he suspected, she was momentarily fixated with Pamela Manners; the phantom relative, the beautiful actress on the cover of magazines and featured in the same periodicals that advertised her books. Perhaps it was because Pamela was known to her and she knew how he had once felt about her. She wasn't sure why she was attacking him, or why she cared so much, except that little else stirred him and this had struck a nerve.

'No. I was going to say I wouldn't know her these days. But you know, I imagine you two would get along.'

'And what's *that* supposed to mean?'

'The f-f-famous actress and the great authoress.'

She sighed, defeated.

Silly quarrels aside, George had something on his mind and he intended to discuss it with Marina. He wanted to know why she refused Daphne the treat of coming home at the weekend. School was not that far away and she could easily take the car to the school or drive to the station to collect her. If he was at home all day he would have spent more time with her but, as he had told Marina when Daphne was small, that was *her* job. And, since they could not afford a nanny or a governess, for the first eleven years of her life, Daphne experienced a semi-feral childhood roaming around High Greenwood, playing on the endless stretch of lawns and shadowing Cook and Gladys; the latter in particular had a soft spot for the girl.

When she was in Marina's care, her favourite thing to do was to say, 'Let's play a game.' And, naturally the child was eager to do so. 'Let's pretend you're a mouse,' she would say.

'Okay,' Daphne would whisper, enchanted by the idea.

'Let's see how quiet you can be.'

'But mummy, mice squeak. *Squeak, squeak, squeak,*' she whimpered.

'You're a mouse and I'm a cat, so you'd best be quiet or you'll be my lunch,' Marina menaced.

He did his best, but his role of father was not nearly as important as Marina's place in Daphne's life, he thought. She ought to try harder.

'You're certainly spending a lot of time at home,' Marina said, disturbing his thoughts.

They were both silent for a moment before George quietly coughed. 'Yes. Yes, I am.'

'Why?'

'I've had a lot of things to do around the house,' seemed a sufficient answer. But it was not what she wanted to hear. 'Actually, I am glad you've brought it up. I'm leaving tomorrow, as a matter of fact. I've some business to take care of in town and, as I imagine it'll run on a bit, I think it's best if I stay there too.'

'Suit yourself,' she shrugged.

*

George took the car and drove into town, the steering wheel creaked as it turned the corner, and he prayed it would not conk out on the journey. 5A Morrow Square, the address was scribbled inside his pocketbook. He had a vague idea of where it was: he recalled it was on the outskirts of town, close to the river. It took forty-five minutes to drive to town and a further ten to look for the flat.

It was a five-storey townhouse overlooking the river, as he had thought, and Louisa's flat was on the very last floor. He opened the stained-glass doors and walked along the empty hallway, his shoes clicking on the parquet floor. A dog barked from behind a closed door as he climbed the stairs, looking out for number 5A. There it was. A brown door with the name Miss L. Greenwood written on the postbox, in the hallway. He thought about running back down, going outside and finding a phone-box to telephone first. Before he could put his plan into practice the door opened. 'I'll schedule a lesson for next Wednesday,' a middle-aged woman said as she left.

He thought he had stopped at the wrong flat. The sound of Louisa bidding the woman goodbye confirmed it was the correct one. 'Hello,' he called out, rapping the opened door.

Louisa walked into view. 'Oh,' she said, 'what are you doing here?'

George looked around the room. It was a hexagon shaped flat, with high ceilings and bay windows. A woman's overcoat hung on the hook behind the door and a tea set was on display on a sideboard behind the sofa. How ordinary it all looked.

'So...,' she lit a cigarette and pushed open a window. 'What brings you here?' She kept her eyes on the street below. Smoking and flicking the ash out the window, keeping her back to him at all times, waiting for him to reveal why he had come.

'I've got to talk to you, Louisa.'

'Yes?'

'It's all so awful. So bloody awful.' He stood before her, cap in hand, his shoulders slumped.

She turned to look at him. 'What is it?' And, before he could reply, she pointed to the sofa. 'Take a seat.'

He sat down, keeping his cap in his hands. His coat hung over the edge of the sofa, how small and frail he looked. 'I've made up my mind. I am g-g-going to sell High Greenwood.'

'Oh?'

'My God, if I don't act now I'll drag everyone down with me. I have a few schemes up my sleeve but, regardless, the house must go.'

Louisa appeared calm, in spite of the news. He had not meant to blurt it out, but he was relieved it was out in the open.

'I haven't told Marina.' Panic appeared in his voice. 'I don't know how I *will* tell Marina. Christ, putting a gun to my head would be kinder on them all, at least the insurance would pay out.'

'Not for suicide, darling.'

He put his head in his hands and took three deep breaths. 'I c-c-can't sleep. I lie awake at night wondering what will happen to the house. Two centuries of custodians and I mess everything up. I've gone through most of the money, after mother died I had to get rid of the staff. I've had the paintings valued to see what they'll fetch. The Gainsborough will be sold to a museum.'

'The Gainsborough?' she appeared concerned.

'Oh don't worry, Louisa, I'll see that you get your share. Why do you think I've come here?'

'I don't know. To tell me about the house.'

There it was, his old foe the stutter. Don't think about it, he told himself. Breathe, don't think about stuttering. The Australian chap who taught him his exercises was very good, but an expense he could not justify. But he reminded himself of the advice he had given him. He took a deep breath, and paused before he began.

'To tell you that I can't go on paying you.' He noticed her eyes narrowing with resentment, he knew she would begin to berate him, to threaten him. 'S-S-So, you may go ahead with your long-standing threats to tell Marina what happened. It's what you've been longing to do, isn't it?'

She stared at him, speechless.

'Isn't it?' he demanded.

She pursed her lips and turned her head away from him. 'You had better go,' she said. 'Joan will be home any minute.'

*

When the girls left for the weekend it was only Daphne and Celia who remained behind, except for Marianne the Roman Catholic boarder who disappeared to the school chapel for a rigorous weekend of praying and penance. They spent the long, drawn-out weekends indoors in the cold dormitory or walking around the silent grounds, but never too far, as that was Miss Fag's rule. She allowed them to dine with her and the three or four teachers who did not visit friends or family. And every other Saturday she would drive them into town in her rickety Morris motorcar.

'Have you written to your mothers?' Miss Fag asked on this particular Saturday.

'Yes,' they replied without looking up from the bag of marbles Miss Fag had bought them.

'I don't know why I bother,' Daphne said as she picked up a Devil's Eye marble. 'She never bothers to write back.'

The sleeve of Celia's coat slid back and Daphne could see the gold bangles glistening in the sun. She had asked Celia if she could try them on, but Celia said no: they were a secret and not even her mother knew of them.

'Your mother's frightfully busy. It's not easy being a novelist, you know,' Miss Fag reminded her.

'Maybe she's up the duff,' Celia's eyes twinkled with mischief. She intended to shock Miss Fag, and it seemed to work for the old woman pushed the gear stick until it made a cranking noise and she accidentally hit the window wipers as she turned the corner.

'What's up the duff?'

'Oh you know, pregnant.' Celia held a marble to her eye and studied it. 'It can make people sort of silly.'

Daphne pulled a horrified face and turned to look out the window. She recalled hearing the word, only once, when her father told Marina that his sister was pregnant again. The emphasis was on again. It certainly wasn't a word she'd ever heard on the BBC. Making a mental note of this strange word, which she gathered related to babies, she had trotted off to the library and rummaged through the sagging shelves to find an encyclopedia. A quick glance down the index told her to turn to *R* but the pages about reproduction were torn out. It was Sybil who had removed them, hoping to preserve her daughters' modesty, especially after that ghastly business with her youngest daughter Louisa, whom they all agreed had been the victim of a sick perversion.

Perhaps Celia's statement was not so far-fetched. Marina had been extremely nice and motherly to Celia when she had the nightmare. Celia told her it had something to do with seeds and how they scattered and grew. Daphne thought of George's self-seeding plants growing in the flowerbeds at High Greenwood and how Marina hated them, she preferred bulbs because at least they stayed in one place. She liked things to be tidy, manageable, like an instant death or dying on one's birthday. That was good form, she thought.

Miss Fag interrupted this imagery when she swooned, 'He who has a garden wants for nothing. That's a quote by Cicero, you know.'

The girls made an unattractive hissing sound as they stifled their giggles. Miss Fag was beginning to wonder what sort of homes they came from. They appeared to her not as two well-bred girls from good homes and decent parentage, but as two foundlings thrown together. Thank God they have each other, she thought as she flashed them a smile through the windscreen mirror.

They returned to a letter from Mrs Hartley, the first in two months. Celia snatched it from Miss Fag's hands and ran to the bench below the cluster of willow trees.

'Sorry, dear,' Miss Fag put her hand on Daphne's shoulder. 'None for you.'

Daphne gave her an apologetic smile, she felt sorry that Miss Fag was disheartened by Marina's lack of interest.

'Daphne, come here,' Celia ordered. She walked to the bench and pushed the wet leaves out of the way and sat down. Celia looked at the letter and then at Daphne. 'Mummy says she has taken a house in town and that as soon as Pitā gets here we'll all live together.'

'That's good, isn't it?'

'It's rotten.' Celia scrunched the letter into her fist and dropped it next to Daphne.

'Oh, look,' Daphne unfolded the letter. 'She says you three can take a holiday.'

There were tears in Celia's eyes. She rested her head against the trunk of the tree and took a deep breath before letting out a sigh.

*

Marina was a firm believer in the philosophy that it took a lifetime to build something and only a moment to tear it down. It had been months since the upheaval of George's coming and going, his frequent trips to town, his disappearance without warning and the unpredictable pendulum of his mood-swings governing the atmosphere at High Greenwood.

The paintings left the house and were sold at auction or to private buyers. The money they fetched was decent but it was swallowed up by the mounting debt. An ornate clock was sold to a Swiss baroness, one of the more valuable spoils of war from the Battle of Waterloo, and a Louis XVI table left the house. George did not clarify if the table was sold or not, or where it went to, only the physical emptiness of where it had once stood was a reminder that it was gone. Marina asked what on earth he had done with the money. He said it was paid into the bank account he used to run the house and that it went towards paying off some debt. Still, in the midst of his shameful estate sale, she pressed on with her book.

Louisa wrote to him at High Greenwood, a daring move, for they had once struck an agreement that she would disappear from family life altogether. He could not chastise her for it, he had broken the agreement when he telephoned her all those months ago. Where was her money? she demanded to know. He slipped off to the library to telephone her to say he was waiting for a cheque to clear. 'Liar!' she accused. 'You're fobbing me off. You're stringing me along!' she wailed. After threatening once again to come to the house, he gave in.

He asked Marina to loan him a few quid until the phantom cheque cleared. It was an embarrassing thing for him to have to do and, although she had sighed and rolled her eyes, she agreed and it bought him some time. If only he could wait until they were out of the house he might get away with cutting Louisa off once and for all.

'Daphne will be coming home soon,' Marina said as she opened her cheque book, poised to write the figure he had asked for.

'Oh, good,' he said, keeping his back to her.

'She did ask to spend the holidays with that ghastly girl... what's-her-name?'

'I know who you mean.' He looked out the window and pretended to watch something in the distance.

Marina shook her head as if to say 'look at how exasperated I am'.

'Come on,' he turned to look at her. 'She's not that bad. I recall the last time she was here, she was quite lively. Made us all laugh.'

'She told Daphne about S-E-X.'

'No? Oh God,' George was horrified. Not his little Daphne. 'What did she tell her?'

'Nothing, really. Nothing accurate, thank God. It was more of a lesson on photosynthesis and something about sculptures at a Sun Temple, in India, that is.'

George blinked and raised his eyebrows and looked down at the floor. He was troubled by the thought.

'So, we agree? No trip to Dieppe with the Hartleys?'

'Over my dead body,' he said.

At least they could agree on something. She passed him the cheque and he glanced at the figure and folded it in half. The ink was barely dry when he put it in his pocket.

'What's it for?' Marina asked before he left. She watched as his back stiffened and he hesitated before answering. He had told her to leave the cheque blank except for the figure, he would fill in the rest.

He was ashamed he had not thought up a good alibi, so he lied. 'You... you remember Mr Roper?' He paused for a moment before continuing with his deceit. 'He sent in his bill.'

That old chestnut, she was tempted to say. She meant the lie, and not the man.

Chapter Six

The school holidays had begun and Daphne returned home looking as though she had grown a foot taller, which quite unnerved George who longed for her to stay little forever. The oppressive feeling that she was once again backed into a corner overwhelmed Marina. The blissful warmth of summer could not silence the whispers of war. It loomed in the air, signalling a calm before the storm. The heat and humidity of late August ached with lethargy, and George and Marina lazed around the house, snapping at one another and suffering long silences, punctuated by her sighs.

Celia came to High Greenwood for a week before she left for Dieppe with her mother and father. She stropped around in a surly mood. She told Daphne she hated the new house that her mother had chosen for them, how it was much more comfortable than High Greenwood but not quite – there was not one servant except for a daily helper who tidied the house and irritated Mrs Hartley by putting everything back in the wrong place. Her father had taken a job at a tea factory in town, where he sat on the board of directors. It was a step down, Celia complained (in her mother's tone of voice, no less) but she said, as she rolled her eyes to high heaven, 'We're all together.'

The cheeky, boisterous outbursts that were once funny had become cruel and callous, even Marina noticed there was a hardness to Celia. She thought it was her age, all sweet young girls cross that threshold sooner or later. Their behaviour suggested this, and they hung around the house, their bodies draped across the furniture.

'Go outside,' Marina ordered them. She could not stand their constant presence.

Celia dragged behind Daphne as she walked to the woodland. She was tired and had no enthusiasm for anything. 'Let's go swimming,' Daphne said, knowing how much Celia enjoyed the lido in town.

'I don't want to,' she moaned, then her voice quickened to a dismissive shrill, 'besides, that's for babies!'

'You never minded before.'

'Yes,' Celia snapped. 'But I'm bigger now, and older. I'm older than you, remember. You've yet to catch up with me.'

Daphne wondered if Celia's churlish mood had something to do with the fading bruises on her bare arms, close to her shoulders. They seemed to travel up her body, the rest were probably hidden by her clothes.

'What happened to your arms? Did you fall?'

'Of course not.' Celia tugged at the sleeve of her dress. 'Stop asking me boring questions.'

Daphne asked what Celia would like to do instead of swimming. 'Nothing,' Celia replied. 'Where is your bicycle?' she asked after a moment of silence.

'In the garage, why?'

'I'd like to cycle to the station.'

'I could ask Gladys for hers and we could go together.'

'No, you stay here and swim. I want to go by myself.'

Daphne felt hurt by Celia's blatant rejection. It pierced through her heart, wounding her completely. 'Okay,' she tried not to cry.

'Great!' Celia leapt to her feet and made for the door. 'If you're especially nice to me I'll tell you a secret. But not now.'

Hours had passed and the sky blackened, there was a distant rumble of thunder before a torrential downpour. Nobody appeared to notice that Celia was missing, and Daphne remained in her bedroom awaiting her return. Finally, she heard the gravel crunching beneath the bicycle and looking out the window, she saw Celia pushing it up the driveway, soaked from the rain. Gladys let her in, and she came to Daphne's bedroom, her hair dripping wet, and demanded a bath but Marina had used the last of the hot water.

'No matter.' She pulled off her wet cardigan and threw it onto the bed.

Daphne fetched her a towel and she dried her hair. 'Where did you go? You were gone for ages.'

'Oh, you know, I went here and there,' Celia sighed. 'Is this new?' she asked as she picked up an amethyst coloured bottle of scent. Before Daphne could reply that it was a cast-off of Marina's, Celia sprayed the scent onto her wrist and made a petulant face at its smell. 'I've got a boyfriend, he's awfully nice.' She put the lid back onto the bottle and pretended to read the label. 'That's where I went to. I went to see him.'

Daphne thought Celia was joking. She laughed and asked, 'Really? Where did you meet him? We don't know any boys.'

'I met him a while ago. Remember that time you were sick and Miss Fag sent you home? I went home for the weekend and that's how I met him. His mum works on the radio.'

'Is she a singer?'

'A singer?' Celia closed her eyes and giggled. 'No! She's the tea lady. Mummy would have a fit if she knew.'

The entire foundation on which their friendship was built began to disintegrate. Theirs was a friendship that was formed on an exclusive, affectionate bond toward one another, for they had nobody else, nor did they want another friend intruding on their tight circle. Daphne was speechless, she tried to speak but the words would not form. Her neck tensed up, the shock of which made her feel light-headed. She wanted to verbally react but her brain would not engage with her mouth.

'What's up?' Celia asked with a friendly, understanding smile. A patronising gesture that served to make Daphne feel worse. 'Don't cry. Here.' She pulled off her bangles and threw them in Daphne's direction. 'You can try these on. Go on, I allow you.'

'You're a vain, selfish little tart and I hate you!' Daphne screamed as she fled the room. She ran downstairs to the drawing room, she did not intend to go in but she wanted to leave her bedroom to escape Celia.

George stood up, thinking something terrible had happened to her. Marina remained seated, but looked up from her magazine. She told them how Celia had sneaked into town to meet her boyfriend. The words came out so rapidly that she gasped for breath, the tears streaming down her face. Marina did not appear to be fazed, but George walked to Daphne and said she had done the right thing by telling them. He explained that something bad might have happened to Celia and how it would be their responsibility if it had happened while she was their guest. The best thing to do, he said, was to ring Mr and Mrs Hartley and send Celia home.

Daphne blinked and looked at the carpet, her mouth twitched downward. She sniffed and took a deep breath and looked up when George came back into the room.

'It's all settled,' he said. 'I'll drive her home. I would've put her on the seven o'clock train but who knows if she'd actually go home.'

Daphne sat on the armchair, from where she had a view of the hallway. She could see Celia as George picked up her bag. Their eyes met and Daphne looked away. Judas, she thought she heard her say.

They heard the front door closing and the car engine starting. Marina blew out a heavy puff of smoke, as though she had been holding it in until they left. Or to punctuate the melodramatic scene. Daphne sighed, quietly, her shoulders sloping forward.

'You'll see her after Dieppe,' Marina said.

'She had bruises on her arm,' Daphne said, still believing the bruises were to blame for her odd behaviour.

'Where did they come from?'

'I don't know. She has them, sometimes. Do you think somebody harmed her?'

'You know her better than anyone. What do you think?'

Daphne shrugged.

*

It was a scorching day, the hottest it had been all summer or as long as Marina could remember. She and George sunned themselves on the lawn, barely speaking a word to one another. The heat made her irritable, and she pushed her hair, which had gradually lost its wave, off her face. Daphne appeared in view, trudging in their direction.

'Please drive me to the station,' she asked George. She sounded exasperated, which Marina sensed was put on.

'What for?' Marina asked.

Daphne glanced in her direction. The sight of Marina, reclining in a green bathing suit, filled her with an unexplainable rage. Its elasticated material flattened her chest and skimmed over her hipbones, and Daphne could make out the dent of her bellybutton. 'Because I want to see Celia,' she snapped.

'Let me fetch the keys,' George was about to get up.

'No,' Marina said, firmly. 'It's too hot. Besides, I thought the Hartleys were in Dieppe.'

'They don't leave until tomorrow.'

Marina said no. She was concerned that the hot roads would burst the car's tyres. The thought of becoming stranded on a roadside, and bearing the expense of new tyres, was too grim to bear.

'Fine, I'll cycle to the station.'

'Don't contradict me,' Marina said.

'Your mother's right,' George agreed with her sentiment, but not her delivery. 'Besides, I'm sure the Hartleys have a lot to do for their trip. Packing and so forth. You don't want to intrude.'

Daphne stormed off and went into the house to change. She re-emerged with a book and a blanket. Choosing a spot within their view, she fell onto the grass, dramatically.

'For God sake,' George said as he caught sight of Daphne in her old summer clothes. 'Buy the girl some decent things, will you?'

Marina lowered her sunglasses to the tip of her slender nose and peered over them. Daphne was oblivious that they were scrutinising her appearance. The top she wore, smocked-by-hand by Gladys, was tight against her torso and crept up her midriff.

'Well,' she fixed her sunglasses, 'if you're so concerned, you buy her something.' She made a flippant hand gesture in Daphne's direction, 'Besides,' she told George, 'it's just puppy fat, but if you want to waste your money...' She turned onto her stomach, exposing her pale back to the blistering sun. 'Shall I leave my cheque book out for you?' She had meant to wound him.

'No need,' he turned to her, inadvertently placing his hand on her leg as he did so. He meant it as a confiding gesture. 'The Aubusson rug f-f-fetched quite a ransom.' He knew she liked that rug and for a moment it gave him great pleasure to tell her. He could pay Louisa for three months, at least.

'Well,' she sighed, 'you're the boss.' She pushed her arms forward, and twisted her wrists as she stretched her fingers. 'Do me a favour, George?'

'Yes?'

'Remove your hand from my leg.'

*

Daphne went to bed filled with resentment for her parents, her mother in particular. In her mind she called Marina an evil bitch, a nasty bitch, a bitch in general. Celia had taught her such words. She thought of school starting and how excited she was to return to normality. How she could see Celia every day. She got up and went to her dressing table, lifting Celia's bangles off it. Celia had urged her to return them at once, but how could she when George refused to drive her to the station? She slid them onto her wrist and, raising her arm to admire them, they fell towards her elbow. Three types of gold, as Celia had pointed out; the platinum was the last one she had received, before they shipped her off to school. It must have been a going away present. Daphne felt envious all over again. Celia had told her that Uncle Christopher had said she was a special girl.

George hovered behind Marina's door, of two minds whether to enter or not. The ghoulish moaning of the door caught her attention and she turned around, quickly.

'You made me jump,' she said.

It was an odd night, pitch black with a moonless sky. She had been listening to the cry of a vixen which, before moving to High Greenwood, she had mistaken for a woman screaming. It was a sinister sound, and she still felt a rush of panic whenever one cried out. 'Help!' it seemed to screech.

'The, ah, the Aubusson rug,' he began, 'you're not very c-c-cross, are you?'

She could tell he was nervous or upset, but she cared little. Without answering she went to her dressing table and sat down. She reached for her hairbrush and began to drag the bristles through her hair.

'Because I could, I could…,' he stopped to gather his composure. 'I could get it back.'

'Don't bother.' She held out her wrist for him to unhook the clasp of her bracelet. He did so, without speaking. 'It's only a rug,' she shrugged, hoping he would go away. He placed a caring hand on her shoulder. 'Careful,' she flinched. 'Sunburn.'

'Well,' he kissed her on top of the head, 'goodnight.'

*

It was a long, drawn-out day. The sunless sky reflected the pessimistic tone of High Greenwood that morning. George entered the room just as Daphne ate the last of the three biscuits Cook had given her. Lately, she felt constantly hungry and Marina said she ate like a horse. George looked at her and although not meaning to wound, he said, 'I shouldn't eat that, if I were you. You're getting tubby, darling.'

'God,' Marina spat, her eyes wincing with hatred. 'You really are a bastard, aren't you?'

Daphne blushed from the swear word, and from the ridicule. She felt a pang in her heart and wanted to cry.

'Do you need me to do anything?' he asked in a tiresome voice. 'I mean, around the house or...,'

'No, why?' Marina talked over him.

'I suppose I'll go fishing, then.'

'It's going to rain,' Marina said, accusingly.

He left, and Marina sat in silence for a few moments. The ticking of the clock was the only sound until Daphne sighed.

'I don't feel well,' she said, her mouth twitching downwards.

'Go to bed,' Marina ordered her.

Daphne had a dull headache, a heavy feeling lingered in her body; she was exhausted and irritable, and too wound up to sleep or take a nap. She went up to her bedroom and lay across the bed, but time went just as slowly, and she silently wished summer would speed up so she could escape her mother and the house. She wondered if that thing would happen again: the *thing* Marina had told her to expect. It was something disgusting, Marina had warned her, something to do with having babies. Her mind turned to Celia's seed theory and how she said everyone had seeds inside of them, like apples. 'In school chapel,' Celia had once said, 'why do you think Miss Fag says fruit of thy womb?' Even Daphne thought this revolting and on par with Marina's disgust.

Downstairs, Marina smoked and contemplated the scene which had played out. As she exhaled the smoke, it dawned on her why Daphne felt ill. It made her feel conspicuous, but inconvenienced all the same. She emitted a deep sigh as she stubbed out the cigarette, and she slowly got up and walked out of the room, feeling quite light-headed.

Marina climbed the stairs and caught Daphne as she walked stiffly across the landing. She stood several feet below her, the dynamic was off. 'Daphne,' she said, stopping her in her tracks. 'Do you feel sick?' Daphne nodded. And then, in a low voice, Marina asked, 'Is it your... that thing I mentioned?' She could not bring herself to say the word and she loathed hinting and talking in riddles.

She shook her head, her cheeks burning. Marina knew she was lying or adhering to the secrecy that had now been instilled in her. She narrowed her eyes, but Daphne did not relent. Clever girl, Marina thought.

The ringing of the telephone took them by surprise. How Marina loathed the sound. She glanced over the balustrade, and from her bird's-eye view she wondered if Gladys was going to come out and answer it.

'Oh I forgot to tell you,' Daphne did not make eye contact. 'Gladys had to nip out. She told me to tell you, but I forgot.' She walked away, saved by the telephone.

The ringing continued and Marina let out another deep sigh and rolled her eyes, pointless since Gladys was not around to see how annoyed she was. She walked down the stairs and pulled the phone off its dial. 'Yes?' she said as her earring bashed off it.

It was a telephone call from town and Marina agreed to accept. 'Mrs Hartley,' she said, quite surprised as she had very little to do with the woman and thought she had left for Dieppe. She had spoken to her about five times, if that. It was an odd experience, for as awkward as Marina felt talking to Mrs Hartley, she could not process the information she had been told. Celia was dead. Celia Hartley, the plump, irascible, spoilt, uppity little madame – all those things she had once called her – was dead. Mrs Hartley told her in the most cordial manner, only once did her voice wobble, towards the end, at the word dead. She seemed to be holding her breath, and only spat the word out to stop herself from making an unattractive squeaking sound. Marina said how sorry she was and to ring if she, or Mr Hartley, needed anything. What could they possibly need?

When the phone call was over Marina kept her gaze on the corner of the hallway where the umbrella stand was, and noticed her brolly was missing. Then, the chiming of the clock coming from the living room brought her back to the present. In a split second everything became frantic. She moved to the bottom of the stairs, she did not rush but she seemed to react quicker than usual.

'Daphne,' she yelled. 'Daphne,' her voice became more urgent.

Upstairs, Daphne flinched at the sound of Marina calling her name. She had never heard Marina scream, or shout, or raise her voice. Her heart started to race and her blood pounded in her ears. She imagined she had a dam inside of her, filled with blood, and ready to burst.

'Yes?' Daphne called in a forced, casual voice. 'What's the matter?' She got up, her legs shook as she walked to the staircase, where she sat down on the middle stair, peering at her mother through the gaps in the balustrade.

'Come here.' Marina held out a spidery hand. 'Come on, come here,' she coaxed.

Daphne could tell she had suffered some sort of shock; her breathing was short and rapid, and she had tiny beads of sweat on her forehead, between her eyes.

Marina took a deep breath and stopped. She felt like saying something else, something to deviate from the truth. She rubbed her forehead with the front of her hand and, pressing her knuckles down the bridge of her nose, she closed her eyes for a second.

'There's been an accident...,'

She thought it was her father, and she predicted from the pained look in Marina's eyes that it had been fatal. 'No,' she said in a panicked voice. Her leg shook as she made a quivering sound, trailing off from the 'no'. She tried to hold her breath, to gather her thoughts and imagine what her reaction should be.

'Celia's...,' Marina said, her voice punctuated with a regretful sigh. 'Celia's dead.'

For a moment Daphne did not comprehend what Marina had said. When the cloud of disbelief lifted from her brain, she could see Marina far more clearly. She noticed the look of pity in her eyes and the concerned expression across her face. That's when it hit Daphne and she felt as though the floor had been pulled from beneath her feet, as though she were falling and could not stop. Everything was light; she was disengaged from her movements, floating outside of her body, watching the mirage that was Marina, the scribbled lines of her arms moving from side to side.

'How,' her mouth opened to speak. Hysteria choked her every word into a series of incomprehensible gasps. 'How... how,' she tried to speak. 'How,' she tried once more.

'How did she die?' Marina finished the sentence.

For a few seconds, which seemed like several minutes, she watched her mother's lips move without hearing a sound. Her long, thin arm reached out to grab Daphne as her legs buckled.

'She was crossing the road...' She held Daphne by the shoulders and looked into her eyes, willing her to calm down. 'She was hit by a car.'

'A car?' Daphne closed her eyes to stifle the tears, her voice was shrill.

'Yes. It happened the night before last.' Marina's voice trailed off, Daphne could no longer hear it. 'Mrs Hartley just didn't have the courage to tell you. And she's sorry about that.'

Hours had passed since Marina had broken the news of Celia's death, though to Daphne time was of little consequence. They sat in silence, with Marina letting out small sighs as she looked out the window.

'I do know how you feel,' Marina said carefully, as if she did not know what to say at all. 'I was quite young when my mother died, but it's not the same as a friend, I do realise.' She thought her grief far more superior, more intense. 'There's no point dwelling on it.' She reached across and patted Daphne's hand. 'You can't change anything.'

George walked in during their exchange, timing was not his forte. He entered the room and was surprised by the sight of Daphne lying across the sofa with Marina sitting on the edge. Perhaps sensing he was about to make a joke, Marina stood up and stretched out her arm, as though to ward off a blow. In her gentle voice, she told him about Celia, which, despite the content, the sound was oddly comforting to Daphne.

'Oh my,' George swallowed before finishing his sentence. 'Poor thing.'

Daphne sat up and looked at her father, she knew he was going to cry; she could tell by the quivering of his mouth and how he coughed profusely as he spoke.

'How did it happen?'

'She was knocked over,' Marina's voice was so low it was a whisper. 'A terrible accident, really.'

'Yes,' George agreed, though he appeared agitated. 'A terrible, terrible accident.'

*

'When can I see her?' Daphne asked over breakfast. George was at work, and Marina came down to the breakfast table, despite not eating anything and only drinking black coffee which made her heart palpitate. And then she added, 'Can I see her?'

'I'm not sure,' Marina began slowly. She did not know if it would be an open coffin, or if the Hartleys wanted Celia's body to be viewed. The accident, her being hit by a car. 'It might not be pleasant, darling.' She did not want to elaborate why, but she sensed Daphne understood.

'I think I can handle it.' She had become hardened to the news, was putting on a bravado. Marina knew from experience that this was shock.

Marina took another sip of the bitter coffee. 'Well, I'll give Mrs Hartley a ring this morning.'

'What does a dead body look like? I mean, I know they're supposed to be sleeping. Isn't that right?'

'Well it depends on the circumstances. Celia... Celia was knocked over. She might,' she paused, searching for the right words, 'her injuries could mean the coffin isn't open. It might be best if you remember her the way she was. So pretty, and so full of life.'

Daphne sighed and looked down at the edge of the table. She wanted to accuse Marina of talking her out of it, of making life easier for herself so she would not have to ring Mrs Hartley.

'But,' she began once more, 'if it is an open coffin then I'm sure her injuries have been fixed up. They cover them in make-up, and other things.'

'Like when Granny Sybil died?'

'Well...,' Marina forced herself to remember that awful day. 'Yes. But she died of the consumption so she looked quite unpleasant in general. It wasn't... it wasn't a nice thing, really. I'd rather forget it.'

As it turned out, Mrs Hartley telephoned High Greenwood and was greeted by the unfamiliar voice of Gladys, who took a message. Celia's body was at the chapel of rest in town and she invited the Greenwoods to view the body, if they cared to. This saved Marina the effort of not only gathering her nerve to make the call, but the forced sincerity she would have to evoke. Not that she wasn't sorry, she was just hopeless at that sort of thing.

Marina decided it would be best to go in the late afternoon, and they took the train into town. All the way there, she hoped Daphne would change her mind and not want to see the body, though she realised if that was the case, she'd tell her off for causing all this fuss. She wore a new cardigan that day, and she cursed herself for doing so because the wool was scratchy, and the sunlight beating through the carriage window made her unbearably hot. She would have taken it off but was afraid of leaving it behind, and so she suffered in silence.

'You don't have to do this,' she told Daphne. She could tell Daphne wanted to cry, or was on the verge of tears, because she took short, deep breaths. 'Where did you get those bracelets?' She pointed to Celia's bangles on Daphne's wrist.

'They're Celia's, she left them at the house on the night...,'

'Right, well I suppose you can give them to Mrs Hartley at the...' She also gave up, she could not say the word. Instead she smiled at Daphne and eyed the bracelets, which she knew at first glance must have cost a small fortune.

The walk from the station to the funeral parlour struck Marina as odd and overwhelming. She had not noticed before how busy town was on a summer's day. It was an unremarkable observation, but that was how she felt. Everything felt intensely alive; children in sun-hats and women in sundresses, people sitting on walls and benches and loitering outside shops, complaining of the heat and eating ices. She shivered as they went down the side-street to the funeral parlour, it was dull and shaded from the sunlight.

The door creaked as Marina pushed it open. The funeral church smelled of beeswax, dust and floral wreaths. 'I think she's in there,' she said as they approached another door.

'How do you know?'

'Ah, Celia Hartley. I was right.' Her name was on the door.

'You go first,' Daphne said.

Marina pushed the door open, enough to catch a glimpse of Celia and to slam it shut if the sight was an unpleasant one. She almost sighed with relief when it was not.

'It's all right.' She stepped forward. 'Daphne, it's all right.'

But it was not all right, and Daphne sheepishly entered the room with her eyes fixed forward, in Celia's direction. The coffin was on a stand, a fair haired girl was inside it. She let out a piercing wail, followed by incoherent screaming. 'No!' she yelled, over and over. Although Marina had not been expecting it she reacted by pulling Daphne close to her, and forcing her head to turn around, against her chest, to avoid the sight before her. It was not an awful one; she merely saw a dead body with no sign that anything untoward had happened, or that the death had been a painful one.

Daphne was still hysterical when they left the funeral church and her wailing echoed through the side street. Marina was certain people would assume she was being attacked and she urged her to take a deep breath, to sit on the edge of the pavement. To throw up. Anything, to stop the awful racket.

Their plan was to call in on George at the office and go to tea. He wanted to know how Daphne had got on, perhaps he felt Marina was inadequate in comforting the girl. Instead, Marina made the decision to return home immediately, and she found a phone-box and called George. Daphne waited outside the door, but she could hear her mother's voice travelling through the glass.

'Awful,' Marina said. 'Awful.'

*

They had an early night on the eve of the funeral. Daphne walked ahead without speaking to her parents and went to her bedroom. Marina was about to call out, to remind her to have her bath before bed and not in the morning because that's when she wanted one and there might not be enough hot water to go round. The moment was lost and Marina did not pursue it.

'Well,' she said to George, 'goodnight.'

Before he entered his bedroom, he said, 'It was a terrible thing that happened to the girl, wasn't it?'

Marina knew it wasn't a question as such, but she agreed with him. 'Dreadful, I am sure. I was...' She looked down the landing at the strip of light below Daphne's door. Then she looked at George as he opened his bedroom door. Following him inside, she said, 'Gladys was talking to Mrs Hartley, the mother.'

'Oh yes?'

'She said Celia was knocked down by a taxi.'

'By a taxi?' he repeated.

'Quite. Apparently she was out gallivanting at ten o'clock at night. If you ask me, she was asking for trouble.'

'Do you mean to say you think she deserved it?'

'To be killed?' Marina asked. 'No, of course not. What a disagreeable thing to say.'

'I apologise.' He sat on the edge of the bed. 'I'm so terribly fraught. Have you been sleeping?'

Marina was caught off guard by the sudden shift in conversation. 'Yes, quite well,' she lied. 'And you?'

'Not a wink.'

'I am sorry.' She sat down next to him. 'Is anything the matter? What can I do to help?'

'To help?' He shook his head. 'Not a thing.'

'You are all right? I mean, there is nothing you wish to tell me?'

They sat next to one another, on the edge of the bed, like conspirators. If she stayed with him long enough he might tell her, she hoped. But he did not. He took her hand in his, kissed it and said goodnight.

'I do hope whatever is troubling you leaves you alone.'

'Thank you,' she said, though she was not sure what he meant.

*

On the morning of Celia's funeral everything appeared dark and lifeless. It was half-past-eight in the morning when they set off, and there was frost on the car. George held out his hand and said, 'Feels like winter. Autumn's just around the corner.' Marina skirted past him and got into the car. When they were seated she turned to Daphne, who sat quietly in the back.

'Ready?' Steam came out of Marina's mouth when she spoke.

No, Daphne wanted to say. She nodded, her body shivered from the cold.

They stopped off at a shop close to the church so Marina could buy cigarettes. There was a quiet, solemn atmosphere on the street, as though everyone had known a child had died. It was in the local newspaper and various girls from the school offered a snippet, a quote, about Celia. 'She was so nice', 'A lively girl', 'Gone too soon' – the clichés were endless.

When Marina stepped outside she saw a hearse driving behind a bus. She quickened her pace as she went to the car. When she got in she stuffed the magazine she had bought under her seat. It seemed a thoughtless thing to do, as though she were going to the hairdressers or anticipating a long, boring wait. She passed an apple to Daphne.

'Cook said you didn't have breakfast.'

'There wasn't time.'

Marina shot her a look and felt like asking her whose fault it was. Daphne did not have her bath the night before and decided at the last minute, half-an-hour before they were due to leave, that she would like one. So, Marina had to get out of the bath and give her her water. Sensing an argument was brewing, George said, 'All set?' as he started the car.

When the car stopped outside the church, George gripped the steering wheel for a moment before turning off the engine. 'The girl, Celia,' he said as he looked at the coffin in the back of the hearse. 'So young... so terribly young.'

Daphne glanced in its direction and turned away. Her heart began to race and she wanted to grab on to the back of Marina's seat and plead with her not to make her go inside.

Marina put on her gloves. 'Is that the father?' she asked, offhandedly. She thought him terribly handsome with his swarthy skin and dark hair, greying at the temples.

George let out a great sigh as though he had absorbed Mr Hartley's pain and was exorcising him of it.

For the duration of the service, Daphne was flanked by the backs of people in mourning clothes and barricaded by their arms and legs. She felt like a tiny child, trying to jump up and down to see over the tall grown-ups. What was more astonishing to both Daphne and Marina was how George had burst out crying. Marina was mortified, she jabbed him with her elbow and told him to go outside. He leaned over the pew, his head in his hands, crying at the sight of the small coffin.

'What's wrong with you?' Marina hissed. She caught the eye of the people in the opposite pew, looking in their direction.

Daphne refrained from looking towards the altar, where Celia's coffin stood. As long as she did not see it, did not listen to the service, she could maintain the retched empty feeling she had nurtured for days. She tried to take a headcount of the people present. Who were they? She recognised Miss Fag, discreetly dabbing her eyes with a hanky and wilting in a frock coat, and some girls from their dormitory, but she did not know their parents. And, of course, the Hartleys, who seemed as pulverized as she was.

Behind their solemn faces, Mr and Mrs Harley were bewildered by everything. They only knew Daphne, and Mrs Hartley did not immediately recognise Miss Fag when she approached her to offer her condolences. Holding onto Mrs Hartley's wrist, she spoke of Celia in the past tense. Afterwards, Mrs Hartley stood on her tiptoes and scanned the church for Daphne, but she could not see her, she would have recalled her face instantly, but her brain failed to register any form of familiarity.

'I think Mrs Hartley is looking for me,' Daphne told Marina as they filed out of the church, behind the coffin.

'You stay here.' Marina grabbed her by the back of her cardigan, stopping her in her tracks.

The burial took place at Hawthorne Hill, a graveyard on the outskirts of town that overlooked the neat hamlet below, with its steeples and roofs forming a fortress. The taxi driver who had knocked Celia down arrived with a small wreath of flowers, and at the graveside he hid behind the bushes.

As the coffin was lowered into the ground, Marina said, 'Stay with her, I'm going to the car.'

'Don't you feel well?' George asked.

She did not answer and walked away, past the headstones and to the car. Daphne looked up at George and weakly smiled. He trailed behind her as she approached Mr and Mrs Hartley.

'Daphne,' Mrs Hartley announced in a theatrical voice, her teeth were gritted into a tight smile as she placed a limp hand on Daphne's arm. She was so like Celia; the same round face, snub nose and big eyes with straight eyelashes and thin, over-plucked eyebrows. 'You were such a good friend to Celia,' Mrs Hartley said to bolster her spirits.

'This is my father,' Daphne quickly said, accidentally dismissing Mrs Hartley's compliment. It was a foolish thing to say; they had met before.

'My wife and I are very sorry. Celia was...,' he searched for the right word. 'She was a spirited girl.'

'Your mother, is she not here? I thought I saw her at the church.'

'Yes,' George spoke for Daphne. 'I'm afraid my wife doesn't feel well.'

'Oh, I am sorry,' Mrs Hartley said, concerned.

George and Daphne both radiated apologetic smiles. They were sorry they lied.

Marina sat in the car, watching the pitiful sight. She was about to reach under her seat for the magazine when Mr Hartley walked past her. She heard the sound of his shoes on the stones, and she slid down in her seat to avoid him seeing her. How embarrassing if he did, even though he did not know her. She felt terribly self-conscious about the whole thing. He paced back and forth, turning on his heel as he did so and glancing in the direction of the grave. This struck Marina as odd, and she watched him while he repeated this ritual, placing his trembling hands to his forehead, almost covering his eyes. When the voices of the mourners became audible as they went to their cars and made for the gates, he stopped and took a deep breath, bracing himself for goodbyes.

Daphne and George got into the car. It was over. They drove back to High Greenwood in silence, with George at the wheel. Marina kept her eyes fixed on the road in front, and George periodically let out a quiet whistle before giving up on forming a tune. Daphne sighed a few times.

'Well,' Marina announced, 'I don't suppose you'll be seeing the Hartleys ever again.'

'Why not?' Daphne asked. It frightened her to think of the finality of everything.

'Well, you barely knew Celia...,' Marina tried to explain.

'I knew her for over a year. I knew her for a year-and-a-half!' Daphne shouted.

'Yes, darling. Barely no time at all. It's time to move on, to go back to school and to make new friends.'

George gave her a sideways look. 'Steady on,' he mumbled.

Marina lit a cigarette. 'Ghastly girl,' she said as she exhaled smoke.

Daphne rested her head against the corner of the seat, her eyes were fixed on an angry bluebottle thumping off the window, trying to escape. Would she have to explain herself to anyone who might question her grief? She closed her eyes and slipped her hand inside the sleeve of her cardigan, feeling for the bangles she had inadvertently stolen. All she could hear were her mother and father's low voices, barely a muffle over the growl of the engine.

'I don't know about you,' George placed his hand on Marina's, 'but it makes me terribly glad that we're all together.'

'Do stop it, George,' Marina pulled her hand away, as she turned to look out the window. 'I hate it when you're soppy.'

Chapter Seven

The summer of 1939 was one to be forgotten, its events too traumatizing to trivialise in the months to come. The summer of death, Daphne would call it. They were each given a gas mask; 'A horrible piece of apparatus,' Marina said. She slipped it over her head and pulled it off just as quick, complaining that she couldn't see a thing and that it stank. The blackout had been implemented, and Marina watched as Gladys ran up a mountain of black fabric on the Singer in the dining room. George hammered tacks along the frames of the windows, saying he hoped the wood wouldn't split.

'It looks dreadful,' Marina groaned. 'Worse than dreadful. It looks like the Grim Reaper's cloak.' Gladys found the remark funny and was quickly reminded, by George, that war was no laughing matter.

When news broke that the army had officially remobilised, Marina said they were all tempting fate by taking such measures. She wanted it to be true, and she eyed George as he climbed down from the ladders and dropped the hammer onto the floor. He was useless at this sort of thing.

'Sorry,' he said. He could read her mind.

She shrugged.

'Will you miss me when I'm gone?' he teased her.

'Miss you? Why? Where on earth are you going?' She looked away, hoping he would leave.

He folded up the ladders and moved to the door. 'War is coming,' he said as he left.

*

The same practice of hanging blackout curtains was repeated at school, only with a lot more vigour from Miss Fag, who had appointed herself as a sort of blackout warden. Daphne felt as though she were living in a world of permanent darkness, moving through the shrouds of blackout curtains and dimly lit rooms. She longed for the days of sleeping with the curtains wide open, letting the moonlight spill through the window.

'I've come to talk to you,' Miss Fag said as Daphne stood at the dormitory window, looking out at the willow trees. She had not noticed before, how the catkins touched the tip of the lake. The lido as Celia had called it. *Had*, she blinked hard to stop her thoughts. 'There is a girl,' Miss Fag continued.

'Yes?' she said, not quite catching the first part.

'There is a girl,' Miss Fag repeated, 'who will be arriving today. In fact, is that her car?' She crooked her head forward and stared through the rectangular pane. 'Ah, I think it is.' She looked away from the window, her eyes narrowing at the empty bed. 'She's an English girl, a Leonora Farthing. Her father's a playwright, so I am sure you'll have lots to talk about.' Miss Fag patted her on the back before she left to bring Leonora to the dormitory.

When Daphne did lay eyes on Leonora Farthing she was incredibly sweet, very nice, awfully plain looking with skin like the inside of a seashell and hair the colour of corn hanging over the shoulders. She had scoliosis, though Daphne had never heard of the condition. Miss Fag pre-warned the girls about Leonora's back brace and how it was not her fault and that it was rude to stare or to ask questions.

As it turned out Leonora's s-shaped spine had punctured her lung, the result of which meant that she only had one good lung. Not an asthmatic, but something worse. Daphne wondered if Leonora was waiting for her spine to snap and puncture the good lung. Then what? She knew that Miss Fag meant for her to be Celia's replacement, a well-meaning gesture that unnerved her. Of course when they were introduced properly, Daphne smiled and nodded, and watched as Leonora walked timidly to the bed where Celia had slept and set her suitcase on top of it.

'Your father wrote *Rigmarole*, didn't he?' Daphne asked her as she unpacked.

'Yes, you know it?'

'Yes, my father took me to see it three times last Easter.'

The conversation stalled. Daphne turned away and went to her own bed. She wished they had curtains around their beds, it would have helped enormously when avoiding this strange girl who was about to sit on Celia's bed. Did Miss Fag tell her about the terrible accident? She hoped not.

'It's all right,' Leonora said. 'Miss Fag explained what happened. Celia, wasn't it?' When Daphne failed to respond, she continued, 'I'm sure she was a very nice girl. Miss Fag said she was. I'm sorry she died. My mother is dead.'

71

Daphne wanted to turn around and offer an understanding smile but she remained still, unflinching, and unfeeling.

'We can swap beds, if you want?' Leonora caught her off guard.

'That's very nice, but I'm rather used to this one,' Daphne said, though she wanted to swap. She had become so like Marina and she hated herself for it. She wondered if Marina thought as much. 'How did your mother die?' she asked. Perhaps it was an impolite thing to do, but lately the subject of death was all she could think about.

'My father said she died of a heart attack but I know she killed herself. The maid found her in the bath. There was blood everywhere.'

'Why?'

'I don't know exactly.' The way in which Leonora spoke of her mother's death, relaying the facts so coldly, impressed Daphne. 'I think she cut herself, or something. She must have. Once, I heard my stepmother say that my mother had cut her... arms. That must have been it.'

Daphne gave a slight nod as though she were picturing it in her head.

'But my father wrote a play about it called *Blood in the Bath*. It was for adults only, so naturally I didn't see it. It wasn't allowed to open in London but he's turning it into a book, so maybe I'll be able to read it someday. I don't know.'

'Is your father nice?' Daphne asked.

'Yes, I suppose he is.'

'And your stepmother, is she nice?'

'Yes, she was very polite when I met her. She's an actress, but not terribly famous or anything like that. Before I came here, my little brother and I lived with our nanny in a cottage away from the big house. We moved out after my mother... had her... accident.'

Leonora dropped a small pile of clothes as she unpacked her case. Daphne realised she could not bend to pick them up and quickly did it for her. It was quite clumsy, and she blushed as she handed Leonora the things. She wanted to say that Miss Fag had told them about the brace, and she wondered if Leonora herself would mention it. She did not. Daphne thought of her as Joan of Arc in her armour. It might have been a nice thing to say, but she was too shy.

Daphne was relieved when war was declared two days later. It stopped Leonora talking about her mother and probing her for details on Celia. She had sat along with her classmates in the recreational room, all of the girls from her dormitory squashed together in their navy serge pinafores, before heading to church for their weekly dose of religious indoctrination.

A prefect got up and switched on the wireless with great aplomb; it was viewed as a privilege for the girls to listen to it on a Sunday. The static hissing of the wireless as it searched for the station filled the room until it picked up a human presence. 'We interrupt this broadcast...,' the stern voice echoed through the mesh speakers. The girls groans were hushed by the introduction of Neville Chamberlain's commanding tone. Miss Fag stared at the wireless the entire time, as though Chamberlain himself had been sitting opposite her, in the flesh, engaging her in a deep and meaningful conversation.

When the broadcast finished there was complete silence. The worried faces around the room did not trouble Daphne, she was already thinking of home.

*

Marina was in the drawing room listening to the wireless. From the window she could see George, he was taking great strides across the lawn, pushing the lawnmower and attempting to smoke a cigarette at the same time. The familiar voice of Chamberlain caught her attention and she stopped, before that she had been reaching forward to lift her cup of tea off the table in front of her. Now that war had been declared, she felt sick to her stomach. Gone was the bravado of wishful thinking, hoping that it would take George away so she could live without him in the house and be free to do whatever she pleased. It gave her a feeling of deja vu: the untimely death of Celia, Daphne's grief, and now the war. It made her feel anxious, a sickening knot formed in her stomach.

The door opened, and although Marina's back was to the person entering the room, she instinctively knew it was Gladys. 'Go and fetch Sir George,' she said. 'Tell him it's urgent.'

She watched as Gladys met George as he came closer to the stretch of lawn before the window. What Marina failed to do was to tell her not to mention the war. This, she realised, was a grave error. Observing their exchange, she could see Gladys had told him; she was almost giddy about the news she had delivered.

George looked up, he saw Marina standing in the drawing room, in front of the chair she had been sitting on moments before, staring directly at him with a helpless expression on her face. Without acknowledging Gladys, he walked directly towards the house, keeping his eyes on Marina through the window.

When he came into the room, Marina saw the blades of errant grass poking from the holes in his fisherman's jumper, and the sunburn across his nose and brow. Before she spoke, he took the initiative to begin.

'Gladys told me the news.'

'Stupid fool, I told her not to,' she lied.

'I shouldn't get too upset.' He attempted to touch her as he passed. 'It's been a long time coming.' Lighting another cigarette (she watched him throw the other one down before he entered the house) he added, 'There's something I've been meaning to chat to you about.'

The telephone started to ring, distracting from the matter at hand. 'Ignore it. You were saying?'

'It's all right. It can keep for another day.'

The telephone continued to ring, stopping for a moment before ringing again. It mocked any promise of a conversation between the two.

'Answer the bloody phone,' she snapped.

'So sorry,' he said as he left the room.

Later that night he told Marina that he would be enlisting in the war. She asked if he was too old, and he said yes, technically, but he had offered his services all the same. Marina knew what he was hinting at. He had used his influence, had pulled some strings. Just why he wanted to leave for the battlefields puzzled her. There were fit, healthy young men being conscripted, and besides his age he was married, and married men were overlooked in favour of single chaps.

'I know I'm not clued up on world affairs,' she told him as they drank coffee and listened to the wireless, a foolish thing to do since every programme was dominated by war talk. 'But I do know that your credentials are last on the list. This is not meant to wound, darling.'

Wound him it did. He smiled and said, 'You're sweet to worry.' She was not as charitable as that. 'But I've given my word. I can't back-peddle, besides the rest is just petty bureaucracy.'

'You're quite the rebel.'

George laughed.

His regiment would be posted to Malta, but first he would have to leave for his training camp. 'Malta,' Marina said. 'Well that's hardly dangerous. It's practically a holiday.'

'Not dangerous at all, darling,' he assured her, even though he himself was unsure of the predicament.

In a week George would be off to his training camp seventy miles away. He resigned from the bank, and for one week Marina begrudgingly played the role of a dutiful wife. Six days and he'll be gone, she told herself, five days and he'll be gone, and so forth. She pretended it was an unpleasant sabbatical and that it would soon be over. The only thing getting her through the week was the certainty that he would, in fact, be gone. She slept beside him every night, in his bed. A disagreeable bed that was too soft. With his weight on top of her she felt as though she was sinking through the dense mattress. It was all she could think about, as though she were being pushed further and further under, a slow death until she drowned.

On the last night he told her to go into the drawing room, that he had something important he wished to discuss with her. 'You go off tomorrow,' she said, thinking it was that.

That much was true, but not quite. 'This...this. house,' he said as he paced in front of the fireplace, back and forth, making her nervous and irritable. He struggled to get the words out and he attempted to apologise but could not, and so he smiled and hoped she would understand. Finally, he took a deep breath and managed to say, 'This house has been a beast of burden.'

Marina felt the blood drain from her head to the pit of her stomach. She anticipated the rest, but it was worse than she imagined. As it turned out, George was not the only one leaving. Through his riddles and various pauses and pacing, he told her of his money troubles, but not of Louisa and her demands. He would have to lease the house, meaning she would have to leave and take Daphne with her.

'How long have you known?' she managed to ask, though her voice was shaking.

'A long, long time,' he replied as honestly as he could. Somehow he thought that would soften the blow and make her understand.

'A long time?' she said in a low voice, almost empathetic. 'How long?' This time her voice was harder, a shrill note appeared in it. 'How long?' she demanded once more.

'A year. Perhaps longer.'

The realisation that she had been tricked, that she did not see it coming, infuriated her. It made her feel vulnerable, weak. She wanted to cry.

'Please,' he begged her, 'don't tell Daphne of my money woes. I don't wish to rob her of her happiness.'

George left the next day. Marina spent the night in her own bedroom and she watched from the window, discreetly standing off to the side, as he packed his bag into the taxi. He told her to sell the car, but she knew it was worthless. Neither of them made an effort to say goodbye. George caught a glimpse of her before he climbed into the taxi. He raised his hand and said, 'So long.' Although she could not hear him from behind the glass, she read his lips. She lifted her hand and gave him a feeble wave.

It was up to her to dismiss the staff. This task was made easier when Gladys announced her intention to volunteer for the war effort. The thought of firing Cook troubled her the most. How could she give an elderly woman her marching orders? She thought of writing a letter and signing George's name, but she was not a coward.

'I'm afraid things have been tight,' she tried to break the news gently. 'The thing is… Sir George has advised me to close up the house. I'll be leaving myself just as soon as I can. I'm afraid I can't take you with me.'

The stunned look in the elderly woman's eyes threatened to break Marina's composure. They stared at one another for what seemed like an eternity, and eventually Cook looked away. She was genuinely interested when she asked Cook about her future living arrangements. Cook said she'd go live with her widowed sister and that everything would work out for the best. Marina longed to ask if she had a pension, but that might prove troublesome if she said no, for there was no money to give her.

Afterwards she sat in the empty kitchen long after Cook had departed. Marina offered to pay for a taxi and her train fare, but Cook was too proud. She rested her elbows on the long, narrow bench clouded by traces of flour - it smudged the elbows of her good cardigan but she did not care. As her eyes met with the stove she had an idea. For a moment she thought of setting fire to the house to hurt George. But, as much as the thought gave her a wave of sadistic pleasure, she was not a spiteful person.

When she walked down the hallway to the staircase and up to her bedroom she realised, perhaps for the first time, how alone she was. There was no Cook or Gladys, and no George in a far flung corner of the house. The wind whistling through the cracks in the windows and the shutters banging back and forth frightened her.

George had made all the arrangements, she would not be thrown on to the street or forced to look for rooms. He told her to open up Hiraeth, an old family home in town. Years ago he had threatened to sell it but could not find a buyer, and when he did find a buyer they did not offer him the money he had wanted. Perhaps he did not want to get rid of it. But now, with his money running out, Marina wondered why he had not flogged it to the first person who offered him a price. In his defence, she realised the looming war spoiled any chance of a quick sale, or a tidy return on investments. Then she wondered if he kept the house so he could have affairs in town. Now she was being ridiculous, she told herself.

It was a house she knew well. The interior and the exterior, the walking distance to the shops, the bus route across town. When she had lived in the house it did not have a name, and it was George who, with a degree of hindsight, called it Hiraeth. A longing for a place that was once her home. Her longing for a place that can no longer be.

Chapter Eight

School ticked along as normal, and Daphne's moment as the grief stricken friend was over. She had made no new friends, her fault entirely, and Leonora had fallen in with the older girls who thought her a celebrity. They laughed and called her a hunchback when Miss Fag took her away to remove the brace at bedtime. Despite Marina's literary career, nobody thought Daphne a star, or asked about her mother. But then again, her mother had not written a famous play. 'Pompous in heart and brittle in soul,' Miss Fag said as she loomed behind her, observing the girls fawning over Leonora.

Perhaps the transition from companion to solitary figure would have been easier had they followed the ancient Hindu tradition and burned Daphne alive. But she was not Hindu and she was not a widow, though she felt like one. She was momentarily relieved when she spied George's car on the gravel outside the main entrance of the school.

Marina was standing in Miss Fag's office with her arms folded and her back to the door. She was about to light a cigarette when Miss Fag entered with Daphne, her presence only detected when she coughed. Marina's eyes met with the 'No Smoking' sign on her desk.

'Mother,' Daphne said, surprised to see her.

Marina gave her a similar smile and raised her eyebrows as if to say *this is out of the ordinary*. She was going to leave it up to Miss Fag to break the news, but the intensity of Daphne's stare meeting her own eyes made her blurt out the news. 'You're not finishing the term.' And then, 'You're coming home with me.'

Daphne nodded, she thought it was because Miss Fag had telephoned or had written to Marina to say how miserable she was. She wondered if Marina simply missed her now that George was gone.

Miss Fag's grey eyes misted over as she packed up Daphne's folder. She added a list of the curriculum they would be studying, mainly the books they would be reading and some notes on historical topics, having wrongly assumed that Marina planned to teach her at home. 'It's been a pleasure having you with us,' she shook Daphne's hand as they left. 'Please, don't be a stranger.'

It felt odd to travel in the car with Marina behind the wheel. Daphne could not remember the last time Marina had driven her anywhere, and her driving skills were ropey to say the least. She stalled twice, both at crossroads, and she almost ploughed over the man standing in the middle, directing the traffic.

'Why have I left school?' Daphne plucked up the courage to ask, only to be told everything would be explained properly when they got home. Marina told her to be quiet: talking in the car distracted her.

Obeying her mother, she fell silent. Turning her eyes to the road ahead, Daphne could see two crows in the middle of it, one lying on its side, its wing askew, and the other squawking and flapping its wings, trying to pull its mate to safety. It was unbearable. The living crow gave up, finally realising its mate was dead, and flew away.

*

When they entered the house, Marina took off her coat and lit a cigarette. She cut a wane, mournful figure as the sunlight filtered through the window behind her, outlining her frailness. Daphne noticed the trunks and wooden storage boxes in the entrance hall. There was no sign of Gladys or Cook; she would have liked to have said goodbye.

'We're moving,' Marina told Daphne. 'Go upstairs and pack up your things. I'll be up shortly.'

Daphne obeyed her mother, though she was unsure of what was going on. Marina had left a trunk in her bedroom for her clothes and other necessities to go into.

'None of my clothes are much good,' she said when Marina came to help her.

'None of them?'

'Well,' Daphne threw a threadbare jumper into the trunk, 'this still fits.'

'It's all right,' Marina sighed. 'I'm sure I have some things that'll fit you.' She stuffed Daphne's clothes and books into the trunk and pushed her blanket and pillow on top, forcing the lid down.

There was nobody to help them with the trunks, so Marina and Daphne took a handle each and staggered down the stairs with it. The landing was stripped of its paintings and Marina said, 'Roper certainly cleared us out.'

'What?' Daphne asked.

'Nothing.'

It was almost dinner time and Marina realised she would have to feed Daphne. She asked her if she was hungry, to which Daphne said yes, and she asked what she would like to eat.

'I don't mind,' Daphne shrugged.

The response irritated Marina; she preferred a straight answer. She went to the kitchen and pulled open the larder and looked around. Cook had taken some of the food, at Marina's insistence, but there were jams and chutneys and a loaf of bread. Preparing a meal was not beyond her grasp, but she hated domesticity.

'What did they feed you in school?' she asked as she made a cup of tea, the kettle's whistle screeched over Daphne as she spoke. It always reminded her of an hysterical woman, and she took no notice of it.

'Oh you know,' she raised her voice over the din, 'meat and vegetables. Soup and toast. Whatever the teachers were having, we had some of it.'

'Well take a look in there,' she gestured to the larder. 'I'm sure you'll find something.'

'The last supper,' Daphne said as she emerged with a loaf of bread and a jar of piccalilli.

'Yes.' Marina sipped her tea. But not quite, after all the traitor was absent.

*

Before he left for his training camp, George met with Louisa. He told her as plainly and as simply as he could that High Greenwood was to be let out to evacuees and that Marina and Daphne had gone elsewhere.

'Where?' Louisa snapped, without missing a beat.

'I don't know.' He made an unconvincing liar, so he rummaged in his pocket and retrieved a handkerchief and blew his nose as a distraction. 'She's left me, told me to never contact her again.'

'And she took the girl?' Louisa asked, though it sounded like a demand.

'That's right.' He pushed the hanky into his pocket. 'I... I told her everything.'

'Everything?'

'Yes. Everything. You know... a-a-about Ev...' he stumbled on the v.

'Oh God,' Louisa almost whispered. Her eyes widened at the thought. 'How terrible for you. I'm so sorry, George. I know how you loved her.'

He gave a feeble shrug. 'The thing is, I've nowhere else to go, so I thought I'd lend a hand to the war effort. I'm going to Malta, as a matter of fact.'

'You? You're going to fight?'

'Well, not quite. But what else can I do?'

Louisa looked at him, her eyes were kind and she smiled. Touching his hand, she told him how brave he was. But he knew what was coming, he knew she would ask about the money.

'So... ,' He reached into his pocket and took out an envelope. 'I want you to have this. It's not much, I apologise. But it's yours.'

When they parted George basked in the relief that she had believed his story. He felt like a bigamist, though he realised that was an iffy sentiment given Louisa was his sister. How else could he explain his meddling and keeping secrets and desperation to keep everyone apart, yet provide them with money and a roof over their heads?

Louisa slithered away with her envelope of money. It was not his money, he had stolen a brooch from the small drawer on Marina's dressing table and managed to pawn it in town. He was ashamed but he allayed such feelings when he promised himself he'd buy her a new one, someday. She'd hardly notice, she never wore brooches, and he justified the theft by reminding himself that he was the one who had bought it for her. So, in a way, it was his. Yes, he felt quite clever.

Before he caught the train, he thought about going back to High Greenwood and living there while Marina and Daphne went to Hiraeth. They would never know, and it would be easy for him to remain at the big house and help out with the evacuees. He might even offer the house to the army as a convalescence home or headquarters. And then he thought about going to Hiraeth and living with his wife and child like a normal family, but he knew this was not possible. He hated that place.

But the fact was, he reminded himself, he could not shirk from his commitment. His going to Malta was the best for everyone. There was a method to his impulsiveness and he hoped to be killed in the war. He could no longer live with the shame of what he had done.

Chapter Nine

The taxi stopped at Marigold Square, a small neighbourhood on a sloping hill overlooking the industrial hub of the town centre below. The lead roofs of historic buildings, the domes, towers and bridges, snaked along the river which pushed the boats towards the docks, making for a pleasing panoramic view.

The facade of the red brick houses were uniformly alike, forming a long row, stretching from one end of the street to the other, with cast iron railings on the windowsills and around the edge of the attics' oriel windows. Some houses had been demolished, others converted into small flats, another a boarding house. They stood next to one another, the same height with gaps in between, like splayed teeth.

On the corner was Hiraeth, it was three storeys high and framed by an infectious growth of ivy that crawled up to an arched window sticking out of the slanted roof. A small wooden porch with a pitched roof encased the front door which had panes made from stained-glass in a kaleidoscope of blues, golds, greens and purples.

There was a moment before they entered the house, when Marina stood on the step of the porch, resting her gloved hand against the brickwork covered in cobwebs. Her stomach stirred with anxiety and her hand trembled as she felt for the key in her handbag.

'Hold this,' she said to Daphne as she passed the bag to her. She tutted under her breath and strands of hair came loose from beneath her hat, falling in front of her eyes. The skin above her sparse eyebrows itched, causing her mild discomfort, but she resisted from scratching it as she did not want to smudge the pencil.

'Did you forget the key?' Daphne asked, not because she assumed her mother had but because she felt the need to speak, to ease the tension that was building up inside of Marina.

It served to irritate Marina and she let out a small growl, a sign of anger, before pulling the key from the bag. It had a string looped through the hole in the metalwork and it caught on the button of her glove as she put it in the lock. With a sharp push she opened the door and glanced over her shoulder at Daphne before stepping inside.

It was cold inside; the dust caught in the back of their throats and there was an odd smell, lingering damp. The interior was narrow; the long hallway was dark and frozen in time, a portrait of a daily routine hastily abandoned. There was an umbrella stand tucked into a corner, a large pot where a plant had once been but had since decayed to dust, the earthy smell of the dried soil could be detected.

Marina stood at the foot of the stairs, steps away from the front door. For a moment it felt as though time had stopped and she glanced around the house that had once been her home. Before she had left High Greenwood, when George told her about the move, she anticipated a flood of emotions would come rushing back. But nothing happened, not at first.

'Oh, don't look!' Daphne's voice met her ears, it was loud and gruff, causing her to flinch. She gasped and turned around, quickly. 'Don't look, it's too awful!'

Those words, she had heard them before and it prompted her heart to race.

'Sorry, mother,' Daphne walked from the drawing room. 'Sorry to startle you.'

Marina did not speak, or smile to acknowledge her. She walked into the drawing room, slowly, as if she were in a dream or sleepwalking. There were trunks in the middle of the floor, sent from High Greenwood on the milk train the day before. The delivery man had been given a key by George and he posted it through the letterbox, along with his bill.

'It's just... well, look,' Daphne pointed to a dead mouse on the floor.

The sight did not stir Marina, and she stepped out of the drawing room and her eyes met with the foot of the staircase. I'm so sorry, she heard George's voice, pitched and stuttering as it had been in his youth.

There has been an accident. Don't look. Turn away.

1920

Chapter Ten

It had happened quite suddenly. 'Quite suddenly,' Sybil told Marina. She thought the word 'suddenly' was an unfortunate choice, on par with settee and cemetery. But in this moment, one of crisis, she felt tongue-tied. Blasted George, where did he go to? She stood at the window, twitching the curtains.

Marina looked down at her hands, the skin was sore around her fingernails. She picked at a rag nail until it bled, wrapping it in her linen handkerchief. The blood transfixed her.

'You're not to worry. Not to worry.'

'You keep saying everything twice.'

She did not mean for it to sound critical but it was taken that way. It set the tone for the dynamic between herself and Sybil. Why did bad things keep happening to her. Was she cursed?

'Do I?' Sybil said rather flippantly. The handkerchief caught her attention and she looked down at the spots of blood, disapproving of the small spectacle Marina had created. 'I was talking with George and we think it's for the best if you come home with us.'

'Home with you?' She felt panicked, sick to her stomach. She did not want to leave her home.

'There is nothing here for you now.' Salt had been rubbed into the wound and Marina began to sniffle. 'Sorry, my dear. I did not mean to upset you.'

George walked into the room; he was pale faced and his limbs appeared to quiver. 'Sorry,' he said. He walked to Marina and sat next to her, taking her hand once more. The gesture did not escape Sybil's watch. He had been in the kitchen all this time, listening to the muffled voices as they travelled down the hallway, a hissing sound owing to the small distance between the rooms.

'I was just saying to Marina that she ought to come back with us.'

'Oh yes,' George replied. 'You must.'

'But what will I do?'

He could feel her hand warming up, becoming slippery in his grip. They both looked to Sybil for an answer.

'Do? Do? Why must you do anything.' Sybil was on edge, as though she were waiting for someone to walk through the door.

That evening Marina, George and Sybil motored to High Greenwood. She brought with her a trunk of clothes and some books but nothing of Evangelina's. Not even a photograph. George's younger sister Clara was there, having come back from a tour of Munich, and his other sister, Sadie, was in Paris being finished. Marina suspected she herself was finished in more ways than one. It was a frosty reception and Clara offered a tight smile but little by way of a greeting. She went off with Sybil to the drawing room, leaving Marina to follow George into the library.

'I've got it all figured out,' George said as he stood in front of the fire. He did not stutter, she would learn that he could speak clearly when he felt in control. Somehow he appeared older to her and less endearing. Here he was the man of the house, but not quite out of Sybil's frail shadow. 'Tomorrow we'll go back to town and get a marriage license.'

'Whatever for?'

'To get married, of course.'

'But I don't love you. And you barely know me.'

'Yes, I know all of that,' George said as he threw a log onto the fire. 'But whoever married for love?'

What was it to be? Marina thought. If she refused would he turn her out into the night? If she said yes would he grow to love her? He said he liked her, thought she was charming and intelligent, and anyone should be glad to have a wife like her. But what about Evangelina, she wanted to ask. What if she was just like her mother? Or would George fix it all so she would never have to be.

'Can I give you my answer in the morning?'

'Yes, of course. But don't over think it.'

Marina nodded. Somehow she sensed in the morning Sybil would put a stop to it all and that, in a way, scared her more than marrying a stranger. Yes, she would accept. She was certain of it all now.

'How old are you?' George asked as the train pulled out of the station.

'Nineteen. I'll be twenty in March.'

'Ah,' he said, 'I'm twenty-one.'

They sat in silence, their eyes fixed on the window as it flashed past the greenery before approaching a smattering of industrial buildings.

'Do you have a middle name?' he asked.

'Yes. Alice, after my Belfry grandmother whom I've never met.'

George knew this Alice Belfry, a stately woman with silver hair and blue eyes, who was friendly with his mother. His knowledge of the family outside of his own parents was poor, but he was certain Alice was his father's aunt or step-aunt, by marriage anyway. He pondered it for a moment, trying to piece aunts and uncles together and distant cousins and great-grandparents before giving up.

'Mine is Walter, after my father.'

Marina smiled. The conversation stalled but at least George had garnered a few facts about her.

They stopped off at the bank where George worked, his father had once sat on the board of directors, and his position had little influence over the day to day running of things but the name Greenwood still meant something. He appeared so confident, it was as though Evangelina was not dead at all. It puzzled Marina, and being in his presence made her feel that way, too.

'When they release your mother's body I think it's best if we have her cremated.'

'Cremated?'

There, the topic of Evangelina's death had presented itself and Marina felt wretched all over again. She had not seen the body, not since they had taken her away. She thought it was all a dream; she felt quite unlike herself, as though she had been transplanted into somebody else's life.

'Yes. My father was cremated and it was the best way.'

'But I don't think I like the idea of my mother being burned.' Then she thought of Evangelina's pitiful existence and decided that a cremation was appropriate. Here today, gone tomorrow. 'But who will pay for it all?'

'Don't worry about that.'

'I don't think your mother will approve of you spending your money on my mother. And on me, for that matter.'

'It's my money, I can do what I like.'

'Can you, Sir George?'

It was the first time she had said his name and he enjoyed the sound of her voice reaching his ears. He almost fell in love with her.

'George, please,' he dismissed his title.

After a spell of silence she asked if they could see her mother. 'Somehow it doesn't seem real. I don't feel a thing.'

'I don't think you should.'

'But I want to. Please, George. Please take me to wherever she is.'

He did not know where she was, and he suggested they go back to High Greenwood, have supper with Sybil, and go the next day.

*

'Look at you,' Sybil said with disgust. 'Acting as though nothing has happened.'

The words wounded him and he felt the impact of her disapproval. The false bravado, the act of taking care of Marina, had begun to falter. He no longer felt brave. I killed a woman, those words came back to him. How could he live with himself? How could he tell Sybil that Louisa knew? He had dug a grave for himself in more ways than one.

'So sorry,' Marina said as she walked into the library. 'I didn't realise anyone was in here.'

'People using their library, who'd ever heard of such a thing?' Sybil snapped.

Marina turned around, about to leave, when George stood up. 'Please,' he said, 'do come in. Mother was just leaving.'

'I don't wish to intrude,' Marina said.

'No, we wouldn't want that,' Sybil mumbled as she got up. 'Have you seen Clara?'

'I believe she's in the garden, I thought I saw her from the window.' When Sybil left, Marina turned to George and said, 'Your mother hates me.' He brushed it off and said Sybil hated everyone, it was what made her life worth living. 'You said I could see my mother today.'

'Did I?' George seemed disinterested and distant.

'Yes. I should like to go now.' She was about to add 'before I lose my nerve', but she sensed George might take advantage of those feelings. 'You don't have to go with me. I realise it must have been a shock to find her... to find her like that. But I still don't know where she is, so could you please tell me?'

'Right,' he said. 'I'll ask mother.'

He left the room and stood against the wall, in the hallway. The image of Evangelina, dead at the foot of the stairs, flashed in his mind and he replayed the scene in which he had told the policemen that she was

88

already dead when he got to the house. Or was that the correct story? The lies and scenarios clouded his better judgement and he felt his heart palpitate, his collar tightening around his neck like a noose. I'll swing for this. He thought of telling Marina that Evangelina's whereabouts were unknown but he wanted to stop the lies and put an end to the cruelty. If only she knew the truth she would never speak to him again. Worse. She would tell the police.

Marina stood in the doorway. 'Well, did you ask your mother?'

'I can't find her.'

She pointed to the window. 'There she is.' Sybil was walking across the lawn with Clara, they were in deep conversation.

'Ah,' he said. 'There she is.'

She thought he was acting peculiar, he was less confident and the stutter was there. Perhaps she ought to tell him he did not have to marry her, that she would be all right. She could find work and a room but, really, she had no experience of life. Her mother took care of everything, even if she did resent her for it.

'Mother says she's at O'Brien's funeral parlour but we're not to go,' he said when he came back. That was a lie, he had interrupted them as Clara spoke of her impending marriage to a man she had met in Munich, an American.

'Why not?' asked Marina.

'I don't know.'

'Well, can't you ask her?' She felt like screaming. Tears formed in her eyes and her voice cracked with emotion. 'This is ridiculous. Why can't I see my mother. Where is she, really?'

'Wait here.' He went back outside.

Marina saw Sybil take his arm and speak into his ear. Clara walked away, glancing over her shoulder as she did so. George nodded quickly before racing back into the house.

'She said it's not a pretty sight. That you ought not to put yourself through it. The cremation shall be arranged straight away. You've already identified the body.'

'I have?'

'Yes, when we found her. Remember. Remember the policemen asked you?'

Marina tried to think of their questions. She recalled identifying George as the landlord, but nothing as formal as confirming that it was her mother.

'You see,' George said as he put his arm around her as though they were a real couple, as though they had known one another for ages. 'You see how upset you're getting. Perhaps you should lie down.'

She began to cry and George pressed her head to his chest, touching her hair as she did so. He felt as hopeless as she did but he could not break down. So long as he could take care of Marina he would somehow manage.

He walked her upstairs to the bedroom Sybil had appointed and he willed her to sit down on the bed. He closed the window and drew the curtains, and told Marina to get into bed.

'I'll fetch you a glass of water. It'll help with your headache.'

How did he know she had a headache? she wondered.

Returning with a glass of water, he handed her a tablet and told her it was a painkiller. She took it with a sip of water and got into bed. For two days she had not eaten and the tablet cast a phantom weight on her body and her eyelids closed.

His behaviour was deplorable, he knew, but he had no other choice but to drug her. To help her along, as Sybil would have said. When the tablet wore off it would be the next day and all would be taken care of. He stood at the side of the bed while she slept, her breathing was light at first and her chest went up and down, gently. Since they were engaged to be married he felt it acceptable to take the pins out of her hair and to remove her shoes and open the first three buttons of her blouse. He was making her comfortable, there was no crime in that. Poor Marina, he said to himself as he leaned down and kissed her lightly on the lips, thinking he could go further and she'd never know. He lay down next to her and put his arms around her, her hair touched his face and she opened her mouth and slurred a few incoherent words before drifting back to sleep. Closing his eyes he hoped to evoke a sense of familiarity, the same feeling he had felt with Evangelina, but there was nothing. That was good, he did not want to see Evangelina each time he looked at Marina. It felt as though nothing had happened, nothing untoward had taken place. If he could keep her at High Greenwood, and not go with her to town or to Hiraeth, or see Evangelina's body, he could hold everything together. He needed her to co-operate; so long as she remained with him and all traces of the past were erased, nobody would get hurt. He fell asleep thinking those thoughts.

'George?' Marina said as she woke up, feeling the pressure of a person lying next to her, almost draped across her. She was still groggy and her voice was hoarse. She wondered why he was next to her, why they had fallen asleep in the same bed. 'George, wake up.'

He opened his eyes and looked at her. His mind scrambled to recall what had happened, to think of an excuse as to why he was there.

'What's going on?'

He yawned loudly, resisting the urge to go back to sleep.

'Why are you in my bed?'

'So sorry,' he yawned once more, turning onto his side. 'We came up here because you weren't feeling well.'

She tried to follow his story, tried to remember if she had felt sick. 'Was I ill?'

'Yes, you had a headache.'

'I did?'

'We began to talk. We must have fallen asleep.'

Her eyes narrowed as she jogged her memory. 'What did we talk about?'

'Your mother and other things.'

'What did I say?'

'Lots of things. That you didn't want to go back to the house.'

There was a gentle knock on the door before it opened. It was Clara, she was holding a tennis racket. The sight of George lying next to Marina startled her and she stormed off.

'We're in trouble,' Marina said. 'Your mother won't stand for this.'

'It's all right, I'll talk to her. We didn't do anything.'

That made Marina blush, but she was glad to hear it. Her mind felt stuck, as though she could not make the wheels turn to form a thought. What had happened before she had fallen asleep? Somehow George's story did not strike her as familiar. She was certain they did not have a conversation, and she was sure she would not have permitted him to get into bed with her.

He got up and went to the door. He was still fully dressed, though his clothes were dishevelled and his hair stood up.

'Don't come down 'til I send for you.'

'What am I to do?'

'Read a book. Anything to pass the time.'

She nodded.

'Oh, and Marina.'

'Yes?'

'You know what this means.'

'What?'

'We'll almost certainly have to get married now. Can you imagine what people would think?'

A feeling of dread washed over her, she felt caught up in something she had no control over. Two days ago her mother had been alive and they quarrelled about Marina wanting to cut her hair. Silly things, ordinary things, which had always ended with Evangelina's temper breaking and her striking Marina, or insulting her. Now she was dead and nobody would take her to see the body, and nobody spoke of things like a funeral or even the inquest. And now she was going to marry George, someone she barely knew, and become Lady Greenwood and live in this big house. She leaned back against the headboard, and looked up to the ceiling. Was this how it was for most people; they simply found themselves in predicaments that only marriage could cure? Is that what had happened to her mother? She knew so little about her father and nobody seemed to offer any information except that his parents were respectable and rich. Who was George Greenwood, anyway? And why was he being so nice to her? Was this what they called love at first sight?

*

Marina had only been at Hiraeth for a day before she realised it had all been a mistake. She had come back with her mother's ashes; Evangelina had been cremated before the funeral and Marina did not think to ask why or wonder if this was standard procedure. The service was short and the vicar kept harping on about repenting in this life. George said not to go there alone, though God knows he did not want to go back with her. Sybil said she was a foolish girl and mumbled something about ungrateful children and serpents' teeth. Clara gave her sideways glances and made a point to ask George about Cousin Pamela, whom she thought very pretty and a catch.

The nights were on the turn and at six o'clock, as darkness fell, she found herself overwhelmed by the silence and the static feeling that she recognised in the house but could not piece together fragments of her life there. For the past three years, since her lessons had stopped, it had been the same day in day out: running errands for her mother and working as a typist when she could, usually in smart homes, typing letters and memoirs for people who paid her a flat fee, regardless of the time she spent with them.

She tried to remember her childhood, spent in the makeshift schoolroom in the attic where she was taught by an ill-tempered Yugoslavian woman whom her mother knew and felt sorry for. 'She has a glass eye,' Evangelina told Marina after she had caught her staring at the faux brown eye mismatched with the blue one. 'It's rude to stare.' Up in the attic, nestled beneath the eves, she learned how to spell and to write her name and read books and do sums.

The solitary feeling struck her with a sense of familiarity and despite being surrounded by houses, the neighbours did not speak to them. They whispered about her mother, who had been orphaned as a child and taken in by Evangelical Christians, hence her name. Bad luck followed her, they said. That's because she's a gypsy, said another. She was small and slight, with black eyes and brown hair. 'And so beautiful,' Marina once heard a neighbour, an older woman, say as though all whores were supposed to have impetigo, a limp and missing teeth from syphilis and scurvy. She drank, heavily, but did not have the appearance of a drunkard except for a bloated face. 'Wouldn't you do the same if you had to touch Walter Greenwood and have *him* touch you?' Evangelina said as her pale hands shook over a bottle of gin. It was an extraordinary thing to ask a child.

*

The following morning, after a sleepless night in her old bedroom, there was a knock on the door. Marina stood up, the blood rushed from her head and she felt faint. She walked down the stairs, her footsteps heavy with exhaustion.

'George,' she said as she opened the door.

'I've come to take you back,' he said. He did not come into the house, and stood steps away from the front door. 'It's no good you staying here alone. I'm going to sell the house.'

'Sell my home?'

'Yes. It's not much of a home any more. The place is a wreck, I can't afford its upkeep.'

There was an urgency in his voice, and she was certain he would reach forward and drag her away with him. He shifted from foot to foot, looking up to the upstairs window and then over his shoulder after the breeze caused the gate to creak.

Louisa had come to High Greenwood and, knowing her stubborn nature, he predicted she was still there. They had exchanged bitter words in the hallway, before Sybil came out of the drawing room to investigate the noise.

'Joan's going to the police!' she said.

'Will you shut up,' Sybil hissed.

'You must stop her!' George said just as loud.

'I can't!' Louisa menaced.

'Do stop it, Louisa. Stop this melodramatic hysteria.' Sybil reached forth, attempting to grab her before George stepped between them.

'What will it take?' he said.

'She *wants* money. She says we *need* money.'

'To go away?' George asked.

'I think so. Yes.'

'She's acting,' Sybil raised her voice to an unbearable shrill. 'She's always acting.'

George said he would get the money from the bank and come back at once. He ran from the house, taking the spare car keys from the box next to the front door as he did so. As he drove into town he wondered how much it would take to silence his sister and her, whatever she was, friend. He could not fathom any of it.

Bypassing the bank, but heeding Louisa's threat, he drove straight to Marigold Square and stopped outside Hiraeth. The engine was still running when he left the car. Although done in haste, Marina thought this quite romantic and, owing to her innocence, she was quietly impressed.

'All right,' Marina finally said. 'I'll go with you.'

He breathed a sigh of relief and held onto the gable of the porch.

'Are you ill?'

He looked up, steadying his breath. 'No, no. I'll... I'll be all right in a moment.'

When they reached High Greenwood, George carried Marina's small suitcase into the house. He told her to go straight upstairs, that he would be up in a moment. She did not want to see Sybil, so she did as he said.

'What's in there? My money?' Louisa said.

'Shut up,' he said as he flung the suitcase onto the sofa. 'I've brought Marina back. We're to be married at once.'

'What?' Sybil sat forward in her chair, seething.

'I'll sell Hiraeth and you'll get your share,' he said to Louisa.

'You're lying.'

'In the meantime can we agree on a figure? A one-off payment?'

'Don't do it, George,' Sybil said.

'How much?' Louisa ignored her mother.

'One hundred pounds.'

'One hundred quid, what do you take me for?' Louisa was becoming hysterical.

'One hundred and fifty, that is all I can give you.'

'Stop this!' Sybil banged her hand off the table. 'You'll not get a penny from us, not one penny for your little benjo.'

'Do you want to hang, George?'

He stopped for a moment and subconsciously touched the back of his neck. Sybil was glaring at them both. He saw the fear in his mother's eyes.

'Enough!' he roared. 'Enough! Get out.'

Sybil's shoulders slumped and she fell back in the chair. She felt relieved, though she would never admit it.

'But George!' Louisa wailed.

He took her by the arm and marched her from the room. She was so light, he could have carried her. She screamed and resisted as he dragged her to the front door. He was certain the entire house could hear the commotion.

'Play along with me,' he said when they were on the driveway. 'Damn it, do as I say!'

'You think you're so clever.' She pushed him, her own strength too feeble to cause even a stumble.

He leaned in, close to her. He knew Sybil was watching from the window. 'You'll get your money. I promise you that.'

'How can I trust you?'

'Have I ever lied to you?'

She paused for a moment. 'How will I get it? I can't come back here.'

'You must promise you'll never come back here. I'll make it worth your while.'

She stared at him, angry tears clouded her view. 'I live at 2B Morrow Place. You write Joan's name on the envelope.'

'And?'

'And I'll talk to her. You'll not hear from us again.'

'Christ,' he sighed, almost falling to the ground. 'Well, what are you still doing here?' he yelled. 'Go on, go away!' he lifted a stone off the driveway and threw it, intentionally missing her. 'Go on!'

She ran away, down the driveway, falling as she did so. Without crying out or looking behind her, she got up and continued to run.

Marina had seen it all. She asked him who the girl was and George told her it was his sister. 'Why did you strike her?'

'She's a vicious, nasty girl. Anyhow, I've given her her marching orders. We'll not hear from her again.' He took her hand and they sat on the bed. 'You're not to be frightened,' he said. He meant it, even though his head raced with a million alternatives as to what Louisa might do. Not Louisa, he quickly thought, Joan. He wanted to wring her neck.

For a moment she thought she loved him and that he would do anything for her. 'Thank you, George,' she said. 'You've been so kind to me.'

'We'll get married straight away.'

'Yes, and?' her voice was almost a whisper.

'And then we can decide what to do, or what might be the best arrangement for us both. It's a formality to make this proper, we can't go on living together.' He became self-conscious and worried that he sounded silly or overly dramatic, and so he added, 'Well you know what I mean. It's not proper to have you here if we're not to be married.' She nodded to make him feel better and he kissed her hand. 'We don't have to... not right away if you don't want to. I don't wish to embarrass you but you know what I mean. You, you know what I mean, don't you?'

She nodded once more. 'You mean sleep together,' she said matter of factly.

He was surprised by her candour, the vulgarity, but he did his best not to react. 'Let's just do the right thing now.'

1939

Chapter Eleven

For the first few days they approached one another and negotiated the smallness of the house like two polite strangers. 'This is not so bad,' Marina had begun to say, over and over, throughout the day. The rooms were not so bad; the weather was not so bad; their being in one another's company was not so bad.

But it was hopeless to pretend that everything would be all right. 'I have this horrible feeling that I am sinking,' Daphne longed to tell Marina. Since Celia's death she felt heavy, an invisible weight pressed against her body, and she had an aching feeling in her chest. She was tired and had no enthusiasm for anything. It had not happened immediately: at first she felt numb, as though she had stepped outside of herself and was observing everything with an air of detachment. It was not how she wanted to feel but it helped, and then an overpowering feeling of guilt struck her. She wanted to ask Marina if it was normal not to cry, but she sensed Marina would say crying was weak. Where were the Hartleys? And how did they feel?

She went to the small jewellery box Marina had given her for her birthday. It was wooden with a sun engraved on the centre of its lid. Inside were the bangles Celia had left at High Greenwood and she was yet to return them to Mrs Hartley, she was still undecided whether she would or not. She could not have guessed the sinister motive behind such gifts, and Celia had always said, in an airy voice, that Uncle Christopher loved her very much. Once or twice Daphne managed to scratch the surface to reveal the sort of love Celia had thought was acceptable, and, perhaps to shock or to appear worldly, Celia said Uncle Christopher had made love to her. Not entirely, she was quick to add, but almost.

The rose gold bangle, the first offering, was to sweeten the alarming fact that Uncle Christopher had set in stone the molestation of Celia. You must not tell anyone, he warned her after he pushed her from his lap, they won't understand and you don't want your father to get jealous, now do you? No, she shook her head; she had seen little girls sitting on their fathers laps before, though she had never experienced anything like that with Mr Hartley, he'd never even hugged her. She thought it innocent enough when Uncle Christopher pulled her onto his lap as he sat on a bamboo chair which reclined slightly. He thinks I'm quite wonderful, Celia had thought at the time, and she enjoyed the attention but felt something was odd when he began to make strange noises and grab at her and hold her tightly to him as he leaned back in the chair. When it was over he issued the warning not to tell anyone, and a day later they went into town together and selected the bangle. 'That's for being a good girl,' he had said.

Daphne neglected the bangles and closed the lid of the jewellery box. Now that she was older and wiser, and somewhat more cynical than before, she began to wonder what else Uncle Christopher had done. She wanted to tell Marina, to get her opinion before she made up her mind to give the bangles back to Mrs Hartley, but she was not sure how she could put it into words. It might sound stupid if she merely said Celia had sat on his lap. What was so wrong about that? It occurred to her that she did not know her friend at all, only the things Celia had divulged and even then Miss Fag and the Greenwoods had dismissed it as fibs and idle fantasies. Would this knowledge somehow taint Celia's memory for her? She hoped not. But already she felt her grip on their friendship slipping away. Another day has passed, a week has passed, a month has passed. Celia, a distant memory, vanishing into the past.

There was nothing there to suggest George was part of their lives. No empty chair, clothing left in the wardrobes, or a missing place at the dinner table. Nothing. Marina did not feel a void where George was concerned, only the unsettling feeling that she must adjust to something new.

In a small way it helped that the house remained unchanged since she had left all those years ago. She cleaned it as best she could, dusting the cobwebs and sweeping the floors, and she placed the china from High Greenwood in the cupboards. If she could manage it, she would see about having the sofa and chairs reupholstered but in the meantime she draped blankets across the furniture. It was not so bad when it was tidied up, but not quite inhabitable. There were two good bedrooms, hers and Daphne's, and the third bedroom remained a wreck with soot blackening the chimney-breast and the carpet dirty and matted; that was where a small fire had been when Marina was young, and they never bothered to redecorate.

Before he had left, George told her not to worry about a thing. But she did. In the dead of night, Marina worried about everything: the bills, the ebb and flow of her income, and the foreseeable future and beyond. Even George entered her thoughts and how she had taken for granted that they would always have High Greenwood and he would pay for the day-to-day running of things. Before coming to Hiraeth she did not have to worry about that. The panic began again, the sickening feeling in her stomach and the inability to think rationally or to dismiss her qualms. The whole country was at war, she told herself, what is the worst that could happen? Timing was on her side; everything was such a mess and everyone was united in their hopelessness, so perhaps she was one of the lucky ones.

'Oh,' Daphne groaned, bringing Marina back to the present. 'I feel so wretched.'

'You do?' she asked. 'Why?'

She knew why, but she wanted Daphne to tell her. She wanted Daphne to speak of Celia and how she felt. Was it wrong to feel comforted by her daughter's melancholy, and how Daphne missing her best friend could make Marina not think about George and all that had happened?

Daphne could not bear to utter the word 'Celia', and so she paused and squeezed her teeth together to stop herself from crying. Opening her mouth, she made an unattractive wheezing sound and then, taking a deep breath, she said, 'No reason.' I miss my friend, she longed to tell Marina; I want my friend back. She did not think it normal to dwell on Celia's death or to talk about it, but she could not stop her thoughts from forming. They crept up on her in the night before she went to sleep, and it was the first thing she thought of when she woke up. It seemed selfish to only think of herself when George was overseas putting his life in danger for their freedom. That might be the trick, Daphne decided, she would think of other things and other people and somehow forget about Celia.

'Everything's a hell of a mess,' Marina said. 'But somehow it will be all right. I know it will be all right.' She switched on the wireless and Ambrose spilled into the drawing room, live from a supper-club far away.

With her half-hearted determination to forget about the dilemma they had been thrown into, Marina tried to find pleasure in her everyday pursuits. She listened to the news broadcasts with a lot more vigour than before and, with a morbid curiosity, she sometimes listened to Lord Haw-Haw's speeches lamenting the Nazi cause, but never in front of Daphne. She thought of Hitler and all the bad men of her generation. It gave her something to think about, something other than regressing back to the house and why they were there and she was relieved that Daphne had not asked about it. She seemed oblivious to the fact that Hiraeth had existed all of this time. That was the beauty of grief; it clouded one's judgement.

The girl was a stranger to her, she did not know her at all. And for the sake of saying something Marina sometimes spoke of the casualties she had read about in the newspapers. She spoke of such things as though it were gossip. Romanian prime minister is assassinated; Warsaw falls; British freighter sinks in the South Atlantic.

'Your father wrote,' she said to Daphne, one evening after the second post had been.

'When?' She almost jumped out of the chair. 'What did he say?'

It was a pitiful letter of long-winding excuses, protesting why he had lied and how none of it was his fault. He said he loved her and missed her, and he asked her to write a full account of Daphne's progress and of her happiness.

Marina had thrown the letter in the bin. She would not give George the satisfaction of her writing to excuse his actions, or give him the pleasure of hearing news of Daphne. She rummaged in her dressing gown pocket and took out a packet of cigarettes.

'I'm so bloody stupid,' she said as she put a cigarette to her lips and felt for her lighter. Exhaling a whirl of bluish smoke, she said, 'I should have sent you to the shops. You can go for me tomorrow.'

'For cigarettes?' Daphne asked.

She had not left the house since they had arrived, and the idea of walking out the front door, walking down the street, struck her with a sense of doom. It was a silly thought, she knew, but nothing seemed safe. If Celia can be knocked down on a road she had crossed a thousand times, then how could Daphne be certain of anything?

Marina viewed her question as criticism. How troublesome girls are, she thought. 'Well, since you're here you ought to make yourself useful.'

The gesture of buying cigarettes for Marina reminded her of Celia and how Celia would steal her own mother's cigarettes and smoke them. Not at school, though. Miss Fag could sniff out smoke a mile away. It was not worth the petty punishment of banging chalkboard erasers outside as the sea air whipped through clouds of chalk, causing a more severe choke than any cigarette, smoked by a novice, could.

There they were: thoughts of Celia. She could not stop them.

They dared to smoke in town, sitting on a bench along a dingy side-street. How arrogant they were, really. When Celia brought Daphne to her house, her father opened the door. 'Your mother's not here,' he said, looming in the doorway, blocking their entry as though she was not to be there without Mrs Hartley. 'Do I smell smoke?' his nose twitched.

They froze.

'I asked you: do I smell smoke?'

Celia's lower lip trembled and she nodded. Daphne looked at the ground, afraid.

Mr Hartley drew back his hand and slapped Celia across the face. 'Get inside.' He closed the door, leaving Daphne on the doorstep.

She could hear Celia's hollow screams as her father hit her. She began to run down the path, scared to stand at the front door, unable to bear the sound on the other side, and afraid that Celia might have known she was there and question why she did not help her. She fell over and cut her knee, and wiped it with her hand, smudging the blood downward, to her shin.

On the train home she thought of the scene between Celia and Mr Hartley. She had replayed it so often in her mind it had become a blur. Marina saw her as she walked through the front door, breathless and feeling sick, having peddled back from the station where she had chained her bike to the railings.

'I thought you were staying over?' she asked. And then, 'What on earth happened to you?'

'I fell over and cut my knee.' She looked down at the wound, it was still bleeding. Marina stared at her, not quite believing her story. 'And Celia's dad hit her. That's why I'm not in town.'

'Hit her?' She stepped back as Daphne climbed the stairs.

'Yes, hard. Across the face.'

'Oh,' Marina said as Daphne walked further out of sight. 'If she were my daughter my hand would ache from hitting her.'

The short, callous statement was oddly comforting to Daphne. Somehow, since Marina had never struck her, she must be doing something right.

*

Marina stood at the drawing room window watching Daphne walk away from the house on her errand to buy cigarettes. It was raining outside but she did not grumble about having to go. Marina had given her enough money for a packet of du Maurier's. 'Ask for the green ones,' she told her. She could not stand to smoke anything except for the menthol kind. George had once asked her what was the point of smoking if she was not going to do it right. There were many things she could apply that to, in his instance, but she refrained from wounding him. Or, perhaps, encouraging him. Practice makes perfect, as Sybil used to say.

Daphne detoured and went to the shop where Celia had once bought the *Beano* and sweets. It was quite a walking distance but she felt the journey was worth it, if only to reminisce. She imagined going inside and finding Mrs Hartley browsing the shelves for her essentials. It made her heart beat faster and she invented a friendly exchange between the two. Oh God, what would she say to her? Should she smile, or would that be too cheery? When she got there the shop was closed, perhaps indefinitely, and she stepped aside as a small crowd of schoolboys in short trousers passed. Their schoolmaster tried to round them up, like cattle.

The chemist on the way back to Marigold Square was open and Daphne went inside. It smelled of TCP and peppermint. She walked up and down the aisles, looking at the quasi medical equipment on display. The bell rang as two chattering girls entered, they made for the make-up counter at the far side of the shop. Daphne watched them as they poked their fingers into the pancake make-up and laughed as the clerk looked up, disapprovingly. She felt a pang in her heart, and was relieved when the clerk suggested they ought to buy something or leave. They left.

'Can I help you, young lady?' he asked Daphne.

'Yes.' She walked up to the wooden counter and looked at the cough sweets and boxes of safety pins and gramophone needles. 'May I have

103

some du Maurier's...' She tried to remember Marina's exact orders. 'The...
the green ones.'

The clerk gave her a reproachful look before he turned to the cigarette
display behind him.

'They're for my mother,' she felt compelled to say so he would not
think her bad.

'I should hope so.'

When she stepped out onto the street she was tempted to steal one of
Marina's cigarettes. She felt flustered and unsure of herself, of anything.
She knew a cigarette would calm her nerves, that's what the
advertisements said in her mother's magazines. Then she realised she did
not have a lighter or a box of matches or enough money to buy some. So
she went home.

'Oh, there you are,' Marina said as Daphne walked into the drawing
room, her hair was wet from the rain. 'Got the cigs?'

Daphne rummaged in her pocket and brought out a crumpled packet of
du Maurier's, slightly soggy from the rain seeping through the thin fabric
of her coat. Marina despaired at the idea of having to buy her a new one.

'Take off that coat, just sling it over the bannister and it should dry out.'

She pulled the coat off and did as Marina said.

Marina was pleased with the cigarettes, and that first morning smoke
caught in the back of her throat as she inhaled. This was routine, Daphne
was not.

'Have you had any breakfast?'

Daphne shook her head. She was going to say that Marina hadn't made
her any but she realised it made her seem like a baby, so she shrugged
and said she wasn't hungry.

'I don't know how anyone can eat in the morning. Makes me feel sick.'

Daphne sat on the chair in front of the window. 'Have you heard from
my father?' she asked.

'Yes. I told you last night.'

'Sorry.'

'That's all right.' Marina did not elaborate about the letter or what she
had done with it. The cigarette burned between her fingers as she stared
into the empty fireplace. They had so little in common, so little to talk
about. 'I'm chilly. Are you chilly?'

'A bit.'

Marina got up and walked to the fireplace. She bent down, still holding her cigarette, as she manoeuvred the poker into the grate, pushing down the lumps of coal that had not burnt. 'Pass me the matches,' she said as she threw a few sticks onto the fire.

'We're going to be all right, aren't we?' Daphne blurted out.

After a slight pause Marina looked at her, her eyes were kinder than before. 'That's up to us, isn't it?'

Chapter Twelve

George dreamt that he was at High Greenwood, in his own bed. The tall windows were open and the voile blew in the summer breeze, it was night-time but not quite dark and Marina was next to him. 'I love you,' he said. 'I'm sorry.' She turns and looks at him, but on second glance it is not her face and he can see that it's not High Greenwood and this is not his bed. He is next to Evangelina and her dark eyes penetrate his soul. It ends, as it always does, with him jumping out of his sleep.

This time he lets out a tortured cry and sits up, fumbling for the bedside lamp. For a moment he does not know where he is, and he scans the bare room for a semblance of familiarity. The single bed, the white walls, the khaki carpet tell him he is at the camp. He rests his head against the headboard, beads of sweat prickle in his hairline and the back of his neck is clammy. Closing his eyes, he moves his mouth and says into himself, 'Let me die, let me die, let me die.' He is afraid; his stomach turns, and he trembles. The death scene he has imagined will be quick: a bullet will get him when he is unaware, in the back of the head, or through his chest. There will be a loud noise, a scrambling of commotion, but he will lie there, on the ground, dead. He imagines the telegram reaching Marina, and her reading it slowly as she does with all of her post. She will clasp her hand to her mouth and shake her head, before telling Daphne the news. It will be cruel, a shock to the system, but they will cope.

He leaves for Malta in two days. The news is that life on the island continues as before, except for the British fleet moving their naval base from Valletta to Alexandria, in Egypt. He sees hordes of servicemen in their safari shorts walking down Kingsway, an outpost of Empire. And the hospitals and makeshift medical camps stocked to capacity with pretty British women, wearing red lipstick and cool, cotton uniforms. Army cars and jeeps move down the narrow streets, against the backdrop of stacked buildings, palm trees, and fishing boats coming into the harbour. Locals swim at St. George's Bay and children play on the rocks, their miniature fishing nets dipping into the shallow pools. The school bell rings, a church bell tolls. There are posters pasted to the walls outside the opera house, *Gone with the Wind* is showing at the cinema. It is a calm, picturesque scene but they have been warned the Germans will attack. It is only a matter of time before the first bomb is dropped on Malta.

*

The night before he was due to leave, George went for a walk. The air was humid and the moonless sky and high walls surrounding the camp made it appear darker than it was. He heard the drone of the jeeps and the scuffle of men coming to and fro, in preparation for their leaving in a few hours. If only he could get out of the gate, if only he could go to Hiraeth one last time, to see Marina and say goodbye to Daphne. Now he was uncertain about everything, a feeling of dread struck him and he felt like running away.

'Greenwood!' came the voice of Stopes, the Lieutenant, startling him.

For a moment he felt the same boyhood uncertainty and fear, that he was back at school, and braced himself for a beating.

'Good evening,' George said.

Stopes stopped, though George did not want him to. He felt awkward in his comrades' presence; he was aware that he did not possess their thirst for war or their masculine bravado. Were they scared, too? Stopes offered George a cigarette. He removed a card from the packet, a portrait of Lana Turner, the sweater girl, and let out a small whistle and studied it for a while. George looked at her apple cheeked smile, her arms raised above her head – he thought it perverted: she's still in her teens; she's still a child, he wanted to say.

'Anyone coming to see you off?'

'No. My wife and daughter recently moved away.'

'I see.' There was silence before Stopes added, 'There'll be a lot of women and children killed in this war. The people's war.'

The colour drained from George's complexion and he felt as though he had made a grave mistake.

'What's up?' asked Stopes. 'Looks like you've seen a ghost.'

He thought of how he had moved Marina and Daphne from High Greenwood, a safe distance from town, and had placed them at Hiraeth, in harm's way. He was so stupid, he quietly berated himself. In his haste to cover his lies, he had not thought of their safety.

'You remember the Zeppelins from the last war? The baby-killers?'

George wanted to grab him by the scruff of the neck, to tell him to shut his mouth. He felt the cigarette burning his fingers as the paper disintegrated. He thought of Marina and Daphne, blown to pieces in their beds.

'The night raids,' he said. 'I remember it wiping out a family on my road. Mother and baby, gone. Boom! Just like that.' He threw his cigarette over George's shoulder. 'They say the Luftwaffe can blow up an entire town in one go.'

George felt hot, he wiped his brow. He wanted to say it had all been a terrible mistake, that he ought to leave before morning. He was there on good faith, his father had known the Major General and they had taken him to make up the numbers. It was only a desk job, anyone could do it. The drill sounded and a jeep approached, its lights blinding him.

'That's us,' said Stopes. 'We'll be on our way, shortly.'

'Good luck to you,' George held out his hand.

Stopes cast him a reproachful look before accepting his handshake. 'And to you,' he said.

Chapter Thirteen

The wind howled, hurling the heavy rain against the windowpane. The blackout curtains blew back and forth as the draught crept through the gap of the closed window. As Marina lay on top of the bed, she thought of her mother and the past. She wanted to picture the familiarity of her mother's face, how she would walk into a room, the expression she used when happy or sad. The stinging feeling after Evangelina had slapped her across the face and called her a bitch.

An insecure aura surrounded her mother, Marina always felt it and she never understood, not completely, until she had Daphne. She knew her father must have promised Evangelina the world: Larry Belfry, with his background and breeding, was an irresistible combination to the eighteen-year-old girl who had no parents and no money of her own. Her life wasn't always like that; she wasn't always selling her body to make ends meet, but she was always at the mercy of others. To Larry, she was the opposite of what his mother had expected him to marry and so this enhanced her appeal. A vortex in the Belfry family. Walter knew her too, he egged him on to marry her, or to at least flaunt her in front of his family. You're a man, Walter had said, you can do as you please. And so he married Evangelina; he'd got her pregnant first, and made a great show about doing the right thing. His mother, a widow, cut him off. With no money and no prospects, Walter threw him a bone and let him live at Hiraeth, then a nameless house, but he always did have a hand in their life. He stood back, observed, solicited advice, and waited for Larry to fail. He began to drink, more than he could handle, and gamble more than he could afford, and he dropped dead in the middle of the street one afternoon when Marina was a baby. His family did not approach Evangelina, if only for the sake of the child, and she was once again entirely on her own, and Walter knew this and waited until she was desperate.

A gust of wind bursting through the window startled Marina. For a moment, she stood at the opened window, looking out at the silent street below. The darkness was heavy and it hurt her eyes but they became used to it and she could see threads of light as she blinked: the outline of unlit lampposts and the spidery lines of tree branches as they shook in the wind. She felt as though somebody was watching her, and she stepped back out of direct view but close enough to the window to see if someone should make a sudden movement or sound. She thought it might be George; she felt his presence and how he lingered from a close distance before approaching her. Stop it, she told herself, stop being ridiculous. Another gust of wind slammed her bedroom door shut, interrupting her foolish thoughts. She closed the window, the glass trembled as she slid the hatches across.

*

Daphne climbed out of bed and opened the curtains; the sun was coming up, and she shivered as she crept across the cold bedroom. She changed out of her nightgown and hung it on the hook behind her door; she would not have dared to leave it on top of her bed or under her pillow, for Miss Fag had drummed into her the risk of bedbugs crawling into the nightclothes.

She managed to slip out of the house before Marina woke up. She had been in charge of her own identity card since they were issued the month before and she kept it in her coat pocket at all times. As she walked along the tree-lined pavement of Marigold Square, she hugged her jacket around her as the breeze picked up its pace. The frost in the air nipped at her face and she lowered her head as her eyes watered in the sunlight. The hissing of a bus's brakes caught her attention and, aching from the early morning drowsiness which had not quite left her body, she was tempted on board. The fare made short work of her pocket money, most of it was gone, but she felt frivolous and, as it were, selfish.

As the bus chugged down the street, Daphne rested her head against the window. She looked out at the schoolchildren walking along the path and women beginning their daily work, she saw the occasional soldier on leave and nannies in pristine navy uniforms, pushing large buggies on their way to the park. In the silence of the half-empty bus, quiet before the chaos of the morning rush, her mind drifted to Celia and the last time they had seen one another. But she could not bear to replay that scene, so she thought of nothing. The bus stopped at Hawthorne Hill, across the road from the graveyard.

How different everything looked with a clear head. The events from Celia's funeral existed in tiny fragments, like shards of broken glass, every so often she'd try to piece the memories together but nothing seemed to fit. She could not recall the size of the graveyard, nor did she remember the exact location of the burial. She had taken nothing in: she could still feel the tightness of George's hand as it held hers, the hot sun on her dark clothes and the burning sensation as her eyes stared at the hole as Celia's coffin lowered out of sight. A white marble headstone glistened in the bright October sunlight, flickering in her peripheral vision. Tread Lightly; She is Near, read the engraving. 'That's Oscar Wilde, you know,' she heard the invisible voice of Miss Fag.

In the silence of the graveyard, Daphne became all too aware of the parallel realm between the living and the dead. The grass had grown quite neatly around what was once freshly dug earth concealing the tiny corpse inside. Celia was encased in the ground, never to grow old or experience the trivialities of an ordinary day. Daphne would age, that was inevitable. It had already been two months since Celia's death, and in that time she had lived and edged closer to her own mortality. She turned and walked away, with every step she could feel the dent of the soil containing a body.

It had been a mistake to go there, she felt nothing and that made her feel worse. She thought she might cry, or that it might trigger sorrow, but instead it made her feel confused, and the ache in her chest intensified. Her heart palpitated and she felt dizzy. Sitting on the edge of the wall, next to the bus stop, she kept her eyes fixed on the graveyard across the road. She could see Celia's headstone staring back at her, defiantly. Look at what you did to me, it seemed to say; look at what happened because you told on me.

Was it her fault? It had never occurred to her that she was to blame for Celia's death. She had told her mother and father about Celia sneaking off to meet her boyfriend, she did not stop George from driving her home. And then she died. A sickness overwhelmed her, adding to this feeling of hopelessness. She's in India, pretend she's gone back to India, is what Marina had told her to do. 'She's not there,' she said aloud. She had a life before she had met Celia, and she had somehow managed before. Yes, she thought: trick the mind and trick the heart. 'She's not there,' she said once more.

She could bear to wait for the bus no longer and, wanting to be away from the graveyard, she walked back to Marigold Square. It was not a long walk, and she was ashamed at having paid for a ticket when it was only two stops away, but that morning she had felt tired and lazy and could not be bothered putting much effort into anything. She reached the main road which led to a parade of shops dotted along a market square.

'Daphne,' a familiar voice called after her. 'Daphne,' it continued.

She looked up and flinched at the sight of Mrs Hartley standing before her. 'Oh,' she gasped. 'Mrs Hartley, you made me jump. I'm... I'm just out for a walk.'

Daphne felt her skin burning; she ran her hand across her forehead, pushing her hair off her face. They stared at one another for a moment, with Mrs Hartley's eyes taking in her appearance. Could she see her spots? Did she look different? Was her nose running from the cold?

'This is a surprise,' Mrs Hartley said.

'Yes,' she grinned, her top teeth biting down on her lower lip.

'Won't you have a cup of tea with me?' She must have noticed a reluctant look on Daphne's face, for she added, 'Please say yes. I've been so longing to see you.'

She wanted to go home, to be with her mother. She had become oddly attached to Marina, even if she seldom showed it. 'Yes, okay.' Her heart was thumping.

'Good.' Mrs Hartley stood on the spot staring at her. 'We'll pop over to Lyons, it's very nice.' She put her arm around Daphne as they walked to a Lyons Corner House. Daphne wanted to wriggle free, but she could feel Mrs Hartley's fingers pushing into her shoulder and she did not want to be rude. 'Don't you go to school any more?'

'Oh, no. I left ages ago.'

'Ah, because of the war?'

'No, my mother withdrew me before we moved to Marigold Square. We left High Greenwood a while ago.'

She guided Daphne to the green door of the Lyons Corner House. 'Do you come here with your mother?'

'No, she hates it,' Daphne said, though she wished she hadn't.

The tearoom was a hive of activity, with a mass of people moving around in a chaotic attempt to find an empty table or to queue for food. Marina had been right: it was headache inducing. A Nippy showed them to an empty table close to the front door, a poor choice since there was a stream of people moving to and fro, and Daphne sensed Mrs Hartley was irritated by the traffic.

'You know it has been two months since Celia left us,' Mrs Hartley said as she poured the tea.

Was it quick, did she suffer? Daphne longed to ask. Instead she said, 'Really?' although she knew the exact time, day and month Celia had died. She could have tallied it up to the exact minute, had she been challenged to do so. She hated herself for acting aloof, that was her mother's influence, and she wished she had remained silent. The bangles were on her mind and she was going to mention them but somehow never got around to it, and the timing was never quite right.

'I went to a fortune-teller the other evening. No, sorry,' Mrs Hartley shook her head. 'A medium, it's very rude to call them fortune-tellers, she gave me an awful telling off for it.' She rummaged in her handbag and retrieved a newspaper clipping. 'Here you go.'

Daphne glanced down at the newspaper clipping. Contact the dead, it read. It promised a ninety-nine-percent accuracy providing the correct details were given. You could even send a postal order and a note to its premises on Kingpin Road. God, it sounded like one of Marina's books.

'Do you believe in all that?' she asked, quite astonished.

'Not before, no. It's against the Bible, you know. But I was passing a few shops the other day and I suppose curiosity got the better of me. There was a sign, Madame... oh, I forget her name.'

'Was she accurate?'

'On some things, yes. She said that I had taken a new path and that the future looked uncertain. That I must seize the day, do what I must to be happy. How could she have known that?'

'I don't know.'

The conversation abruptly ended and Daphne felt there was nothing more to say.

The walk home was bitterly cold, it was already past four o'clock and a fog of darkness was filling the dull, mid-afternoon sky. The market traders were packing up their stalls and shopkeepers were preparing to close up. The cobbled ground was littered with debris of roguish brown paper as it escaped from the cashier, and Daphne noticed the fishmonger brushing away the disgusting watered down blood from the fish he had gutted for his customers. She heaved from the potent stench of the fish stall as she passed it.

She rummaged around in the pockets of her coat and pulled out a few coins, not nearly enough for the bus ride home. It was only a short distance but the weather was cutting through her coat. She looked up and down the empty street, hoping to catch sight of Mrs Hartley. What a fool, she should have stayed with her; at least Mrs Hartley would have shared a taxi with her and paid the fare.

As she climbed the small hill to Marigold Square, she could see the smoke puffing from the chimneys of the townhouses, filtering out and evaporating into the heavy night air. She had forgotten how dirty the air was in town; the smoke caught in the back of her throat, causing her to choke a few times, it lingered in her hair and seeped into the fibres of her coat as she walked through it.

Marina heard the key turning in the door. She stood at the bathroom sink, her sleeves rolled up, washing her unmentionables. It was an idiosyncrasy, a silly one she knew, but she was too proud or too prudish to let a stranger handle her undies.

Years ago, when she first went to High Greenwood, she would hang them to dry from the springs of the bed and one day the housekeeper discovered this unusual habit while trying to coax Sybil's cat from beneath the bed. She did not say anything, but Marina knew by the look on her puzzled face that she had not seen anything like it before. Everything else was sent to the laundry, and she continued to send her own and Daphne's things out to be laundered.

Footsteps bounded up the stairs as she hung the underwear on the clotheshorse in her bedroom. She had made it to her bedroom just in time with her loot of wet laundry.

'Sorry I stayed out so late,' Daphne loomed in the doorway.

Marina turned around, blocking the view of the clotheshorse. 'That's all right. Where did you go?'

'I...,' She wanted to tell her mother about the graveyard but she felt silly. 'I bumped into Mrs Hartley in town. She invited me for tea. I couldn't say no.'

'Naturally.'

Daphne knew of her mother's odd habit, and so she began to walk away, sensing that Marina did not want her to linger in the bedroom.

'How is she?'

Daphne stopped, and turned to face Marina. 'I can't say. She said she's been to see a fortune-teller. A medium, I mean.'

Marina raised her eyebrows, perhaps in disbelief, but she did not say. 'And?'

'And I think that helped her. I don't know.'

'Silly to grasp at straws,' Marina said. 'It would be better to accept what has happened. What I mean is, she can't change anything so why torture herself?' She gave a little shrug and went back to the clotheshorse.

There was a knock on the door and Marina looked at Daphne, signalling that she ought to answer it. As she left the room, Marina fiddled with the laundry and inspected the hems of a few slips as they hung like bunting. How ordinary her life had become, and what about her book? Her mind ticked over, thinking of her ridiculous characters and approaching deadline.

'It's a letter for you,' Daphne said.

Marina took the letter, she recognised George's neat handwriting on the envelope. 'Go put the kettle on,' she dismissed Daphne. She wanted to be alone to read it.

Daphne left the room and Marina could hear her thumping down the stairs: she was so tall, so slight, and yet she had little grace. She sat on the edge of the bed, the letter pressed in her hand. Well, at least I know he's not dead, she thought. The envelope was ragged, and she gave herself a paper cut as she tore it open. Specks of blood dotted along the seal.

George had written the letter in the dark, on the boat train. The writing, small and neat, was less assured than before and it appeared as a brief note rather than a farewell letter. 'Going to Malta today,' it said.

The name of the camp had been omitted by the censors and so Marina had no idea where he was exactly, except that he would be on his way. The whistling of the kettle sounded through the house, screeching like a grenade. It made her think of George, surely in Malta and facing God knows what. Was he scared? She remembered the day he told her he was leaving for the war and how blasé she had been about it all. Did he want her to say, no don't go, and for her to beg him to stay? Should she have told him what he wanted to hear? Was this an act that had gone too far?

In the kitchen, Daphne poured the boiling water into a cup and strained the tea leaves. She recalled how Cook had not only taught her how to make a cup of tea, but how she would save the tea leaves and feed them to the house plants. Or read Gladys's future. She saw a man in uniform and said that Gladys would marry him. Now there's a war, what were the odds? Silly thoughts, really. And then she thought of Mrs Hartley and their encounter. She felt as though the moment was lost, she would never again get the opportunity to ask about Celia. Perhaps she only wanted to make herself feel better, to settle her conscience. She was so confused.

'Tea's ready,' Daphne shouted.

'I'm coming,' Marina called back.

Both of their thoughts had been interrupted, and all sentimentality was lost.

Chapter Fourteen

The sailing was delayed by two days, and George and the regiment were billeted to a boarding house close to the docks. The winds were too strong to set sail for Malta, and Stopes said they ought not to risk it. They were willing to regardless, but Stopes planted doubt in their minds and sabotaged their efforts. Now was his chance to run away, he braced himself for making the break. He did leave that night, after everyone in the room had gone to sleep. They were sleeping six to a room, with George opting for the floor. Crude jokes prevailed.

It was a long walk before he could see a taxi, driving very slow with its lights off. The street was in darkness; prostitutes plied their trade, and he passed punters pressed against lampposts and walls, like dogs marking their territory. He didn't have much money on him, but thankfully the taxi driver took pity and thought it his patriotic duty to ferry him to the bus stop from where the all-night bus departed.

He walked the rest of the way, about two miles, before he reached Marigold Square. The blackout made it easier for him to remain unnoticed. He could see Hiraeth, in darkness, and he stood steps away from the small park in the middle of the square, under a tree, watching the house. The wind whipped around him, lifting the tails of his army coat. He wanted to be brave, to have the courage to walk up to the door and knock on it until somebody answered. 'Daphne, let me in. It's father,' he imagined calling through the letterbox. He heard a small thump, and then he saw Marina. His eyes had become accustomed to the darkness and he could see her silhouette, standing by the window. He watched her, knowing she could not see him. Should he call out? He was about to find the courage to do so when she pulled the window shut and disappeared from view.

His brief escape had happened two days ago. Now he was on the ship to Gibraltar, from where he would take a smaller boat to Malta. The sky was clear and the sea was calm, he stood on the deck looking up at a flock of seagulls overhead. The sea was crowded with ships, and they were warned of German U boats and the possibility of an attack from below. They were told to expect dangerous conditions as the ship approached the Strait of Gibraltar. English evacuees were being moved from the island to further afield and the RAF had set up a base there. But George looked up to the sky once more and thought of the ships as cruise-liners and imagined he was going on holiday. All of the nervousness left him and he enjoyed the cool sea air on his face.

Later, he went inside as it began to get dark. The sky had become overcast and fog closed in, a darkness came over the ship and he felt tired from the sea air and the journey. They were not quite on their final stretch, and the men were asleep; a quietness fell over the cabin. The sea sloshed against their backs, its impact was strong and it dislodged a few sleeping bodies from their place on the wooden bench. George smoked and looked around. An unexpected blast of a ship's horn startled them and he scanned the cabin, feeling disorientated. His eyes focused on Stopes, who was looking around as the dim lights flickered, all he could see were the glowing tips of cigarettes.

There was a thud and an explosion, the boiler blew up. The ship jolted, almost tipping on its side and hurling the men across the cabin, like ninepins. Water rushed in, a powerful torrent split the ship in two. There was silence as the ship creaked and the men found their bearings, and then screaming and scrambling ensued. George thought, this is it; I am going to die. He remained still, allowing the water to overwhelm his body and push him under. Those who had put on their life jackets beforehand bobbed to the top, but men were pulling at their limbs and dragging them down. George wanted to cheat fate, and so he opted not to wear one. He felt calm, a numbness passed through him and he allowed himself to sink.

Everything became dark and there were strobes of light as he felt himself float upward. His body shutting down. It was peaceful and he was not afraid to die. He tried to think of Marina and Daphne but his mind was blank, it was an effort to form a thought and it made everything seem forced and attached to his physical being. And so he thought of nothing, except the process of dying, and that filled him with peace.

Chapter Fifteen

I am going overseas and you must not be afraid. I am going to fight so all the little Daphnes in this world can be safe forever. Marina crumpled the letter in her hand, holding it in her fist. She resented George's words to Daphne; he was the one who uprooted them from High Greenwood, he was the one who chose to go to Malta. The letter had arrived that morning and Marina sensed he was already in Malta, and thought it best not to mention it to Daphne.

'Would I know if my father had died?' Daphne asked as Marina made a cup of tea.

Their lives had become a monotonous routine, day in day out, sitting at the small table in the kitchen or in the drawing room, while Marina read her magazine or scribbled in a jotter the ideas and thoughts for the book. Daphne tried to keep quiet, she tried to not trouble Marina. She realised that she was intruding on her mother's life, and she felt that Marina was a poor companion in comparison to Celia. Life was somehow going on, and she had fallen out of the here-and-nowness of it all.

Marina put the kettle down and abandoned her tea-making. 'I don't know,' she said, feeling guilty that she had destroyed the letter. Should she forge another?

'Would I know if he'd been killed?' her voice cracked a little.

'I don't know,' Marina said once more. 'What do you think?'

Daphne felt silly; she held onto the edge of the table and pushed the chair back, balancing on its back legs. Her mind had been on Celia's death, not the breaking of the news, but the feeling she had experienced beforehand, before she knew what had happened. Perhaps in a way she did sense that something awful had happened; she recalled the strange atmosphere that night, and the static, sickening feeling she had felt hours before Marina had broken the news. So yes, she would know if something had happened to her father.

'No. I don't think so. I think he is all right.'

Marina herself wondered if she would feel something was amiss, if she could predict something terrible had happened to George. She had detached herself from her feelings and had isolated herself from others for so long that she wondered if she was capable of empathy at all.

*

The first thing George saw when he regained consciousness was a nurse standing over him, arranging his pillows. Her blonde hair was crowned by a Red Cross hat and she smelled of Floris soap. Each time she leaned closer, the tinny smell of blood and gore was vanquished.

'Marina,' he said, his vision was hazy and it hurt to speak. 'Marina,' he croaked once more.

'Stop it,' came a stern voice, not soft like Marina's. 'If I've told you once, I've told you a thousand times I'm not called Marina.'

In that moment he could not remember anything, or how he came to be saved. Often something small and insignificant piqued his memory, and his mind recalled a black hole, the night sky, the dark sea, and the feeling that someone was grabbing him, pulling him upward. 'Get off me.' He struggled from their grip. 'Let me go, you bastard.' He tried to hit out, to punch the good Samaritan. A passing ship came to his rescue and pulled him from the mass of bodies floating in the Strait of Gibraltar.

'You're one of the lucky ones,' the doctor had told him, when he awoke in the hospital. 'Over three-hundred men died and as many are still missing.' It was of little consequence to George, he wanted to be one of the fatalities. The doctor said he was suffering from delirium, the result of being in the water for too long. 'You're lucky you didn't die,' he said. 'You've certainly defied the odds.'

The nurse said it would be a good idea to write a letter to his next of kin, to explain that he was alive. 'The newspapers will have reported on the collision,' she said. 'It will be a worrying time for your loved ones.'

Now was his chance to lie and say he did not have anyone waiting back home. He said to write to Louisa, it was his opportunity to show her how desperate he was; to keep up with his lie that Marina had left him. Surely she would not expect him to continue with their arrangement, not now that he had lost his home and his life was on the line.

'Louisa?' asked the nurse. 'Is that your wife?'

He tried to sit up and in doing so he let out a cry; he had broken his ribs. 'No,' he wheezed as he fell back.

'Your daughter?'

He cried out once more, each breath knifed through him. The doctor said to leave him alone, they would come back in the morning.

*

Marina had read about the collision in the newspaper. It did not occur to her that George was on a ship headed for Gibraltar, her geography was so askew that she assumed he could sail directly to Malta. 'Poor buggers,' she said as she skimmed the article, reporting that the ship went down in fifteen minutes and the handful of survivors were at an army hospital in Gibraltar.

Everything had been calm, not much rattled her except for the government's new taxation policy, and she worried that her money from the books, their only income, would be swallowed up before she could cover their expenses. She would have to talk to her editor, Gerald, about it but she loathed to see him and avoided him as best she could. The newspaper also wrote that schools were re-opening and that the evacuees from the city centres were returning home. The Phoney War, they called it. As far as the home front was concerned, very little had happened and all of the excitement seemed to be contained to the air and the seas.

There was a knock at the door and Marina got up to answer it. A postmistress stood on the porch, holding a telegram. 'Lovely day,' she said.

The bright autumnal sun blinded Marina and she put her hand up to shield her eyes. 'Yes,' she said, her eyes watering.

'Are you Lady Greenwood?'

'Yes,' she said once more.

'Telegram.'

Her hand trembled as she accepted it, she could barely utter a word by way of thanks. The postmistress walked to the gate and took off on her bicycle. For a moment, Marina stood in the doorway, looking out at the empty street with the sun beaming through the tree branches. A dog barked over and over. Daphne was upstairs. She sensed history was repeating itself. She felt warm, and sick crept up her throat. She knew George was dead.

'Daphne,' she called out. 'Daphne come here.' She stood at the foot of the stairs, the front door was ajar, and the dog continued to bark. She heard a bicycle bell and the rumble of a car's engine, a rare sound since petrol rationing had been enforced. It was an ordinary day.

'Yes?' Daphne's eyes lowered, she focused on the unopened telegram in Marina's hands.

'Remember when you said you'd know if your father had died?'

'Yes?'

'This just came.'

Daphne stood on the spot, thinking Marina was playing a cruel trick; a guessing game. She managed to nod. She took a step back and sat down on the stairs, her hands gripping the balustrade.

'You haven't opened it,' she said.

Marina looked down at the telegram and ripped it open. She glanced at the brief sentence, and then let out a sigh. 'Oh, thank God.' She felt for the bannister and steadied herself.

'He's not dead,' Daphne blurted out. She had been holding her breath and expecting the worst and hating Marina for keeping her in suspense.

'He's not dead,' Marina repeated. 'He's not dead.' There was an element of disbelief in her voice, as though she could not fathom how or why George had been so lucky.

Daphne picked up on this and gave her mother an inquisitive look. It validated the mixed feelings she felt towards her, which had intensified since she had come home from school and they had been in one another's constant company at Hiraeth. She took the telegram from Marina's limp hand and read it aloud. 'Sir George Greenwood. Stop. Is alive. Stop. Causality of *HMS Bombardier* collision. Stop. Details to follow.'

Now that she knew what had happened and that George was involved, Marina read the newspaper article once again, this time paying attention to every detail.

Lurking behind the chair, from where her mother sat, Daphne noticed the name of the ship and asked Marina, in a critical way, why she did not associate George with the disaster.

'I did not know which ship he was on. He did not tell me,' she snapped.

'Poor father,' Daphne wistfully said.

The thought of him being afraid and almost drowning sent a cold chill to Daphne's heart. In a way she liked hearing bad news, it relieved her from feeling selfish and wallowing in her own self-pity. Celia was dead; George was injured – she had every right to feel downtrodden and without hope.

*

A letter arrived from George to say he would be leaving the hospital in a day or two, they needed the bed, and that he would be coming home. He kept to the facts: he would be sailing home on a hospital ship and that he had broken three ribs, but nothing too serious. He said he missed Marina and Daphne, and that he was anxious to see them. He knew the ship was at risk of torpedoes but he did not mention this in the letter, he did not want to worry them.

Marina assumed they would all be leaving for High Greenwood whenever George came home. She knew about the money and how he said they could not afford to remain there, but he did not elaborate on what he was going to do with the place. It was probably an army base, or something along those lines. God forbid.

It all seemed like a farce; he was so anxious to leave and to be of use, and he did not see battle and was injured on his way to Malta. That was usually how things worked out for him, he was defeated before he had the chance to prove his mettle.

Chapter Sixteen

Marina looked out the window as the bus drove down the high street. It was a sorry sight. Pregnant women long past their confinement were everywhere, out and about, unashamed of their condition. Men and women, boys and girls, pressed against the corners of shops and the high walls outside houses, kissing and grabbing at one another as though their lives depended on it. It was like Dante's Inferno, the ancient city of Babylon, the pits of hell.

'I thought we'd take a taxi back from the station,' she said. 'We'll see what your father says.'

Butterflies fluttered in Daphne's tummy. She tried to imagine what it would be like to see George for the first time in months. He did not say goodbye to her before he had left, and so there was a lack of finality to his departure. Just like Celia. The hissing sound of the brakes brought her forth from her daydream. She looked at Marina, her gloved hands were firmly clenched around the seat in front. She could see her mother's chest heaving up and down, and she sensed the panic longing to escape from her slender body.

When they walked into the station, Marina felt knots forming in her stomach. She stood on her tiptoes and tried to find George in the sea of people, moving like ants towards the platform. 'Can you see him?' she asked Daphne.

'No,' Daphne said, 'can't see him at all.'

'Oh God,' Marina whimpered. She spied George sitting on a bench, his shoulders slumped and his cap resting on his lap. For a moment she felt like she wanted to be sick. And then picking up the speed of her walk she darted forward, her shoes clicking loudly on the floor of the station. Her voice echoed as she called his name.

George stood up, slowly because of his broken ribs. They had taped him up before leaving the ship and he wrapped his arm across his front, holding his side.

'I...,' he meekly said, his eyes glistening. 'I hope I'm not an unwelcome sight?'

'No,' Marina quietly said. 'We're happy you're home. Aren't we, Daphne?' She stepped forward and kissed him on the cheek. He turned away, slightly, to avoid a collision with his ribcage. Taking in his appearance, she thought him frail and aged; his heavy army coat hung from his bones and there were deep lines etched across his forehead and bags under his eyes. You look terrible, she almost said out loud.

'Hello father,' Daphne said, overcome by shyness.

He looked at her as though she were a ghost; he never imagined he would see her again. The words he wanted to say, to greet her warmly, did not come.

Marina interrupted the moment. 'Come on, let's get you out of here.' She took him by the arm, causing him to take a deep breath and then exhale slowly. The pain came in spurts, and he apologised for being incapacitated.

'I'll get the suitcase, shall I?' Daphne picked up George's small case.

A pigeon flew across the station, narrowly missing the heads of those passing through. George flinched and drew back, as though he were dodging a bullet. He made an unattractive noise, a menacing scream, and people looked at him. Daphne avoided eye contact with them. Marina pulled on his arm and hissed, 'What is wrong with you?'

There was an unspoken tension between Marina and George. She thought he resented her for taking a taxi, and he thought she was being aloof and more distant than before. Daphne sat on a small seat opposite her parents, her hands clutching the sides to stop herself from falling off. She wondered why her father had not spoken to her, or made his usual cheerful small talk, the way he always did when Marina was radiating an imperiousness which threatened to undermine them all.

Each time George took a breath, Marina shifted forward, awaiting his remark. But nothing happened. He saw Hiraeth in the near distance, as the taxi approached, and he felt imprisoned in the back seat. There was a sense of entrapment to his coming home, but Marina appeared oblivious to any reservations he harboured.

'Here we are,' she said.

George reached forth and rested his hand on the door as he stood up, his knees cracked and he was unsteady on his feet. Daphne glanced down and saw his bones poking through the flesh on his hand.

'Well, what do you think?' Marina asked as she walked behind him. 'Still looks the same, doesn't it?'

'Yes,' he quietly replied.

'Right, shall we go inside?'

The house to George smelled musty and damp, though Marina and Daphne had since become used to it. He coughed loudly, his narrow shoulders wracking back and forth, a breathless yelp as his ribs gave him trouble. Standing in the hallway, steps away from the foot of the staircase, he looked up to the landing and was transported back in time, back to when he was a young man and he had loved Evangelina. He could see her, small and dark, walking up the stairs ahead of him. In her efficient way, she'd warn him that Marina would be home soon. He would have done anything she said, she had that power over him.

'Now,' Marina called from the drawing room, where she began to light the fire, 'I hope you're not finding it too bracing.'

He walked into the drawing room to find Marina on her knees in front of the fire, arranging a smattering of sticks, ready to set them alight. The burgundy wallpaper, rippling from the damp, and the bronze light hanging from a chain above his head brought it all back to him. He saw the sofa, covered in a blanket, and could envision himself and Marina all those years ago, sitting hand in hand, and his mother hovering by the window. The crackling of the fire startled him and he turned around, to face Marina.

'I said, I hope you're not finding it too bracing.'

'No.' He looked around once more. 'No, not at all.'

'I suppose this seems strange to you. Coming back here, I mean.'

George nodded. He did not want to protest too much, as it was his fault they were there.

'There are a few things I must discuss with you.'

Oh Christ, not Louisa, he thought.

'I hope you're not too put out but we have to share a bedroom.' She felt embarrassed and foolish about broaching the subject of their new sleeping arrangements.

There was a time when he wanted nothing more than to be close to Marina. Her news should have pleased him, but he felt bewildered. He yawned and it had the desired effect.

'You're tired,' she said. 'I'll show you which bedroom is mine…ours…and help you get settled.'

As they approached the landing, he felt panicked but it did not show. He heard the thumping sound as Evangelina tumbled down the stairs, the swift snapping of her neck. He trembled, but Marina thought it was because of the pain. Thank God it was not Evangelina's former bedroom, he could not have coped.

'The one next door is a shambles,' she said. That was the bedroom which he knew well. 'So, I have this one. And Daphne has the one down the landing.' She opened the door. 'This used to be my old bedroom.'

It was pretty and girlish and it warmed George's heart to see it. She must have been a wonderful girl, just like Daphne. There was a small double bed with a brass headboard, and the wallpaper had a trellis print, it had since faded with age and sunlight.

'I was thinking, if we're to be here for any length of time I'd like to paint the walls. But we can talk about all that when you're better.'

He gave a feeble smile and sat down on the bed. She moved to the window and closed the curtains and turned on the bedside lamp.

'I brought the bedding from High Greenwood, and the china and cutlery too. All of our home comforts.'

'I'm sorry I didn't give you enough notice.'

She did not acknowledge him, or smile to make him feel better. 'You ought to get some sleep. Do you need help undressing?'

'Only with the coat, if you don't mind?'

'Of course.' She unbuttoned his woollen coat and gently pulled it from his arms. 'I'm sorry. I forgot to bring up your things. I'll go fetch them.'

When she left the room, he let out a sigh and remained seated on the edge of the bed. He looked around the room and tried to imagine Marina as a girl and how she felt when Evangelina had entertained his father. He knew what sort of man he was, and how little compassion he had for anyone, let alone a child. The things she must have endured. He was glad Evangelina's room was uninhabitable, he was not tempted to open the door and look inside. He pressed his hands on top of the mattress and lifted himself back against the headboard.

'Oh,' she quietly said as she came into the room.

He had closed his eyes and was feigning sleep, hoping she would leave him alone. She put down his suitcase, and then looked around the room.

He heard the rustle of her clothes as she moved to the foot of the bed. Reaching for his army coat, she gently draped it around his shoulders and lingered for a moment before walking away.

*

'Why is he so strange?' Daphne asked as she entered the drawing room. It was dark outside, the room was lit by a single lamp, and she sat down in front of the smouldering fire.

Marina looked up from the pages on her lap; she had been staring at the same paragraph for what seemed like an eternity. The Russian book was long gone and she was rushing through another, a story about a thief who falls in love with a dying heiress.

'What I mean is, he's usually so talkative and, well, different.'

'I imagine he is tired, and he's had such a shock. He almost died, you know.'

'Yes, I know,' Daphne said too abruptly, as though she were dismissing Marina's remark. 'Do you think Celia's father feels the same way? He's also had a shock.'

'Well, yes. But I suppose it was a different shock. He will be grieving. Your father is …your father is probably traumatised. Time will tell.'

Daphne hated when her mother did not agree with her; she was never on her side. She sighed and leaned back in the chair. Marina looked up once more, wanting her to see that she was busy and that she ought to go away. She pored over the words with a pencil in her hand. The only noise was the fire crackling as the sticks gave a burst of light, then died, and Daphne's stomach rumbling. Nobody had fed her, there was so little to eat.

'There is a loaf in the cupboard, and some jam,' Marina said without looking up.

'No thank you. I'm not hungry.'

'Suit yourself.' She set the pages to one side and stood up. 'I'm going upstairs.'

When she left, Daphne got up and went to the pages. She glanced at Marina's hare-brained notes and scrutinised her punctuation. Any idiot could do this job, she thought. It made her feel smug and quite superior, to think that her mother was not as clever and composed as she pretended to be. *Silly bitch*, Celia's voice rang in her ears. *Yes*, Daphne mentally answered it. She wondered if Marina's manuscript contained such naughty words. She was tempted to throw the pages onto the fire, just to teach her a lesson. Instead, she went to the kitchen and made a sandwich.

*

Marina gently pushed the door open, careful to not open it the entire way, as it tended to creak. With the blackout curtains drawn it was impossible to see anything and she was reluctant to turn on the light. The quiet snores of George filled the room, punctuated by him holding his breath and then letting out a squeaking noise. She made her way to the bed, holding out her hands as to not bump into the furniture.

'Sorry,' she whispered as she turned on the lamp, not realising that George had adopted her side of the bed. 'Sorry,' she said once more.

He mumbled something incoherent and turned over, continuing with his snoring.

She took her nightgown and went to the bathroom to change. When she returned, he was sprawled across the bed. 'George,' she nudged him. His frailness was deceiving and it was impossible to shove him over to his own side. He was always deceptively heavy, she remembered. It was cold and she wanted to get into bed. Pulling at the blankets, she managed to slip into bed and lie close to the edge. He flung his arm across her midriff, almost winding her, but she lay perfectly still, so as to not disturb him.

When morning came, George yawned loudly and woke Marina up. A coldness had set in across her shoulders, where the blankets did not cover, and she shivered. Her eyes were closed, but it had not been a proper sleep. She yawned, too. He took in her appearance; her face devoid of make-up, her blue eyes heavy with sleep.

'Hello, Marina.'

She looked at him; he seemed changed. It was as though the past had been erased and they had begun anew.

'Hello, George,' she said.

Chapter Eighteen

There was a distance between Daphne and George, and she could not fathom why. She felt so hopeless and miserable that she thought the problem must be with her. I'm the one who's changed, she thought. I'm the one who's different.

George thought so, too. 'You've certainly sprouted up,' he said. 'You're almost as tall as your mother.' Daphne blushed as she ate her toast. He looked at her intently, taking in her appearance. 'Don't you think she's awfully like Pamela?'

'Who's Pamela?' Daphne asked.

'I wouldn't know,' Marina said from across the kitchen. She was taking an inventory of the larder and making a list. 'What I mean is, I've never met her.' She wished George would stop talking about Pamela Manners. 'She's an actress,' she called to Daphne, as to not appear jealous. 'A famous one, I think.'

'Well, who is this Pamela? I'd certainly like to meet her.'

'We must go to one of her plays when she's in town,' George smiled. Daphne was delighted by the idea, her eyes widened as she chewed her toast. 'Not only is she my cousin, but she's the sister of your mother's editor.'

'Christ!' Marina screeched as she knocked over a bag of flour, quite deliberately to make them shut up. It put an end to the conversation but not to Daphne's curiosity. She ran and fetched Marina a brush.

'I'm terribly sorry,' George said. 'But I'm feeling rather fatigued.' An anxious feeling caught him off guard and he felt suffocated by their company. He wanted to flee the room, to leave the house. 'Do you mind if I go up?'

'Stay there. Daphne will bring you a cup of tea,' Marina said.

George watched the scene unfolding; they seemed far away, as though he were watching them from behind a glass wall. Their voices were loud, unbearable for him to listen to, and the kettle's whistle startled him. He broke into a cold sweat, he tried to speak but could not engage his thoughts with his mouth. Marina walked to him, carrying the tea. He jumped up, spilling it down her arm and onto himself. She screamed from the boiling water hitting her skin. He pushed the chair back and jumped up, the pain from his ribs doubling him over. The cup and saucer hit the floor, smashing into pieces. It was a delayed reaction; it happened in slow motion. He saw her face wince from the pain, slowly, her eyes creasing and her mouth opening to let out a cry.

Daphne walked towards him, saying, 'Are you all right? Are you all right?'

Marina held her scalded arm against George's torso, like a barrier, and said, 'Stand back. I'll clean it up.'

You killed a woman, he heard Louisa's shrill voice inside his head. 'I'm no good,' he said out loud. He pushed Marina away, and she stumbled.

'Careful!' Daphne called.

He ran out of the room, clutching his side. The door slammed and they were left in the kitchen, tidying up his mess.

*

Home was not a place where Daphne wished to be, and her father was not a man she recognised. She wanted to run away, far away and disappear forever. She thought of her plan: it would be an entire day before Marina would realise she was missing, and in that time she'd have pawned Celia's bangles and caught a ferry to Ireland where there was not a war and she could live happily at one of the orphanages she'd read about in the newspaper. The orphans did all kinds of things in return for their keep, and she was strong and healthy and could easily pay her way.

The morning was dark and cold, and she walked in no particular direction. She stopped at the river and sat on top of the stone bridge and looked down at the older children casting around for fish. Something indescribable came over her and she threw a stone into the water, scaring the fish and interrupting their sport. 'Swine!' yelled one of the boys. She hopped off the bridge and walked on, pulling the collar of her coat up to fend off the chill.

As she was crossing the busy road, someone touched her arm and she looked up, thinking she was being robbed. 'Daphne,' said a voice from the cluster of people waiting to cross. 'We're destined to meet again.' They looked at one another for a moment until the crowd began to cross the road and they were swept along without speaking. Finally, when they reached the other side of the road, Daphne said, 'Sorry. I was miles away.'

'I'm just heading home. Won't you come with me? We can have a cup of tea and a chat.'

She must have purposely walked there without realising it. 'Yes,' she said. 'I'll go with you.'

*

When Marina entered the bedroom George was lying on the bed, curled up like a small boy in spite of his injury. For a moment, she thought he was sobbing but realised he was breathing heavily because of the discomfort. She sat on the edge of the bed, keeping her back to him, and asked, 'What happened to you when you were on the ship?'

In his mind he heard the explosion of the ship's engine and the screams of the men. Then the image of Evangelina falling down the stairs flashed between his thoughts and he blinked hard to forget it. 'Nothing,' he mumbled.

'Fine,' she shrugged, hoping to provoke him into telling her. When George did not fall for her trick, she stood up and walked to the door. Before leaving, she turned and said, 'If you don't like Hiraeth just say so. After all, it's your fault we're in this mess.'

It was a callous remark, she realised this on reflection as she sat in the kitchen, warmed from the heat of the stove. Sitting at the small table, she smoked and dwelt on the outburst. Living in the close confines of Hiraeth with no staff, little money and lack of personal space was bound to magnify any little quarrel or qualm. Having Daphne at home would only add to the problem. It would be a matter of adjusting, she thought, as she stubbed out her cigarette on the ashtray. And then it occurred to her: Daphne was not at home.

*

Inside the drawing room, Mrs Hartley poured the tea and fed Daphne some biscuits which had been Celia's favourite. It pleased her to treat her to a biscuit and to give her her share of sugar for the tea. 'I know you children like your sweets,' she said.

Daphne looked around the room; little had changed since her sporadic visits with Celia during the school holidays. The portrait of Celia was still on the wall, she was small with bobbed hair and wearing a party dress with cap sleeves and a sash. Mrs Hartley looked up at it too.

'I do miss her,' she sighed.

'Me too.'

The reflective silence was comforting and it reassured Daphne that Mrs Hartley wanted to speak of Celia. They sat next to one another on the chintzy sofa, its rose pink cushions perfectly fluffed and the furniture tightly sprung with no signs of anyone having ever used it. Daphne often forgot that, aside from her parents, Celia had no one else to whom she could turn except for Uncle Christopher, but he was in India. Now that she was dead, Mr and Mrs Hartley were entirely alone.

'You know when it happened, when she...,'

'When she was knocked down?'

'Yes.'

'Yes?'

'What happened?'

Mrs Hartley took a deep breath and clenched her teeth together. Daphne looked down at her hands gripped around the teacup, her knuckles white from holding on. Something was stifled, she seemed afraid to speak what was on her mind. Perhaps she was afraid to cry.

'Because I've been thinking about it and I can't picture it.'

'There was a taxi, she did not look before she stepped onto the road.' Her voice wobbled and she took another deep breath. Exhaling, she said, 'And she was hit by the car.'

'Was it quick?'

'Her death?'

'Yes.'

'Yes. Yes, I suppose it was.'

'Who told you?'

'Who told me?'

'That she had been knocked down.'

Mrs Hartley paused, then she abruptly said, 'I can't remember.' She placed a hand to her temple and lowered her head. 'I'm so sorry. But it's been a long day.'

Daphne stood up and reached for her coat. 'I should go.'

'I don't mean to chase you out.'

'No, it's all right. My mother will be wondering where I am. My father is home and everything's at sixes and sevens.'

'He is home? Is he hurt?'

'Yes, but not badly. He was in an accident, but I think he'll get better and leave soon.' She walked to the front door with Mrs Hartley trailing behind her.

As Daphne buttoned up her coat, Mrs Hartley reached out and touched the collar, pulling it up around her neck. 'You ought to wear a scarf. It's so chilly outside.' She held onto the thin coat, feeling sorry for the girl. 'Wait here.'

Mrs Hartley went upstairs and Daphne stood in the hallway, next to the door. She felt the draught around her ankles and she wondered what was taking so long. She was worried that Mr Hartley would come home and find her standing there, and there would be a scene the way there had been when he caught her and Celia smoking. She was afraid of him even though she hardly knew him.

'Here we go.' Mrs Hartley held out a green tartan scarf as she approached Daphne. 'It was Celia's, but now it is yours.'

'I couldn't take it.'

'Please. I've been meaning to sort out her things, but I can't bring myself to get rid of them. I want you to have it. You can call it a keepsake, besides it'll keep you warm.' She fixed it around Daphne's neck, though Daphne wished she hadn't, and she kissed her on the forehead.

'Thank you.'

*

There was a blast from a ship's horn followed by a blinding searchlight sweeping across the dark sea. George felt the rough impact of something snatching him from the water and dragging him upward. He yelled out and fought in his sleep, his limbs thrashing around as he pleaded to be left alone.

'What is it? What is it?' Marina shook him. She looked at the tormented expression on his sleeping face and tried to steady his head as he shook it from side to side. He pulled his arms back, digging his elbows into the mattress. Thinking he was trying to sit up, she said, 'Don't move. You'll hurt yourself.' She was holding him down when he pushed his arm forward, his fist driving into her face.

The noise alerted Daphne and she ran to the bedroom. 'Don't turn the light on!' Marina yelled. She abandoned George and rushed to Daphne, pushing her through the door.

'You're bleeding!' Daphne cried, concerned for her mother.

Marina felt her face and drew her hand away, there was blood on her fingertips. He had split her lip open. 'Your father was having a nightmare. He hit me. Accidentally.'

Daphne could not look away. Frozen, she kept her eyes on Marina.

'Go on, go back to bed,' Marina ordered.

She returned to bed, knowing deep down that it was not her father's fault. She knew that he must be ill.

Marina opened the blackout curtains and leaned against the windowsill, smoking. The moonlight spilled through the window and she could see George's silhouette on the bed. When he woke up, after hitting her, he was not coherent and she looked into his vague eyes. She began to think of various situations, and how they could drive a person crazy.

*

The next morning Marina telephoned Doctor Glendinning and asked him to visit the house. She knew George was told to go to the army hospital to have his ribs checked over, which should be in a week or so, but this was urgent. The doctor was put out by the request but he did not feel he could turn her down. It would have been unpatriotic, and perhaps she had over-exaggerated his military prowess.

Doctor Glendinning took the train into town and walked to Hiraeth from the station. Marina offered to reimburse his ticket but he declined and she knew he'd include it in his bill. She led him upstairs, sensing how irate he felt by the visit. He offhandedly said something about High Greenwood being overrun with evacuees, who had come as paying guests, and how good they were to make that sacrifice for the boys and girls. Marina knew nothing of this venture but she smiled and played along.

Inside the bedroom, George lay in bed, half awake, without much awareness. Marina walked to the window and pulled the curtains open. She began folding clothes, putting them on the chair. Anything to pretend that everything was normal.

'He's been terribly disorientated. And confused. I'm afraid you won't get much sense out of him.' She looked at the doctor for reassurance, but he gave none.

Doctor Glendinning slapped George on both cheeks and pulled his eyelids up. 'Sir George,' he said in a loud, stern voice. 'Sir George, do you know where you are?'

'Of course he knows where he is,' Marina interrupted.

'Please, Lady Greenwood,' the doctor impatiently responded. He felt George's pulse, monitored his heartbeat, and then turned to Marina. 'This chap has suffered a shock,' he announced in an almost light-hearted tone, as if it were the most ordinary thing in the world.

'What do you mean a shock?'

'I was a military doctor in the last war. I still recall the vaguest of symptoms. Shell shock. Trauma. The horrors of war. Call it what you like. It's still a shock.'

'But how can you be sure?'

'Fatigue, night terrors...,'

'Yes, I think so.' She knew he was looking at her lip, the wound striped down the middle. 'He has only been home for a few days, but he was at a hospital in Gibraltar before that. The ship he was on went down and he almost drowned. He hasn't seen battle, or anything like that.'

'I see,' he said in a monotonous tone, giving the impression he was pondering something. 'Well, I can make certain arrangements.'

'Like what, exactly? A hospital?'

'Don't be silly, Lady Greenwood. The hospitals are needed for the wounded and the dying. It won't be long before the Huns begin bombing our cities.' He said it so casually that it turned Marina's blood cold. 'I would suggest a nursing home. Somewhere to recuperate.'

'May I have time to think about it?'

'Of course.'

They left the bedroom and passed Daphne, who was standing in the landing. She backed up against the wall, tightly stepping sideways to look through the crack in the bedroom door. George was lying in bed, she sensed the doctor must have administered a sedative, for he looked peaceful. Slowly passing the door, trying to step over the creaking floorboards, she tiptoed downstairs.

'It will be a tremendous adjustment, Lady Greenwood.' Daphne heard the doctor's voice from the other side of the drawing room door.

"How... how long will it be before my husband gets better?'

'I can't say.'

Daphne slumped against the wall in the hallway, neatly falling to the floor. She felt as though her entire world had crashed around her. What now? she wondered.

'Get up off the floor,' Marina said.

She defied Marina's orders and remained on the floor, watching her mother bid farewell to the doctor. 'He's going to die, isn't he? Daphne asked.

'Who's going to die? What are you talking about?'

'He's going to die, that's why he's been sent home.'

'You silly girl,' Marina said, her stare firmly fixed on Daphne. 'Of course he's not going to die. Not unless I murder him!' She meant the latter as a joke, despite it sounding like a callous threat. 'Now run along upstairs. I've had quite enough histrionics for one day, and it's not even lunch time.'

She watched Daphne walk up the stairs to the chorus of George's snores echoing down the landing. Her eyes stopped at the foot of the stairs, where Evangelina once lay. He took care of me, all those years ago, she said to herself. Charitable, she was not. But she sensed if she could make him better, he would leave sooner, and she could get on with her life.

Chapter Eighteen

It was Christmas week, though there was not a hint of the festive season at Hiraeth. Marina did not care for Christmas trees and George stayed in bed, repeating the usual routine of sleeping all day and climbing the walls at night. She thought she could get to the bottom of it, thinking something dreadful had happened on the ship, but her patience was running out.

Daphne felt as desperate as ever, and she missed Celia more with each passing day. She felt tearful and at a loss, and in this state she wished she could feel numb again.

'Are you sending the Hartleys a Christmas card?' Marina asked her.

'I don't know. Should I?'

'It's up to you.'

There was a thud on the floorboards and Marina instinctively knew it was George. Doctor Glendinning had left a supply of sleeping pills and she was happy to sedate George throughout the day, even if the nights were unbearable as the pills wore off.

She went upstairs and found him on the floor, face down. He must have been sleepwalking. Poor tortured soul, she said to herself. When she tried to coax him to get up, he opened his eyes and reached for her shoulders. He pulled her down to his level and said into her ear, 'It was an accident.'

'What was?'

'I didn't mean to do it.'

'You've been dreaming,' she said.

He covered his face with his hands and began to sob. Her heart softened and she looked down at him.

'I mean it. You must believe me. Say you believe me.'

'All right,' she played along. 'I believe you.'

'I didn't mean to do it. I didn't mean to kill her.'

Her. I didn't mean to kill *her*. She drew away from him and stood up, unsteady on her feet. She was not scared, but she felt cautious and wanted him to stay away from her. He lay there, on the floor, sobbing and repeating himself.

Perhaps it was all a game, an act to prevent him from going overseas again. She had read about a young man who had feigned shell-shock until his mother came home and caught him sitting in the drawing room, laughing at a comedy programme on the wireless. The woman had informed on her son and he was imprisoned in a military gaol for desertion. This snippet was followed by a strict warning from the Home Office, that traitors walked amongst them and that everyone must 'do their bit'. Could she turn him in, if she had to? She had never given it much thought. Could she betray her husband?

*

Daphne walked to the Hartleys house and rapped on the door, her hands were shaking and her heart began to pound. She felt brave in spite of the sickening feeling forming in the pit of her stomach. Mrs Hartley's face lit up when she opened the door. 'Daphne,' she said.

'Hello,' Daphne said, her heart still pounding. 'I, uh, I hope I'm not interrupting because... because I can go away if I am.'

She held the door wide open, gesturing for Daphne to walk inside. 'You're not too cold, are you?' Mrs Hartley rubbed Daphne's arms. 'It's quite mild today.'

'Yes, too warm for the scarf you gave me.' It was a quick and clever thing to say. She had purposely left the scarf at home, hidden away in her bottom drawer.

They walked along the hallway and Mrs Hartley stopped at the drawing room door. 'Go on, take a seat, dear. I'll go fetch the tea. Go on, go sit down,' she encouraged her.

Daphne walked through the large, hexagon shaped drawing room with its bay windows and high ceiling. Her mind felt clearer than before and she longed to take everything in: the chintzy sofa with the multi-coloured fringes along the footboard, the wallpaper with cabbage roses, and the cream carpet with the long pink rug running parallel in front of the fireplace.

'Well, how is your father getting on?' Mrs Hartley cheerfully asked as she entered the room, carrying a silver tea-tray.

'I don't know,' Daphne truthfully answered. 'The doctor said to keep him sedated.'

'Well, that's too bad,' she said as she sat down to pour the tea.

A moment of silence passed with neither of them willing to initiate a conversation. Mrs Hartley seemed content to stare at Daphne, which made her uncomfortable.

'Is Mr Hartley in?' Daphne asked.

'Oh yes, he's upstairs in his... sitting room.' She moved to the edge of her chair and, lowering her voice, she confided, 'Since the... accident... we've not really seen eye to eye. He blames me for what happened. But, you don't think it was my fault, do you?'

Daphne felt confused, why should it be Mrs Hartley's fault? She said that she did not think so, and she asked why Mr Hartley felt that way.

'Lots of reasons. I gave her too much freedom.' She stopped talking and looked in the direction of the doorway, where Mr Hartley stood.

'Merry Christmas,' Mr Hartley said as he passed.

Daphne asked to use the lavatory and Mrs Hartley said of course. As she walked up the stairs she could hear Mr Hartley's wireless droning from his sitting room. She saw Celia's bedroom, the door glaring at her, drawing her forth. The rose coloured walls with the tiny, white floral print, the bed under the window; the familiarity of such a scene wounded her and she felt the room spin beneath her feet. Catching her balance and turning slowly, she walked to the dressing table and ran her hand across its dusty walnut top. The sound of Mr Hartley closing his sitting room door startled her. She walked from the bedroom, slowing down at the lavatory door to disguise the fact that she had not been where she had said she was going, and made a dash for the staircase.

'I'm sorry, I have to go,' Daphne said to Mrs Hartley.

'What's the matter dear, don't you feel well?'

'Yes, I feel sick,' she said as she made her way to the door. Putting a hand to her forehead, she mumbled, 'Must be flu.'

'Hmm you do look a little peaky,' Mrs Hartley said. 'Would you like me to see you home? You're not liable to faint, or anything?'

'No. I'm sure I'll be fine.'

*

For hours Marina sat downstairs, thinking about George's outburst. She wondered if there had been women onboard the ship and that, perhaps, something had happened in the water and in a way George blamed himself. Was he guilty he had lived when so many had died? Yes, she was certain that must be it.

She went upstairs, hoping he would be awake. 'George?' she called out.

'Hello,' he said. He was sitting up in bed, looking out the window. He focused on a chaffinch perching on the windowsill.

'Makes you think of High Greenwood,' Marina said as she stood in the doorway.

He smiled, content to watch the bird.

'I was hoping you might join us downstairs for dinner tonight. That is, if you're feeling up to it?'

He nodded. His demeanour was calmer than before and his eyes were clear, but Marina still sensed a barrier between them. It was not like before, when she felt that things were strained. She thought George was entirely changed and she had not yet figured this new person out.

'I've been thinking...,'

'Yes?'

'That I ought to plant a kitchen garden, If... if...' The stutter was beginning to reveal itself. 'If you think it's a g-g-good idea?'

'Yes, it's a lovely idea. It'll give you something to look after.'

He smiled once more, fooling her into thinking he was better. 'I could go up to the house. Bring some gardening things back with me.'

Yes, what a good idea, she leaned forward with anticipation. She was excited at the thought but did not show it. They could go together and she could see what had become of High Greenwood and question him accordingly. She felt so clever; that she could make him do whatever she wanted. Fragments of their old selves were coming back, and it pleased her.

'Whatever you think is best, darling.'

*

They appeared as three strangers sitting around the dinner table. Marina had cooked hare, and Daphne had never had it before and she did not like it, so she pushed it around on her plate. Marina did without, out of principal; far from admitting her loathing of meat, she made a grand gesture of sacrificing it for their dinner and for tomorrow's lunch and, perhaps, supper. She ate only the potatoes and a forkful of carrots. Daphne suspected the quality of meals would get worse.

'Where did you go to earlier?' Marina asked.

'To see Mrs Hartley.'

'Oh? Did you give her a Christmas card?'

'I took one with me but I didn't give it to her. I... I... I just felt silly.'

'The poor old dear, her first Christmas without Celia.' After a moment of silence, she asked, 'Did you ever give her those bracelets back?'

'The bangles?'

'Yes. Bangles.' Really, she did not see the difference and hated Daphne correcting her.

'No. Not yet.' She took a forkful of potatoes to avoid speaking about them. Then, she said, 'Celia said her Uncle Christopher had given her them. He wasn't her real uncle, but her father's friend.'

'We should all have an Uncle Christopher. How lucky.'

'No, that's not what I mean. He um, she said he... they had secrets with each other. That's why he bought her the bangles, so she wouldn't tell.'

'He behaved badly?' she asked. Then it dawned on her what Daphne was trying to say. She looked at Daphne and said, 'If I were you I'd give the jewellery back. Why would you want to hang onto it anyway, if that's the case? The dirty old bugger.'

George spilled his drink. 'Jesus Christ!' He ran his hands down his front, where his shirt was wet.

Daphne was shocked, she felt like crying. Nothing was familiar to her any more: Marina's concern, George's behaviour, the unpredictability of the future.

'It's all right,' Marina got up and went to George. 'It's only water, no need for hysterics.' She used her napkin to mop it up.

'I... I think I'll go up now. I... I'm s-s-sorry I s-s-spoiled dinner.' He walked out of the room, his shoulders slumped and his head down. He was ashamed of himself; he caught the look of fright in Daphne's eyes and it pierced through his heart.

He climbed the stairs, thinking that he ought to do them all favour; that he ought to put an end to this once and for all. Opening the bathroom door he stumbled inside and fell to the floor in front of the lavatory, thinking he was going to be sick. Instead, his chest became tight and his throat felt as though it were closing over. He rolled his head from side to side, willing himself to snap out of it. It's a heart attack; I am having a heart attack, he thought as he got up and felt for the sink. He held onto the edge of the sink, taking shallow breaths which emitted a hollow sound as he exhaled, like a dog being choked on its lead. The whistling of the kettle downstairs irritated him, and he whispered, 'Shut up, shut up,' but his voice was hoarse and he could barely speak. Then he began to cry, he held his breath as the tears flowed from his eyes, his mouth twitching at the sides as the sound threatened to escape. Glancing at himself in the mirror above the sink he recoiled at his image, his face contorted into something quite ugly and unrecognisable. If he were to stagger into the kitchen he would surely frighten Marina and Daphne, for he had frightened himself. It lasted for twenty minutes, and when it was over he continued to feel the tremor of tears; a build-up of emotion.

'There is something I must tell you,' George said as Marina walked into the room.

'I want to talk to you too,' she said.

She assumed that he wanted to talk about the ship and what he could remember from its sinking and his being saved. And that was the nature of the conversation she wanted to have.

'You'll never forgive me,' he quickly said. He stopped for a moment and took shallow breaths, his face entirely readable. She knew he was coaxing himself to speak clearly, to kill the stutter before it came out.

'I already know. You think you are responsible for someone who was on the ship. Isn't that right? You blame yourself for her death.'

Her death; *her* death, Marina's words rang in his ears. He put his head in his hands and began to sob. Why did she not think the worst of him? Why did she not think that he could be responsible for her mother's death?

She placed a limp hand on his shoulder and said, 'You can't go on like this, driving yourself into an early grave.'

'I deserve it,' he said through convulsions. He flung himself into Marina's arms, and she jumped back a little, surprised by this gesture. 'Oh God, I deserve it!' His tears soaked her blouse and she slowly raised her hand, patting him on the head. She was hopeless at comforting people in distress.

'We've all done things we're not proud of,' she said. Please don't ask me what, please don't ask me what, she said to herself. She pulled away, and he did too, and they sat next to one another. Marina was more composed, but she always was better at putting on a front.

He drew away and sat on an angle, with his back to her. His chest heaved and sobs escaped with every second breath. 'If I told you,' his voice shook, 'you would never forgive me.'

'Well then,' Marina stood up and walked to the door. 'Perhaps it's best if I don't know.'

A weakness gripped him and he could not speak, his mind was blank and his body numb. If he had the strength he would have jumped up and grabbed her by the shoulders and told her that he had killed her mother. But he was not brave, and he was not strong. Instead he let her leave the room, as ignorant as she had been when she entered it.

1925

Chapter Nineteen

Nobody expected Sybil to die, and so it came as a shock when she did. It had happened quickly and without warning, the old lung complaint which ran in the family struck her that winter. They were having dinner when she coughed, spluttering blood all over the napkin, and George ran to telephone Doctor Glendinning, who was not surprised by this brittle woman haemorrhaging blood. Apparently she had known for some time but did not want to worry them.

In the last year of her life, she was always wheezing, coughing into her handkerchief and leaning on an ivory cane. Her icy blue eyes were fixed in a permanent stare that was as unnerving as it was beguiling. As her illness wore on, the eyes became grey with a navy ring around the iris – the haunting look of someone dying from consumption but still plodding along in the living realm. Marina resented this self-appointed martyrdom, but in time she came to admire it. Never complain; never explain.

George took it badly; he loved her the most. His only experience of love had come from Sybil, who controlled him all his life. And so he thought by suffocating Marina with this version of love, it would prove to her just how deeply his feelings ran. Her own mother did not love her, she was certain of that. She was scared of Evangelina, scared she was just like her.

Sybil was given six weeks to live but died in five. It was Marina who had found her; she had died in her sleep without much fuss. It was all very quick and clean, and George said: 'But she can't be dead. She was only fifty.' To Marina, it seemed like a disastrous age: the threshold of how one's old age would peter out. Sybil was proof of that. With her crumbling bones and bleeding lungs, she would have suffered and so death was a blessing. Was it that way for Evangelina: was death a release for her too?

Even in death Sybil intimidated Marina. She lay on the bed, her thin body laid extremely flat, her nose seemed larger, her mouth almost hollow and the hood of her beautiful eyelids had sunk into her skeletal face. As Marina's eyes burned through the body, she heard a small clicking noise, magnified by the silence, which caused her to jump.

'So sorry,' it said.

Her mouth hardly moved when she answered, 'Quite all right.'

It was the first time she had met anyone from George's extended family. 'You're George's wife,' he said as he entered the room. 'You must be relieved the old bitch has finally croaked it.' He reached into his trouser pocket and retrieved two pennies, setting them on Sybil's eyelids. 'It's supposed to bring luck.'

She laughed and looked at the ground, feeling quite ashamed by the act and overwhelmed by his arrogance. 'Yes,' she agreed, hoping he might introduce himself.

'I'm Sybil's nephew. Her sister is my mother.'

'I haven't seen you at High Greenwood before.'

'First time I've been back in years.' He lifted the pennies from her eyelids and flipped one into the air. It was clear to Marina that he was playing a game of heads or tails. 'I live in South Africa, but I was in town doing a bit of business. Read about her death in the paper, so I thought I'd swing by.'

'What kind of business?'

'Publishing.'

He moved to the closed window. 'Christ, does it stink in here,' he pushed the window open, the icy air slipped into the room. 'Here,' he picked up Sybil's stiff ankles, 'you take the arms and I'll take the legs and we'll move her to the icehouse.'

Marina watched as the flimsy blanket covering Sybil's body moved upward, exposing the ankles, blackened by the natural rhythm of decay.

'Christ!' he said once more, before dropping her legs.

George lurked in the doorway, coughing to make his presence known. 'I see you've met Cousin Gerald,' he said with an air of disapproval.

Marina glanced at Gerald, who had moved to the window, keeping his back to George. 'Only briefly.'

'I was saying what a shame it is that Aunt Sybil has been taken from us.' He turned to face George. 'She was... so full of life.'

'She is at peace now,' George coughed to steady his emotions.

'You will stay with us, won't you?' Marina said. 'It seems a shame to travel all the way back to town only to have to return for the funeral.'

She would never have been so bold when Sybil was alive; she never felt it was her house and that she could ask people to stay. She only asked him because they became silent and she did not want George to break down.

'Darling, I am sure Gerald has made plans.'

'I should be delighted.'

They left High Greenwood for a breath of fresh air and to escape the heavy silence of George and the shallow conversation of his sisters, punctuated with acid remarks about intruders and those who did not know their place. Digs at them both, they imagined.

'Two bitches in one day, and a dead one upstairs,' Gerald said. 'I'd call that penance.' Marina followed him to the small woodland behind the house. 'This is where Walter died,' he pointed to the jagged rocks where the soil sloped to meet the stream.

'Heart attack, wasn't it?' She stared at the water resting between the reeds and the flies bubbling on the surface.

'Something like that.' He looked up at a flock of birds flying overhead. 'They say the mad daughter did it.'

'Louisa? Surely not.'

'I'm only teasing.'

The sky became dark and there was an unexpected rumble of thunder. It startled Marina and she moved closer to Gerald, accidentally brushing against him. 'What was that?'

'Thunder.'

She moved away from him, smiling awkwardly as she did so. She was saved by a sudden burst of rain.

'Quick,' Gerald pulled her by the arm and led her into the old, dilapidated icehouse.

The roof was intact, though trickles of rain slipped through the stones. She stood in the middle, finding her bearings. The old stone shelves had moss growing on them and spiders' webs were spun across the walls.

Gerald walked to the opening that was once a small window which had eroded through time. 'We'd best stay here 'til it passes.'

Marina smiled, she placed her hands on the rocks beneath the window. 'George will be wondering where I am.'

'He's too preoccupied with the others.'

'So, this is the icehouse?'

'I'm sure George has told you all about it.'

'No.'

'No?' He whistled, knowing it would prompt Marina to press him for more information. She did. 'This is where he corrupted my sister.'

'Your sister?'

'Yes, Pamela.'

Ah, *that* Pamela. She felt odd, it wasn't jealousy but an intrusive feeling. She wished he had not offered the information.

'Sweet, really.'

'It's called incest,' her voice was harsh. She turned her back on Gerald and began to fidget with a loose stone.

'I didn't mean to upset you.' He placed a hand on her shoulder, tightening his grip as he moved closer. 'I shouldn't have said anything. You won't hold it against me, I hope?'

Marina shook her head.

'You're terribly unhappy, aren't you? I can tell.'

She looked at him and nodded, bursting into tears as she did so. 'Sorry,' she sniffled.

'It's this place,' he said. 'I hate it.'

She dried her eyes with the sleeve of her coat and took a deep breath. 'I suppose I'm picking up on George's mood. He loved Sybil so much, I know he's devastated in spite of his brave face.'

'Don't cry.' He put his arm around her. 'I didn't mean to upset you. Please forgive me.'

She leaned against the wall and gathered her composure.

'Feel better?'

She nodded and offered him a smile. He put his finger under her chin and she sensed he was going to kiss her. She stepped sideways and moved away from him.

'We ought to get back.'

For a while they walked in silence. Marina tried to make sense of what had happened; she felt silly for crying and for her mixed feelings about George and Pamela. Surely all that had happened so long ago that it was ancient history. She felt pangs of envy that George had felt love for Pamela, and had experienced excitement and what it meant to fall for someone, and for that person to reciprocate those feelings.

Then, thinking that Gerald cared for her, she pushed those thoughts out of her mind and realised that she liked him, too. It was a pure feeling, like meeting the person who would become a best friend and the thrill of discovering that you shared everything in common and that, somehow, time was running out and there were not enough hours in the day to talk and to be in one another's company. She wished she had let him kiss her in the icehouse, then she wondered if he was really going to or if she had imagined it. If he kisses me now I won't reject him, she thought.

'Is your mother alive?' she asked him as they trudged across the lawn. She liked him taking her arm in his, escorting her back to the house. They looked like a married couple, lord and lady of the manor. Their tangled arms, the way he looked down at her when he spoke, and how she liked being next to him, and listening to his voice.

'Just about.' Noticing Marina's curious look, he elaborated, 'She, too, has a lung complaint. It runs in the family, apparently. Bad blood, and all that.'

George met them in the hallway as they came in from their walk. He looked down at their inappropriate footwear and asked, or rather scolded, 'Why didn't you go to the boot cupboard?' He did not notice her bloodshot eyes or that she had been crying. All he saw was fault.

'Sorry, George,' Marina said as he helped her out of her coat. 'We acted on impulse.'

Gerald pulled off his jacket and cap, throwing them to one side. They were George's best tweeds. He resented how Gerald helped himself to his things, and then discarded them at his leisure.

*

There was a frosty silence throughout dinner. It was the night before Sybil's funeral and none of them had much of an appetite. It was late, and Gerald said he had work to do and slipped off to the library, leaving them alone. Clara made a snide remark about him going to inject himself with morphia or smother himself with chloroform.

'But it's so fashionable, darling,' Sadie giggled.

'Fashionable? Abusing one's body is fashionable?' George asked, sounding like a puritan.

'Shut up, George. You sound like an R.C.,' Sadie said.

'Jolly old chlorers,' Clara joined in with the giggling.

'Shall we go up?' he asked Marina. She nodded. She knew as soon as they left Sadie and Clara would talk about them.

George was in a state. He pulled at Marina, holding her by the wrists, sobbing incoherently about putting Sybil in the ground. Her first instinct was to slap him hard across the face, instead she glanced over her shoulder. How shameful if anyone saw George in hysterics. She pushed him along in the direction of his bedroom and she forced him through the door.

'Calm down,' she said.

He stopped, taking a deep breath that convulsed as the air went in. She stayed while he changed out of his clothes and prepared for bed.

'Don't go,' he pulled at her sleeve as she was about to leave.

'I'm just going to change into my nightdress.'

'You'll come back?'

'Yes.'

Marina hated desperation; she hated to see him beg and plead. He was in bed when she returned, and she drew back the covers and climbed in beside him. 'A good night's sleep will help you,' she said as she turned out the lamp. 'You're overtired and overthinking things.' She was oddly authoritative, and he appeared to her as a small boy, vulnerable and crying for his mother. It was an inconvenience to sleep in his bedroom; she disliked his bed and the room was always much too cold. Her shoulders ached from the chill that had set in, spreading across her collarbone and rising up to her neck.

He closed his eyes, it was comforting to listen to her breathing. They were silent, the rise and fall of their breath was out of synch. The agitation began once again, and he turned onto his side. Marina kept her back to him, her eyes were closed, she was drifting off to sleep. She felt him pressing against her, pushing himself close to her.

'Stop it,' she whispered with her eyes closed. 'Go to sleep.'

'Please,' he begged through his sobs.

The rest was incoherent as he buried his face in the crook of her neck and pulled at her nightdress. She fell silent and he held his breath. The silence preoccupied her, and she listened to the empty din that surrounded them. There was a quick stabbing feeling and then the abrupt heaviness of George as he collapsed on top of her. She did not move and he pulled away from her, she thought he might turn over and resume sleep.

'I'm sorry,' he sobbed, she felt his tears on her shoulder, his chin pressing into the flesh of her upper-arm. 'I'm sorry,' he said once more. 'I'm sorry. I'm so sorry.'

'It's all right,' she whispered.

She was unsure if he was apologising because of what he had done, or because he could not follow through. It must be the former, she thought; poor George had a conscience. She raised her hand, uncertain of her movements, and reached up and touched his face. She was unmoved, perhaps she felt some pity, and the words of Sybil came back to her: that somehow it was all right for them to force you into it, even if you didn't want to. She had numbed herself to all of that, so long ago.

In the morning before everyone awoke, Marina went to her own bedroom. She sat by the window and looked out at the lawn before dressing. The air was misty and a frost formed on the glass. The quietness of the house, the gentle footsteps of Gladys on the landing, and the hum of the hearse as it crept down the icy driveway were the only sounds. Then, she heard various bedroom doors opening and footsteps walking down the stairs. She got up and began to dress.

The door opened and George came into the room. He was embarrassed about the night before and apologised profusely but Marina told him not to worry, that grief was unpredictable. 'Besides,' she added, hoping to ease his guilt, 'hardly anything happened.' After she had said it, she realised the blow she had dealt him.

'Right,' he said in a rigid voice. 'Do you... do you mind if I wait here while the... while the undertaker...,'

'Yes, of course,' Marina said.

'I didn't want to be in the room when they... when they p-p-put the lid on.' He sat down on the edge of her bed.

Marina nodded, she was lost for words. They heard the faint banging on the nails as the undertaker attached the lid to the coffin. They heard the scuffling as the coffin was taken down the landing. 'I suppose it's time we...,'

'Yes,' George said before she could finish.

They gathered at the small plot of land behind High Greenwood to bury Sybil. Sadie and Clara circled the grave, moving in close to George to purposely usurp Marina from his side. She stood behind Sybil's children, in the same small row the servants had formed.

As Gerald walked past, he offered his arm to her and she slipped her hand through the gap. 'I thought the other girl would have been here,' he whispered.

'Who?' Marina asked, and then remembered, 'Louisa?'

'That's the one.'

'Whatever happened to her?'

'Ran off, eloped, with an old school chum.'

When everyone returned to the house for tea, Marina's position in the family was made clear to her. George, his sisters and their husbands, who had come down for the funeral, stood by the fire, greeting the few guests that had made the pilgrimage to High Greenwood.

'Such a shame mummy had the bad luck to die in January,' Sadie said.

'Yes, such filthy weather we're having,' Clara replied in the American drawl she had picked up from her husband.

'I believe a terrible frost is headed our way,' George said.

'Oh, I hope not. I'll never get home,' sighed Sadie.

Marina left the room before she had to endure any more small-talk about the weather. She went to her bedroom, took off her mourning clothes and got into bed with a book of verse. It seemed a frivolous thing to do, given the circumstances. The door knocked and, dressed only in her slip and a heavy cardigan to keep the cold off her shoulders, she ignored it. The handle twisted, and the door opened.

'What's the matter, Ge-' she stopped. 'Oh,' she said, pulling the cardigan across her chest. 'George is downstairs, I think.'

'Oh yes, I know. He sent me up to fetch you. Care for a spot of funeral tea?'

'No, thank you. I'm not hungry.' She felt horribly self-conscious and wished he would go away.

'What are you reading?' he asked as he gently closed the door.

She looked in the direction of the closed door. 'Gunga *Din*.'

'*Though I've belted you and flayed you, By the livin' Gawd that made you, You're a better man than I am, Gunga Din*!' he recited from memory in an atrocious cockney accent. He walked to her and, looking at the book, he rolled his eyes. 'I can't stand the Raj.' He sat on the edge of her bed and took the book from her lap and threw it across the room. It landed under the window, making a thud on the floor.

'What do you like to read?' she asked.

'Hmm,' he thought for a moment. 'As a matter of fact I loathe reading. But I do love writers, they fall into two categories. Either they're wildly fascinating, wonderful eccentrics etcetera, or they're terrific bores and only write because they've nothing else to do.'

'Which category do you prefer?'

'I think the terrific bores. They're less trouble.'

They both laughed. She had felt so wretched, the death of Sybil filled her with dread; she knew George would have no distraction, and they would somehow be thrown together more than they had been before. How could she live like this? She often thought about running away, but she had no money of her own. She thought of death: the options, of which, were many. She would lie face down in the stream behind High Greenwood. She would fall from the balustrade, landing head first on the tiled floor. The list was endless, a quick and easy way out. But she lacked the courage to do so.

Gerald kissed her, quite unexpectedly.

'What are you doing?' She broke away, her heart was pounding.

A nudge from her conscience told her that things had gone too far, or they were about to. He grinned and told her it was what she wanted.

'Yes, and then what?' It was a bold thing to say and she did not mean to blurt it out.

'And then what.' He let out a ridiculous laugh as he pulled her towards him. 'And then what.'

The mood changed and she realised it was not what she wanted. 'No, stop,' she said, hoping he would. She was certain he would. But he did not.

'Don't worry,' he said. 'I'll leave the church before the sermon.'

When she attempted to protest once more, to tell him to stop, he pressed his hands against her shoulders and pinned her down. She felt the pulse of his thumb beating off her bones. His aggressiveness intrigued her, she felt ashamed.

She told herself it was her fault: she had led him on. She had been so nice to him, and he to her, for the past few days that it seemed natural he should expect something in return. Wasn't that how it worked? She knew it was no good fighting with him, he was too far gone to listen. She was furious that he had taken such liberalities. Sybil would have said she was asking for it. His sudden cry brought her back to the present.

'Sorry,' he said, his face pressed against hers, 'couldn't wait.'

She had felt nothing, the same feeling she had felt with George. No, she felt worse, the guilt had already set in, and so, in her mind, it had all been in vain. And now what?

He got up and fixed his trousers, the clanging of his belt buckle sounded to her like a death knell. She tried to look away, fixing her slip as she sat up, but she still felt just as exposed. He put his finger under her chin, twisting her head around, and kissed her on the lips. 'I say, you're taking it all rather well. But I suppose you know what to do.'

'Do?' she asked. He did not understand her naivety, or perhaps he did. Is that why he took advantage?

He shot her a quizzical look, grinning once more.

She pressed her fingers against her eyelids and then opened her eyes, she could see him through the slits. This is what whores do, she thought. I can't complain.

When he left the room, Marina made no attempt to get up. What seemed like hours was only minutes between Gerald leaving and George coming to her room. Quietly knocking on the door, he entered before she answered. He looked down at her on the bed. 'What's going on?' His question struck her with a sense of guilt. 'Why aren't you dressed?' She could tell he was scrutinising her appearance. 'Aren't you coming downstairs?'

'I don't feel well,' she mumbled.

'Probably the cold. Look at you, you're half naked.' He went to her and pulled the covers around her shoulders.

'Please don't,' she said without meaning to. 'Please don't touch me.'

The words felt like a knife, and he removed his hands as though he had done something wrong.

She sighed, hoping to break the tension. 'Sorry,' she offered by way of apology. 'I'm not myself. I'm sorry.'

'Gerald's gone,' he said.

Marina looked up at him, she wanted to ask why but she could not find the words.

'Yes. His wife was waiting for him.'

The words sent a jolt through her. 'His wife?' she tried to sound casual. 'He didn't say he was married.'

'He left her at a hotel in town.' He picked up the book that Gerald had thrown across the room and set it on her night-stand.

Marina could not bear to have it near her. 'Sorry,' she said once more. 'Can you take this with you? I believe it belongs to Clara. It's not mine.' How easily she could lie, it was a quality she abhorred in others. Over the period of those few days, of Gerald's coming and his going, she had turned into someone she did not like, or recognise.

'It belongs... belonged to my mother. It's not Clara's book.'

'I'm sorry.'

*

When it dawned on Marina that she was pregnant, she felt a wretched sense of doom. It was such a grotesque transformation; she felt an odd, indescribable static feeling in her stomach and in her head, as though an invisible cord connected the two, sending a biological order out of her control to the thing inside her, saying: 'Grow, grow.' She was certain it was her punishment for what she had done.

'I feel... unwell,' she said at the time, and George, so naïve, would believe her.

'Women are always so much more prone to fatigue than men,' he once said. 'It has something to do with their bones. They're carrying an extra rib, you see.'

She confined herself to her bedroom unless it was unavoidable, she consumed most meals alone, sitting up in bed, and she moved around harbouring a quiet air of determination. She found a handbook in the clandestine section of a grubby bookshop. This book was not for the jovial mother-to-be, it told her of ways and means to rid herself of the tiny intruder inside her body. It mentioned special kinds of pills, made from a concoction of herbs that promised to abort the baby, but she had no idea where to find them. Certainly not at her local chemist. She went for brisk walks and bumpy drives down country lanes. She even considered throwing herself down the stairs but George caught her just before she lunged from the top stair.

'What are you doing?' his voice startled her.

'Oh,' she said, 'just had a dizzy spell.'

'Here,' he put his arm around her, guiding her to the safety of the landing. 'Let's find you a seat.' He walked her to her bedroom, and she pretended to be light-headed and feigned a stagger. 'Shall I ring Glendinning?'

'No, there's no need. I'll go see him myself on Monday if I'm not better.'

Ignoring her wishes, George rang the doctor anyway. He appeared in Marina's bedroom, led through the door by George. She was too stunned to be livid. The jig was up, she told herself. She knew the diagnoses, but played along anyway. She asked the doctor not to tell George of the news.

'You see, I don't want it,' she blurted out.

He knew what she meant. 'I can't help you, I'm afraid.'

Marina was desperate, she wanted to tell him about Gerald and how the child might not be George's and how she could not be certain who the father was. Shame, all she had felt for the past six months, prevented her from doing so.

'I can't help you,' he repeated. 'But I know of some women who go to France. Paris, actually. They have clinics there. Appendix treatment is the usual excuse.'

How will I get to France? she wondered. It was hopeless: she had no money of her own and no way of taking the ferry without George wanting to go with her. She'd never been to France, she had never been abroad. She could not speak French. What was the French word for abortion? She slumped back against her pillows. A pain throbbed in her temples. She would have cried, if she had the energy.

George entered the room wearing a broad grin, and that triggered her tears. 'What's the matter?' he asked her. 'Don't you see what this means? It means we can forget the rotten business of mummy dying, and everything else in between. Don't you see, darling? We can finally be happy.'

*

Daphne was born in Marina's bedroom at High Greenwood. It was a traumatic birth, with Doctor Glendinning arriving too late to give her a whiff of chloroform to knock her out, or at least take the edge off. It was for the best, he said, for there were complications and he needed Marina to 'help the baby along'. Bad luck, she thought. She would have rather died in a pool of blood than push the little beast into the world, giving it life and saving her own.

The beginning of autumn had been unbearably humid and Marina remembered not the long, drawn-out confinement but the influx of wasps at the end of summer. She recalled every unpleasant detail, perhaps something she would not have cared about before. The wasps, the enormous spiders that ran across her bedroom floor every other evening, the rabbit cull and the gunshots that rang out from early morning until dusk. And the pain that struck her, suddenly. She said nothing, hoping it was something abnormal, something life-threatening and dangerous, until Gladys saw her and fetched George. It had been morning time and Marina was lying on top of the bed, drenched in sweat, the bedclothes underneath her were soaking wet and there was blood all over her nightgown, down her legs, and on the blanket where she must have wiped her hands. There were dark circles under her eyes and her skin was grey and clammy.

When it was over, she was dazed from sheer exhaustion and the blood she had lost. She made no effort to sit up or to ask for the baby, who arrived as the sun was coming over the yardarm. She did not care to know if it was alive or not. Somehow, she heard an echoing voice in her head calling out, 'Is it all right? Is it all right?' But she must have imagined this, for she felt no sudden maternal shift.

Dr Glendinning fetched George, and asked Gladys to bring him a brandy. 'The sun is over the yardarm,' he said in reference to the brandy at the ungodly hour. That must have been the origin of the expression Marina had heard when the baby was born. She remembered him announcing that when it came to registering the baby's time of birth.

George came in and Dr Glendinning told him the baby was a girl. He had spoken more enthusiastically about the brandy. 'No, matter, no matter,' he patted George on the back. 'There's still time for a boy.'

The monthly nurse arrived, a fluster of apologies about the train being delayed because of a nasty accident earlier that morning. 'No fatalities, thank the Lord,' she said as she pulled off her coat. 'The coal carriage broke away from the train. There was coal all over the track.' She slipped a starched apron on over her head and tied the strings behind her back. 'So, this is the baby,' she looked into the cot. 'She's a pretty little thing.' She knew it was a girl because nobody had wrapped the baby up. They were waiting for the nurse to do it.

Before Marina knew it, Dr Glendinning was off, George left the room, and Gladys came to change the sheet with Marina still in the bed, though turning her slightly onto her side as she pulled it from under her. As far as she was aware the monthly nurse had not introduced herself. Gladys left, George returned, and the baby was brought to her.

Marina looked down at the baby and to her it did not look like a child, her child, but a freakish being that had been placed in her arms. A cuckoo dropped in her nest; an accident of nature. Its small head perched on the end of a slender neck, the cloudy eyes peering from narrow slits, scrutinising this woman who had given birth to her. She was repulsed by its straggly limbs poking out from beneath the nightgown the monthly nurse had dressed it in. How brittle it was, its feet about the length of her finger, its translucent nails.

'She's tiny now,' George hovered close to the baby, putting his hand beneath its neck for support. 'But Glendinning said she'll fill out in a week or so.'

'Take it away,' Marina said.

'All right, darling.' He walked the baby to its cot, thinking Marina was overtired.

Marina turned her head away from the baby, she could not bear to look at it. When it began to cry she shut her eyes and tried to block out the noise. She wanted it to disappear.

At first, George said he hoped the baby would be a girl because, then, Marina would have a little friend. He hoped the baby would be a girl for his own selfish reasons, too, because it would mean she would have to try for a boy and he would get his wish of having lots of children. Two at the very least, a gentleman's family.

'Well,' George said as he walked to Marina's bedside. 'A little girl.'

'A girl,' Marina let out a sarcastic laugh. All ready she sensed the child was doomed.

'Girls aren't so rotten. And you heard Dr Glendinning. There is still time for a...' He stopped, thinking it insensitive to harp on about a boy. 'For lots of things.'

'I think I'll go to sleep now.'

'Yes, you deserve a rest.'

'I'll wake you when she needs fed,' the monthly nurse called from across the room.

Marina shuddered, and in a cold, domineering voice, she replied, 'I'm not going to feed her myself. There is a tin of perfectly good formula downstairs. Have Gladys send it up.' She began to tremble, but Dr

Glendinning said it would be normal to have chills. He was coming back with a nurse to give her a blood transfusion.

'Nonsense. All the best mothers do,' the monthly nurse said.

'Tell her to go away, George.'

Later that day Dr Glendinning returned, as he said he would, with a nurse and two pints of blood from the hospital in town. George watched from the far side of the room as the nurse felt for a vein in Marina's arm and Dr Glendinning prepared the tube which the blood would travel through. He watched the blood slip through the clear tube, dripping out of the glass bottle hanging above the headboard, and listened to the medical jargon the doctor and the nurse exchanged. He imagined it to be like adrenaline, a quick boost to her body and all of her colour would return, like she had been inflated. But it was painfully slow and the results were not instant.

'Blood makes blood,' the doctor said. 'Let's see how you get on, Lady Greenwood. You'll need a replacement in a week or so.'

Marina looked up at the glass jar above her head. She knew what the doctor meant, how pointless this exercise was: they were feeding blood through her arm and all the while she was still bleeding from the baby's assault.

It was so barbaric, George thought. Poor Marina.

1940

Chapter Twenty

They left for the nursing home on New Year's Day. The cold woke Marina up before the alarm went off, she climbed out of bed and went to the window; the curtains were damp from the frost on the glass and snow covered the ground. To her surprise, George had been co-operative about going to the nursing home and he spoke optimistically about the care he would receive. It would be better for them all if he left, that is what he said, and Marina thought him a good sport and entirely selfless. Dr Glendinning had recommended a convalescent home not too far from High Greenwood, where the cognitive treatment was advanced and he would be offered a reduced fee due to his having served in the war. Well, almost.

'When I come back,' he said as Marina helped him into his coat, 'I'll be brand new.'

She smiled, though the statement troubled her. Would he come back a stranger or would the old George be restored? He was not without fault, but at least she knew where she stood.

Daphne did not get out of bed to bid her father farewell. She was awake, but could not muster the energy to get up and go downstairs. Goodbyes had become the norm, what was one more? They left her home alone, and Marina said she would be gone for several hours. Despite the freezing weather she felt hot, and she kicked off the blanket and lay on top of the bed. She looked around her bedroom, her eyes stopping at the cracks along the ceiling and the cobwebs dangling from the corners of the wall. Then she glanced at the door and thought she saw an apparition, which vanished when she blinked. If she were to tell anyone they would diagnose it as a hallucination or sleep deprivation, the only rational explanation.

Maybe she was dying. Yes, she was quite sure she was. Now she realised that the wretched feeling, which had plagued her since Celia's death, was a sign from her soul that it wanted to be set free. It was the only way to end this suffering. The final blow came when Marina made arrangements for George to go to the nursing home. Where was her help? Why had Marina not offered to help her?

With a quiet air of determination, she got up and walked to the window. The snow was laying thick, and she could feel the icy draught coming through the gaps of the window frame. Coldness thickens the blood, she told herself, and it makes you sleepy.

'Hypothermia' she heard Celia's voice answer. 'It's quite relaxing, once you get into it.'

The street was silent and she had no awareness of her surroundings as she pulled off her clothes. The thin straps from Marina's hand-me-down oyster silk vest slid down her narrow shoulders and she shivered, her entire body flinching from the chill. She walked through the snow, her pale legs turned red as the icy shards stabbed through her feet, it was up to her shins when she decided to kneel down. She scooped up the snow and covered her body with it, her stomach knotted into a spasm as it seeped through the vest and touched her skin. She lay back and closed her eyes.

*

On the way home Marina felt unsettled, she fidgeted in her seat and looked out the window as the train crept along the tracks in the dark. The blackout combined with the snow made everything take twice as long. She thought of all the things she could have achieved that morning had she not taken George to the nursing home. The house will be freezing, Daphne wouldn't have had the sense to light the fire, and she had planned nothing for their dinner. The train screeched to a halt, stopping on the tracks.

'What is it?' a passenger called out to the conductor.

They were told they had to wait for a passing train, it could take half-an-hour, or longer. Now she was getting worked up.

The trip to the nursing home had been relatively easy, with George co-operating and on his best behaviour. They had sat in silence for most of the way, the familiarity of the journey filled them with a sense of nostalgia. Perhaps it pleased him to be so close to his real home. They were met at the nursing home by a doctor, who was quite elderly, with a foreign accent. His name was Dietrich and Marina had said in an enlightened tone, 'Oh, you are from Germany.'

He was put out by this appraisal, and said no: he was from Prussia – the old Empire. He was a specialist and had developed his methods in the aftermath of the last war. 'My studies were captured on film, thirty years ago,' he said slowly but with authority.

In her mind, Marina saw the static recordings of skeletal men, wearing their underpants, falling all over the floor or biting their fingers in a white room, and then, after a moment of flickering darkness, they were dressed in civilian clothing and walking down the street, doing ordinary things.

During the short induction, Dr Dietrich showed George to his room; a small white box with wide windows, overlooking a field. There were meals three times a day, nothing special due to the meat rationing, but he was free to eat in the dining hall or in his bedroom. Solitude was best at first, the doctor advised, for he could gather his thoughts without any intrusion. Marina was told not to visit and to cut herself off from George until he was better. This she did not protest and she was told that he would write a letter, and that would be her cue to restore communication.

It began to snow heavily, and she said that she must go or she might risk not getting home. 'I'll be stranded at High Greenwood. Won't that be a surprise for the evacuees?' It was a snide remark, but it had just slipped out.

George's back stiffened and he looked at her reproachfully. 'I *was* going to tell you,' he said. 'I *was*.'

'It doesn't matter.' She wrapped the scarf around her neck, pulling her hair out from under it. 'I was only joking.'

In a way, he missed her jokes. Jibes at him, jibes at their situation. Somehow, he felt better and that there was light at the end of the tunnel.

As Marina walked towards the house, the snow beneath her shoes sent a cold chill through her body; her ankles felt as though they might snap and her teeth chattered. She was looking forward to changing out of her things and having a cup of tea. Then she saw an odd figure in the garden, steps away from the front door.

'Daphne. My God, Daphne,' she said. She rushed to where Daphne lay, unconscious in the snow. She reacted quickly, pulling off her fur coat and wrapping Daphne in it, she lifted her body upward and shook it gently, hoping for a response. 'Daphne,' she said over and over. The street was dark and silent, and she looked over her shoulder, hoping to see a passer-by who could help her.

She managed to carry Daphne inside, her half-naked body cradled in her arms. The house was cold, but it was an improvement on the conditions outside. Under the dim light in the hallway she could see Daphne's skin had turned blue, and the vest was entirely soaked through. It was a struggle, but she carried her upstairs to her bedroom and then dropped her on the bed. Panic had begun to set in, she was eerily calm and efficient before. George always said she was good in a crisis and that, despite her faults, she could be relied upon to do the right thing. Then she attempted once more to stir Daphne, to no avail. She knew she was alive; she could see her chest going up and down, and that in itself was a small relief. 'Let's get you out of these wet things,' she said aloud. Putting the fur coat to one side, she peeled off the saturated vest and hung it off the foot of the bed. It was like undressing a small child, and it brought back memories of Daphne when she was little and Marina would often go through the daily motions of getting her ready for the morning. Mostly on Gladys's day off. She did not look forward to such rituals, she did not enjoy any aspect of motherhood or care-giving, but she endured it. There was a practicality to her nature, and George admired it. She knew what must be done, and she did it. She rubbed Daphne's bare arms, feeling the chill through the palm of her hand. 'Nightdress,' she said to herself as she got up to look for one. She chose the warmest one, ashamed of the pitiful state of Daphne's clothes. Then she covered her with the fur coat and pulled the blanket up over it.

Daphne appeared agitated. Her eyes were closed and she mumbled something incoherent. In her dream she saw Celia, who appeared pale and ghostlike; her lips pinched with defiance, she wore a scowl. 'Tell me what happened,' Daphne implored Celia, as she sat next to her on the bench, under the tree at school. 'Tell me what happened.' But Celia remained mute, as obstinate as always. 'Tell me what happened.' She began to shake Celia. 'Tell me what happened. Tell me.' Slumping over Celia's shoulder, with her face pressed down, she cried until she became light-headed, slowly losing consciousness.

Daphne opened her eyes and saw Marina sitting on her bed, stroking her hair, telling her to calm down and that it was only a bad dream. The familiar glow of the lamp on the night-stand emphasised the furniture in the bedroom, its looming shadows draped like heavy veils on the wallpaper. How did I get into bed? How long have I been asleep? she wanted to ask Marina but could not muster the energy to do so. It had seemed real before, Celia was alive and they were together.

'I found you in the snow,' Marina said in a low voice.

'Well then, you should have left me alone!' Daphne fought back tears.

'Leave you alone?' You would have died! It is freezing outside.'

'That's what I wanted!' Daphne yelled.

'You wanted to die? Why did you want to die?' Marina yelled back at her. She was furious with Daphne, and the response surprised her. Why did she want to die, what was so terrible about her life? Marina quickly wiped a tear away. 'How do you think I would have felt if I'd found you dead?'

'You would've been pleased.'

'Pleased? Pleased that my only child is dead?' Marina's voice cracked with emotion, she sniffed to stop the tears. She wanted to fight back, to argue that Daphne was a selfish, stupid girl. But then she stopped before she said another thing. She stood up and took a deep breath, steadying herself. Looking down at Daphne, her face etched with misery, she thought of how frail she appeared.

Years ago, when Daphne was a few weeks old, Marina walked to the cot, from where she screamed her head off. Daphne was not a placid baby, she was always howling and nothing could appease her. Despite her protests about feeding Daphne herself she had relented, but she was so weak after the birth that her own milk had dried up. And that added to her list of personal failures. The baby was sickly, the formula she fed her was soon vomited back up, and Daphne wailed from hunger. One day Marina had had enough. She looked down at her screaming baby, its face soaked with tears, its mouth wide open emitting the piercing sound. She pressed her hand to Daphne's tiny face, holding it firmly against her mouth and nose; the baby's spit soaked her palm and she felt her breath, rapid and then shallow. Then silence. Marina withdrew her hand, slowly, as though she could not believe what she had done. After staring at Daphne for what seemed like an eternity, the child resumed its screaming. She sighed with relief, holding onto the edge of the cot, standing over the baby. But it was a different kind of screaming, this time Marina knew that her child was reacting to what she had done. And she began to cry too, silently wiping the tears away, because she knew she was a failure. Daphne had not asked to be born, Marina had no choice in conceiving her, and so they were trapped.

'I know you think...,' Marina paused, unable to continue. 'I know you think that I don't... care for you. But you are quite wrong.'

Daphne turned her back on Marina and let out a petulant sigh. 'Go away,' she said. She reached under the blanket and pulled off the fur coat. 'And take your stupid coat with you. I don't want it.'

Marina was defeated; George was gone and her child hated her. Wasn't that what she had wanted all along? She went to the kitchen and heated the kettle on the stove. She was livid with Daphne but she felt sorry for her, and angry with herself because she could not tell her that. It struck her that Daphne might try to do something like this again. Was her life so wretched that she wanted to die? The thought troubled her. She felt as though she was losing her grip on everything, and that scared her.

*

'I hear you have a stutter. Can you tell me about that?' asked Dr Dietrich as they sat in his office, an airy room dedicated to order. The books were colour coordinated and the picture frames were level. This was a man who took no nonsense, George thought; he had only been at the nursing home for half a day before Dietrich cornered him. He hated Dr Dietrich, now that he could see things clearer, he hated him because he looked like his father. Freudian, is what the doctor would have called it. Now that the stutter was mentioned, he could not suppress it. Was this a trick to keep him tripping over his words? He felt guilty that Marina's money was paying for such sadism.

'I had a-a-a t-t-therapist,' George said.

'And how did that make you feel?'

Less of a human-being, a weakling. He shrugged.

When he was asked how it had happened, when he first realised he had this speech disorder, he shrugged once more. All his life he had known he was inadequate; his voice was a physical reminder of this. Sybil had always said the stutter manifested after his bout of measles. He remembered asking his mother what Dr Glendinning had meant when he said there could be dire side-effects, detrimental to a young man's life. 'Oh, it means the stutter will never go away,' she said in her dismissive way. But there was more to this tangled web than George had let on. Flashes of memories came back. His father's violence had become the norm, he often remembered a severe beating and the way he had knocked Sybil about. But a darker malice lurked. Louisa was the subject, he paused, forcing himself to remember what had happened from start to finish. She had been sent away to school, which in itself was not unusual as Sadie and Clara had also attended a girls' boarding school. But this was different, she went further away and did not come back during the holidays; she was said to have gone to Sybil's aunt's house close to the Channel. Why had she not been allowed home? George was told it was because she was trouble. Somehow Sadie and Clara escaped Walter's attacks, it was George and Louisa who bore the brunt of it. He recalled a fight which had taken place, and Sybil screaming hysterically, and grabbing Louisa by the hair and slapping her face, wherever she could reach. Afterwards, there was silence and Sybil appeared to have created a barrier between herself and Louisa, there was hatred in her eyes when she looked at her. The rumour was that Louisa had done something unforgivable and could not be trusted ever again, but George did not believe it. Then, when he forced Louisa to tell him what had happened, on the night before she left for school, he learned that Walter had committed the ultimate sin. 'He was wicked to you?' George asked, thinking Walter had done something sinister. Depraved was the word which sprung to mind when Louisa said her father had propositioned her. Somehow, George's thoughts stalled and he could not speak. She had told Sybil about it, but Sybil did not believe her. It was Louisa's fault, she must have done something to lead him on. That is what she had said. George himself wondered if Walter was capable of such a thing, and nobody knew for certain if Louisa had made it up. He wondered if he had missed some of the signs that it was going to happen. Louisa, as much as he loved her, had a cold streak on par with Sybil's, and she said George had known and did not help her. 'How could you have let him do that to me?' she had said, some years later. At the time, perhaps to seek revenge, she told Sybil about Walter's mistress, Evangelina. George had told Louisa, confiding the sordid arrangement he himself had also fallen into. Of course Sybil knew about it, she was not a fool, but she had never been faced with the reality of someone speaking it aloud, and in front of the others. That is what prompted the screaming.

The doctor was told none of this; it was too long and too complicated to relate. Not even Marina knew. Even if he wanted to regress, he could not form the words to do so. The stutter crippled him, keeping him in a state of limbo. If he wanted to go home, he'd have to make progress. But if he wanted to live, he'd have to make peace.

'All right, Doctor,' he said. 'I'll... I'll tell you everything.'

Chapter Twenty-One

The turnaround for Marina's books was quick and she was often given six months to write an entire draft. She was ashamed that many of her ideas were not her own, and she was given a list of possible themes and told to pick one. The Russian one, the one she had submitted before war was declared, had proved mediocre and she just about earned her advance back. This is it, she thought, they've found me out: they know I'm not a real writer. She felt panicked and afraid for the future. The money she was earning, or had put aside, was being used for the running of Hiraeth and for George's stay at the nursing home.

She was relieved when the post arrived, bringing with her a letter from the publishing house. The optimism soon faltered. Gerald wanted to meet with her and she felt put out by his request and berated herself for giving the publishing house her new address. But what else could she do? The cheques had to reach her somehow. She knew Gerald had taken advantage of this and had probably written or telephoned her at High Greenwood only to be told she was not there. On his last visit he had cancelled the week before and his wife, Amanda, had met her in town. Gerald was ill, she said, and was not fit to sail. He only came over once a year, but this annual visit was too much for Marina. She would have quit long ago but she needed the money, and now that George was getting the benefit of this money, it had all seemed in vain.

Gerald had re-entered her life some months after Daphne was born. He had heard through family gossip that his cousin had become a father. When he sent a note of congratulations, Marina tore it up. She thought it was a cruel gesture, that surely he must know that the baby was his. Or was it? She was never sure. He came to High Greenwood with Amanda, a strikingly beautiful girl with black hair and green eyes, who seemed much too young for him. When Amanda asked to see the baby, Marina hesitated and said that Daphne was sleeping and was not to be disturbed. George told her it was rude to refuse their guests a peep of the baby, and so Marina led them to the nursery where Daphne slept. Gerald looked down at the cot, a cigarette clenched between his lips, with the smoke circling above the baby's head. Amanda made pleasing sounds and poked the baby's tummy. A look in her bewitching eyes suggested she wanted one of her own, but Gerald told her not to get any funny ideas.

'Oh, it's too sweet,' Amanda squealed. 'May I wake it up?'

It, Marina thought, far from offended. 'Yes,' she replied, reaching into the cot and pinching the baby's bare arm with her long nails. Daphne opened her eyes, looked up at Marina's face, and began to squeal. 'There you go,' she said.

Amanda picked the baby up and held it in her arms. 'What did you say it was called?' she asked over the din of the crying.

'Daphne,' Marina flippantly answered.

'Gosh, she's not like either of you, is she?' Amanda cast a look at George, and then Marina.

'Marina and I are debating whom she takes after. I said mummy but Marina disagrees.'

Amanda laughed. 'You know when I was born my father accused my mother of having an affair. He said it was not possible that he and my mother, both practically albinos, could produce a black haired child. But... there you go.'

Marina and George politely laughed. She looked down at the dribbling baby and wiped its mouth with her hand. 'Well,' she said with a small sigh, 'once upon a time I had dark hair. *Once*, mind you.'

'Yes, I knew you as a brunette,' Gerald menaced from the far side of the nursery.

'And did she?' George asked. 'Did she have an affair?' he repeated, his eyes glistening with curiosity.

'It turned out she did. Poor father.'

Perhaps Amanda thought they would laugh at her confession, but they remained silent, half smiling and nodding. Daphne howled louder than before.

'Christ, what a racket,' Gerald said. 'Tell it to shut up.'

Afterwards, the foursome sat around the table in the dining room, making small talk and listening to Gerald's boastful tales of his publishing house. Perhaps to irritate George, Gerald suggested that Marina should write books. George scoffed at the idea. Anybody else, who had encountered Gerald in the way that she had, would have declined. They would have avoided him at all costs. But not Marina. Surprisingly to George, she took it seriously and she, at least on the surface, seemed to entertain the idea. She had no passion for literature, she wasn't particularly talented, nor was she a natural writer. But it was a source of income and it offered her an identity away from George and High Greenwood. Maybe she could squirrel enough money to run away.

Daphne interrupted her flow of thoughts, she stood in the doorway and said, 'I'm going out.'

'Where to?' Marina asked.

Things had been strained since their bitter exchange following the snow incident. She had been meaning to sit Daphne down, to talk things over, but she was far too busy. And so the air of hostility had mellowed to a frosty silence and one-word answers.

*

When she got away from Hiraeth, Daphne took off her coat and hoped that she would catch a chill and develop pneumonia. She had not forgotten her wish to die, or at least to scare Marina. A feeling of anger surged through her and she resented anyone who could carry on with life. It was Tuesday and she knew that Mrs Hartley ran her errands on that day, and so she purposely walked past the Lyons Corner House where she hoped she would be. After lingering outside, shivering from the cold, Mrs Hartley made an appearance.

'Daphne,' she said, giving her a curious look. 'For goodness sake, put on your coat. You'll catch your death. It might be spring, but it is freezing.' She thought Daphne much changed; she had a dark look in her eyes and she appeared bewildered.

They went into the teashop and Mrs Hartley found an empty table by the window. When they sat down Daphne sneezed, and then sniffed to prevent her nose from running. It was so unlike her, this little savage sitting before Mrs Hartley in a thin jersey, with messy hair, and without a handkerchief.

'Here you go.' Mrs Hartley passed her a hanky. It had lipstick on it, but Daphne used it anyway.

'My father has gone to a nursing home,' she said. 'I... I had to get out of the house.'

The way in which she said it was unexpected, and Mrs Hartley could only smile. She looked into Daphne's eyes, which stared off out the window, and she touched her cold hand. Mrs Hartley's hand was warm and her smile was kind, and Daphne sneezed once more. She was thinner than before, and her skin was paler than usual.

'You don't look well, dear,' Mrs Hartley said, quite alarmed. The last thing she wanted was to catch the 'flu. 'You don't look well at all.'

'I'm fine,' Daphne said.

The tea came and Daphne asked if she could have a scone or a biscuit. It was a bold thing to do, and she had no money to pay for it, but she could not resist. She felt faint and she had not eaten properly since their last meal as a family. The new rationing law meant little to her, for Marina ate like a bird and did not care if Daphne had eaten or not. They had lived on sandwiches and tea, and at first it seemed like an adventure but now it was like a penance.

'A lot has changed since your last visit,' Mrs Hartley said as she buttered Daphne's scone. She had always babied Celia when they had tea together, and this gave her a sense of purpose. But to Daphne it was achingly slow and she wanted to reach forth and snatch the scone from her. She passed the scone to Daphne and spoke as she wolfed it down. 'Mr Hartley no longer lives here.'

'Where did he go?'

'Back to India.'

It struck Daphne that if Celia were alive she would be experiencing something similar to her, and that made her feel bonded to her dead friend.

'He... he was given the opportunity to help establish a tea exporting firm.'

'With Uncle Christopher?' she asked in a harsh voice.

'Goodness, is that the time?' Mrs Hartley looked at her watch. 'Won't your mother be worried about you?'

'I don't think so. She's so frightfully cross with me, I suppose I might stay out until it gets dark. I'll go home at bedtime.'

She did not mean for it to sound like a hint, and she quickly recoiled when Mrs Hartley announced, 'Come stay with me.'

*

It had been a mistake letting Gerald come to the house, and one that was not entirely Marina's fault. He appeared at the door, claiming he had sent a telegram that morning. It was a fleeting visit, he explained, as he was to sail home to Cape Town the next day. Marina did not believe him,

173

and sensing she remained unconvinced, he told her he had secured passage on a steamship taking evacuees to Australia.

'Come with me,' he said, taking her by surprise. 'Bring the girl.'

She did not say yes or no, or smile to acknowledge his invitation. It was an unnecessary gesture: his showing up, the things that he said.

They spoke of George and his gallantry in enlisting. Marina did not say that he had been invalided home, only because Gerald would have thrived on the news. Once, she would have thought him fun and exciting, but that was only for a brief and foolish moment.

'I thought you would have enlisted,' she said as they walked into the drawing room.

'I could have.'

'Why didn't you?'

'Would you believe me if I told you I have syphilis?'

Yes. Yes, I would. She did not say that, instead she replied, 'How terrible for you.'

*

As Daphne pushed the front door open and stepped inside the hallway, she could see a dim light from beneath the drawing room door, and she heard the soft ticking of the clock. Listening carefully, for a second longer, she could hear the mumbling voice of a man. Everything seemed to fall silent again. The twisting of the door handle alerted her, and the drawing room door opened. Gerald stood next to Marina.

'Daphne,' Marina said. She quickly moved away from Gerald and ran her hand through her hair and pulled at the collar of her flimsy blouse.

'So you're Daphne,' he announced with a wide grin, flashing from below his thin moustache.

She took in his appearance: he had oily black hair that was carefully combed in a side parting, and dark eyes which darted from beneath his bushy eyebrows. He wasn't overly handsome but even with her own inexperience she could sense his roguish air.

'How do you do, Daphne?' he grinned once more. 'I'm Gerald Manners.'

'Oh, you're Pamela's brother, aren't you?' Daphne's eyes met with Marina's, and her mother looked away. She knew Marina was furious, but she didn't know why.

'Such a charming girl,' he said to Marina.

Marina stepped into the hallway and closed the drawing room door. 'And where have you been?' she asked Daphne.

Daphne trembled from the coldness of the hallway. 'I went into town,' she replied. 'I bumped into Mrs Hartley, that's what kept me. She, um, she invited me to stay with her.'

'Why? What have you been saying?'

'Mr Hartley's gone back to India. I suppose she wants some company.'

'Well, we can chat about it tomorrow.'

'I think I'd like to go.' Daphne offered Marina a smile to disguise how pitiful she felt. She could tell by her mother's expression that she was offended by her wanting to leave Hiraeth. Marina simply nodded and then walked into the drawing room without saying goodnight.

'Children are such trouble, don't you think?' Gerald lit a cigarette.

She ignored his remark. 'Would you like some tea before we begin?'

'Tea would be lovely.'

Daphne went to bed, the wretched feeling gripped her more intensely at night. The creaking of the door startled her. Light footsteps crept across the carpet, the distinct smell of cigarette smoke, a heavier kind than Marina's, drew forth.

'Sorry,' Gerald said. 'Was looking for the lav.'

'It's at the top of the stairs,' Daphne replied. He made no attempt to leave, and she reached across and turned on the lamp. There he was, standing in the doorway, smoking a cigarette.

He walked to the window and pushed it open. She watched him take one last drag on his cigarette before throwing it outside. 'Filthy habit,' he said. Closing the window and the curtains, he turned to face her. 'Don't ever try it.'

'I won't,' she fibbed.

'Good girl.'

'Well,' she said, 'lav's at the top of the stairs. Be careful, sometimes the light doesn't work. The trick is to tug the cord lightly before you hear it click and then to pull it once, rather fast. That seems to work.'

'I'll keep that in mind,' he replied. He moved to Daphne's bedside. Her body stiffened and her heart began to race. 'Here, lie back properly,' he coaxed her. 'You'll catch your death sleeping with your back exposed. Go on, do as I say.'

Daphne slowly lay back. She kept her eyes on his face; it was rather pasty with a greasy film around his thinning hairline. She could see the inky black bristles of his moustache and the sparse hairs on the bridge of his nose, between his eyebrows. His eyes were cold and menacing, and when he smiled he had straight teeth with two prominent ones at the front. He began to tuck the blanket tightly around her, pushing it under her arms until she felt cocooned. He leaned closer, his hand reached her cheek and he stroked it for a moment, she could feel his long nails lightly scratching her skin.

'You're very pretty,' he said. 'How old are you?'

'Fourteen,' she whispered.

'Ah, the limbo age.'

She could hear her heart thumping in her ears, and was certain he could too.

'Did you know, in the olden days, girls of fourteen could marry?'

She shook her head.

'I imagine you think boys are disgusting.'

Daphne hadn't really thought about it. She didn't know very many boys, as it were. Only her father, Mr Hartley and Dr Glendinning.

'So, the lav's at the top of the stairs?'

She nodded.

Marina met Gerald as he walked down the stairs. She carried a tea tray and he took it from her as he stepped off the last stair. 'Everything all right?' she asked.

'Yes, why wouldn't it be? Your darling daughter was pointing me in the direction of the lav.'

'Was she?' Marina said as Gerald followed her into the drawing room. He set the tea tray on the table and moved towards the door. 'Leave the door open,' she said rather too quickly. After her outburst, she walked to the cigarette box on the desk and, keeping her back to him, she lit a cigarette. She longed to turn to him and demand to know why he had come. Instead, she quietly sat down on the chair, and he hovered in front of the fire.

'Shall we make a start?'

'On what?'

'The list of subjects I sent you.'

'Yes, of course.' She reached for the pen and paper which she kept on the table next to her chair.

He poured the tea, clanking the spoon off the cup to attract her attention.

'I liked the idea of the thief and the dying heiress. It was on the last list you sent me, before this one arrived.'

'Oh yes?'

'Yes, so I made a start on the first chapter.' She rifled through the pages. 'Ah, here we are.'

'Would you mind typing it out for me?'

'Right now?'

'The thing is, my eyes aren't too good at night and I'd like to read it tomorrow morning.'

'Oh Gerald, must I?' She was sick of his games, she did not want him to linger. In that moment he held the power, she got up and went to the typewriter which sat on the bureau across the room. 'Turn on the light, will you?'

He went to the switch and turned it on. It was more intrusive than the dim light of the lamps and she could see how terrible he looked. He must have sensed this for he turned his back and paced before the fire, pretending to be in deep thought.

'How's George?'

'I can't talk and type at the same time.'

'Of course.'

Her nimble fingers moved across the keys. 'It's only five pages, and it's a rough draft.' She pulled the page free and walked to him.

He looked away as he tucked the page into his jacket pocket. 'Is that the time already?' He glanced at the clock ticking on the wall. 'I must make tracks. Lots to do before the morning.' He brushed down his jacket and straightened his tie. 'I'm staying at the Agincourt Hotel.'

Marina politely nodded.

'I was hoping to be in town long enough to catch Pam in a show. Say, you should adapt one of your books into a play. Pam would be marvellous in... what was the one before the last?'

'Honeymoon in Hove.'

'Right. That one. She could take it on a provincial tour. Now there's an idea.'

'No, thank you.'

She got up from behind the desk and slipped past him. Walking down the hallway, she could sense he was trailing behind her but she was determined to keep going until she reached the foot of the stairs, steps away from the front door.

'Have you lost something?'

'My... I'm sure it was in my pocket.'

'If I find whatever it is, I'll give it to your secretary,' she told him, though she did not mean a word of it.

'Swell.' He took his hat from the hook next to the door. 'Please don't go to any bother or expense. It's just a sentimental trinket from my salad days.'

Chapter Twenty-Two

George liked the nursing home, it was spacious and nobody bothered him. He felt guilty for using Marina's money to pay for the treatment, but he knew if he remained at Hiraeth he would go crazy. Or worse. Dr Dietrich was growing more impatient by the day and with each session he became frustrated, and George sensed he could see through him. He was not well, but he was not ill enough to shirk his war duty and that made him feel quite guilty.

As were the doctor's orders, Marina had not been to visit him and they did not exchange letters, so he had no way of knowing what life was like for his wife and child. Only the doctor could grant him the freedom to leave and to return to normal. Whatever normal was. It was suggested that he should go to High Greenwood for a day visit, to jog his memory and perhaps help him get to the bottom of whatever was troubling him. He knew what the trouble was but could not tell Dr Dietrich, and he fobbed him off with the story of the ship sinking. Just facts, nothing else. He declined the visit to High Greenwood; he was worried that Louisa had been, or would call, and he did not want to hang around the place.

'I have my reasons,' was the excuse he offered.

'Very well,' sighed Dr Dietrich.

They tried a new approach: the stutter was under control and he asked George to talk about what made him happy. What makes me happy? He thought about it for a moment before answering. He tried to be clever about it, tried to give vague answers that required no analysis.

'What makes everyone happy: food, a roof over one's head, love.'

'Ah, love,' Dr Dietrich said.

Yes, love. He thought of Evangelina and how much he had loved her. He was mad about her, but now that he was older and somewhat wiser, he could see that she had merely tolerated him. Their history was too far gone, too complicated to dissect during his hour of treatment with the doctor. He did not want to drag everything up to leave on a cliffhanger and have to dwell on it until the next session.

When he was a boy his father taunted him and said that he was not the marrying type. Not the marrying type, what did that mean? Surely a boy not yet out of his teens was too young for a wife. 'Faggot,' the boys at school had called him. He knew what the term meant, but he was not interested in his own sex. He was not interested in the opposite sex either, he only wanted someone to love. That's what he was missing in his life. There was that word again: love.

He was barely eighteen when Walter took him to visit Evangelina. It was daytime and Marina was off doing her typing at a smart house across town. 'How old is that girl of yours?' Walter asked as Evangelina poured him a drink from the bottle of whisky. George sat on the arm of the chair, watching and wondering if she would offer him a drink, if she would greet him.

'You leave her out this,' Evangelina snapped.

Walter moved behind Evangelina as she prepared his drink, he put his hands around her neat waist and breathed down her neck. 'Like mother, like daughter, eh?'

'You leave her alone, do you hear?' She pulled away from him.

Walter laughed as he drank his whisky, then Evangelina poured him another one.

'What's she called again?'

'Marina,' she said in a low voice.

George glanced in Evangelina's direction and wondered what Marina looked like. His sisters looked like Sybil, so he imagined Marina to be small with her mother's dark hair and eyes. So, it came as a surprise when he first saw Marina and was bemused when this tall girl with light eyes came into the room. What he could be certain of was how Evangelina was determined that Marina would have nothing to do with this life. He sensed that immediately

Those visits were spent in the drawing room, drinking and smoking, and listening to Walter's stories until he drank himself into a drunken stupor.

'What am I supposed to do?' George asked on one of the visits, before Evangelina came down.

Walter gave a cruel laugh. 'Sit here, have a drink. Listen. Watch. You might learn something.'

'Listen? To what?'

He did not know what his father had meant but he sensed it was sadistic. He then knew that Walter meant for him to observe Evangelina, that soon it would be his turn. He felt sick and sordid, and wished there was some way he could blind himself, to deafen himself.

Evangelina came down and eyed the two men in her cynical way. 'Which one of you is coming with me?'

'Both of us,' Walter joked.

Evangelina looked at him, she thought he was serious.

'One day, Evangelina. One day.' He winked at George and got up, following Evangelina out of the room, wheezing as he climbed the stairs.

George sat in silence for a moment, looking around the room. He wondered how long he would have to wait, he wondered how on earth Walter would manage. Would his father die on top of poor Evangelina? Would he have to invent an excuse to Sybil as to why her husband had died in bed with another woman. He wished he would die, regardless of the circumstances. Later, when George was initiated into this secret world but still somewhat innocent despite his fling with Pamela Manners, Evangelina would tell him that Walter struggled most of the time; puce in the face and wheezing, he lay in a heap like a wounded animal. They both laughed at the imagery, and he felt a sense of power knowing that the old man was full of bravado and that, perhaps, Evangelina had the upper-hand.

During one of those visits, a year or so later, he met Marina. The door knocked and he went to answer it. It was Marina, she said something about forgetting her notes. And her key, he presumed.

'Who are you?' she asked.

There was a hint of suspicion in her voice and she eyed him as though he wasn't a human at all, but someone who had climbed out of the gutter. My father's the bad man, he longed to tell her, you can trust me.

'I'm George Greenwood,' he extended his hand.

She accepted his handshake. 'Marina,' she said.

He wanted to offer an apology of sorts, to say how sorry he was that his father was grotesque and stupid, and ugly and decrepit, and that he understood her mother's predicament.

'He's a beast,' George said.

Her eyes were cold, she moved past him without a word. She took the pages and left.

Evangelina and Walter came downstairs, he was flushed and dishevelled. She was as before, if not more bitter.

'It was Marina,' George said.

'Don't speak her name,' Evangelina hissed. 'Don't you ever say her name again.'

Walter drew his hand back and slapped Evangelina across the face. Her head twisted sideways and blood came out of her nose. George felt adrenaline surge through his body, he wanted to hit Walter, to kill him. Evangelina must have wanted to kill him too. She reached for the whisky bottle and smashed it across his head, quickly, before he suspected she would retaliate to his slap. She had done this before, she knew how to take care of herself. Suddenly, to George, she appeared not as a sparrow-like creature but as a tyrant. Blood poured from Walter's head. He fell to the ground, his enormous body thumping off the floor.

Now George was certain that his father was dead; his mouth crooked to one side and his eyes were half open. 'You've killed him,' he said.

Evangelina gave him a little kick. 'He's all right. He's out cold, but not dead.'

The blood continued to drip from her nose, drops landed on her robe and mingled with the busy oriental pattern.

'Are you all right?' George got up and offered her his handkerchief. 'Did he hurt you?'

She took his handkerchief and dabbed the blood. 'I'm used to it.'

George looked away, ashamed. She saw that he was meek and not like Walter in any way, and her reserve softened. She touched his hand and smiled, looking into his eyes. He blushed and pulled away from her, without meaning to.

'You're shy.' She reached up and touched his face. She smiled once more and gave a little laugh, her eyes were kinder this time and George was under her spell. 'Sweet boy.' She leaned forward and kissed him on the lips.

He did not tell this to Dr Dietrich, his only explanation for love was when he spoke of Daphne. 'My only child,' he said, to emphasise how important she was to him.

The doctor turned the subject into that of regret, and he felt angry that he could suggest his daughter was a disappointment. He had risen to the doctor's trick, and in turn Dr Dietrich was delighted to see a semblance of spirit manifest.

'This is the first you've fought back,' the doctor said.

'Yes, well,' George mumbled. 'A man has his limits.'

Chapter Twenty-Three

The idea of staying with Mrs Hartley had played on Daphne's mind all night. In the end, she only agreed to go because she knew it would spite Marina. When had she become so cruel?

'I think I'll go to Mrs Hartley's today,' she said as she stood in the doorway of Marina's bedroom.

'Why?'

'She invited me, remember?'

Marina had been sitting in front of the mirror, brushing her hair. She paused for a moment, and Daphne could see the disappointment on her face. Since Gerald's visit she had wanted to talk to Daphne, but she could not find the words to say to her. She wanted to help her understand Celia's death, to tell her that whatever she was feeling was normal.

'Well,' Marina sighed. 'If it's what you want?'

Daphne nodded, she bit her lip to stop herself from crying. Everything was a mess and she did not know how to fix it. Neither did Marina.

*

As Daphne walked to Mrs Hartley's house she thought of Gerald Manners. Of course she had heard about her mother's editor before, but she had never met him. She wondered why Marina and George had never invited him to High Greenwood, had never really spoken about him. He was her father's cousin, and yet there was nothing there to suggest a familial tie. She had cousins too, and she did not know them. Why? She felt the pressing need to assemble her immediate family, to know who everyone was. She knew of Sybil, but who were her other grandparents? Why did she not know George's sisters. After George had told her about Pamela Manners she waited until Marina was engrossed in her writing before she scavenged through the magazines, looking for a photograph. There it was: a full length portrait of Pamela dressed in jodhpurs, promoting her latest play about a female aviatrix. Her mind turned once more to Gerald. The memory of him coming into her bedroom troubled her and she felt something was not quite right about the entire thing. What did he want? His presence did not make her feel secure, the way

George's did when he used to come into her room during the holidays to check on her before bed, or when she came home from school sick.

Celia had told her about dirty old men and how they liked young girls. She told Daphne that she knew the sort because, in India, there was a dirty old man who had given her wine and tried to have sex with her at a garden party during her summer holiday at Shimla. Not Uncle Christopher, he never tried anything as bold as that. It was a different man, a friend of Uncle Christopher's, who also happened to know Mr Hartley, and she was quite proud of this power which she thought she had over men. Daphne thought of India and its sweltering heat, the death and disease, and somehow this vision of Celia as a temptress on the foothills of the Himalayas did not sit well with her.

It had happened when the snake charmer played the pungi and the others gathered around to watch the swaying cobra, the music hypnotising them too. Thank God Mr Hartley had beaten him up, or who knows what might have happened. There was a big scandal afterwards, and that was why Mrs Hartley had sent her to boarding school. Before she could leave though, Celia had told Daphne that Mrs Hartley had dragged her to a doctor who ordered her to undress so he could examine her. She said she screamed and tried to run away, but Mrs Hartley pinned her down, and that is why she bit her mother on the hand. The scar, Daphne heard Celia's voice inside her head, you *must* remember the scar.

They told her it was a medical examination, something she must do to make her father happy, but instead it felt like an exorcism. 'She's intact,' the doctor had said, but it no longer felt that way. The awful surge of pain, unexpected and intrusive, breached her body. It had gone beyond Uncle Christopher and his perversions, and her father beating her every chance he got.

*

Marina had found Gerald's missing property while she was tidying the drawing room. There it was, behind the cushion of the chair, a small box containing a needle and morphia. Of course she had seen a needle before, but never for recreational purposes, and she did not imagine that people would carry one around in their pockets. The intrigue that it inspired in her was sickening and she picked it up and touched its sharp point with her index finger, careful not to pierce the skin. And so it *was* true, what George and his sisters had said, the fabled Gerald Manners was a drug addict. She should not have been surprised by this revelation but she was; she was saddened by the entire affair. Her mother drank; Gerald drugged. Anything to suppress the pain, if only for a while.

She remembered how desperate her mother became when she needed a drink. The cold sweats, the agitation, the hallucinations. Once, Evangelina had become paranoid and said Marina was plotting to kill her. Another time she swore that a tall, thin man had walked through her bedroom door and held her down on top of the bed, and she tried to scream but no sound came out, and he kept reappearing, night after night, to carry out this sadistic ritual. Only a drink, a swig from the bottle, could cure such terrors.

And so Marina thought of Gerald and how he would be climbing the walls if he could not take his morphia. She telephoned the Agincourt Hotel and asked to be put through to his room. After a moment his voice came on the line and she said she had found *it*.

'It's none of my business,' she said in a nervous voice as though she had rehearsed that line. 'But I can bring it over if you like.'

'Please,' he sounded worn out. 'Oh God, please.' His voice trailed off as he explained that the Egyptian man he usually dealt with had disappeared and he did not know who to turn to.

The secret assignation was carried out quickly and without feeling. Marina walked to the Agincourt Hotel, which she had visited before, and asked for Gerald at the reception. When he met her in the lobby she noticed his frailness and the queasy pallor of his skin; he looked as though he hadn't slept or washed. The case was hidden in her handbag and she handed it over, both of their hands trembled.

'Do you need help?' she asked.

'Marina darling, I'm beyond help.'

She nodded, thinking for once in his life he was being entirely truthful. 'You said you were sailing home today.'

'Did I?'

'Yes. You were sailing on an evacuee ship.'

'Ah yes. Well that fell through. I shall catch the next available ship. You needn't worry.'

He raised his arm and held the case in front of her face as a farewell gesture. She knew he was desperate to go up to his room and inject himself, but she did not want to leave him alone.

'I'll go up with you,' she said.

'You needn't go to the trouble, really.'

She held onto his arm and he walked to the lift, they stepped inside and got off two floors up. The hotel room was a mess, he must have ransacked it when he was looking for the missing case.

'Sorry,' he said as he went to the bed. 'You needn't watch if you don't want to.'

He pulled up his sleeve and felt for a vein, which took longer than Marina thought it would. In the bright light of the room she saw his arms scarred by needle pricks. She had not noticed what a wreck he was before, he was not like that when she had first met him. He appeared so handsome, so confident, or perhaps she had imagined it all. It felt oddly fulfilling to see him vulnerable, and to see him suffer.

The needle went in, and the relief on his face was euphoric as his body absorbed the morphia. It was peaceful; his pained expression was gone, and his eyes rolled back. The clouds floated beneath him as he drifted up and away, his mind a blank space.

The traffic from the street below and the flight of aeroplanes from the sky above reminded her that life went on, regardless. She cast one last look in Gerald's direction and left the room. Joining the noise outside and the movement of bodies on the street, she went home and continued with her life.

*

The mood over dinner was off. The table was adorned with two large and ridiculous candles, leaning to one side on a pewter candelabra, looking as though they might topple over at any given moment and set the tablecloth on fire. The evening news told them about the Jews being expelled from Hamburg.

'I don't care for the Jews,' Mrs Hartley said.

Daphne pushed the flecks of fish around on her plate, hoping to disguise them inside the dense folds of the mashed potatoes. 'Why not?' she asked.

'They're sly, untrustworthy, and they'll take everything you own. If you let them.'

'I don't feel well,' Daphne said with urgency.

'Quick, run to the lav,' Mrs Hartley called as Daphne dashed from the room. She sniffed a forkful of trout, just to make sure.

Daphne lay in bed, her body raged with a temperature and her eyesight was blurry. She could hear the bedroom door creaking open and the light from the landing stabbed through her eyes, causing her to wince.

'Feeling better?' Mrs Hartley whispered.

Daphne groaned.

'I've brought you a drink,' she said in the same low voice as she set the cup on the bedside cabinet.

It hurt to speak and, in a whiny voice, Daphne said, 'I want to go home.'

'You're better off here. For tonight, anyway.'

Daphne closed her eyes, thinking of home.

After an uneasy night's sleep, the morning appeared all too quickly. Standing up, she fell backwards onto the bed, the entire room began to spin and she tried in vain to get up again. She was determined to get dressed and to go home. Glancing at her face in the mirror, she was paler than ever and her blue eyes were darker than usual. She slapped herself, hard across the face, and then back and forth at a rapid pace. It was Marina's trick that she used when she needed to look alive, as she called it.

She stood in the kitchen doorway as Mrs Hartley sat at the small, round table in front of the window. Her glasses slid to the end of her nose and she nudged them back up with the knuckle of her forefinger. Her attention was directed at the butterflies she had preserved in a mason jar. She gently retrieved the dead butterflies, one by one, and laid them out on a piece of paper. They would be displayed under glass.

'Right, I'm off,' Daphne interrupted the scene playing out before her.

'You help me to remember Celia,' Mrs Hartley said.

How could she leave after that? She hesitated for a moment, uncertain if she would leave after all. Then, she said, 'It's been lovely staying here. But I... I have to go home.'

The walk home seemed to get longer and longer, as Daphne dragged her feet along the path towards Hiraeth. She felt warm, her jumper stuck to her back, and she raised her hand to her forehead, which was also clammy. A tiredness swept over her body; she was certain she was sick. It was an unusual fatigue; it made her want to slow down, to lie down in the street and go to sleep. Dizziness overwhelmed her, and a ringing sound in her ears caused her to feel faint. She paused, holding onto the railings outside Hiraeth. Taking a few deep breaths, she straightened up and headed towards the front door. With every step, she felt as though somebody had sliced her open to allow every drop of blood to drain from her.

She collapsed from whatever sickness had been troubling her. It all began just before she went to stay with Mrs Hartley, but she chose to ignore it. A dull ache across the upper mid-section of her back, a freezing feeling, like a block of ice, resting in that one area. There was a sharp pain when she breathed, often causing a pang of nausea. She ignored it, thinking it might be from hunger; she had become used to that feeling.

Marina had been upstairs when she heard the thump. She was combing her wet hair and thinking about Daphne, and wondering if she ought to call at Mrs Hartley's house. She felt something was amiss.

'Daphne, is that you?' she called as she walked down the stairs. 'Oh,' she simply said at the sight of Daphne, face down on the floor. 'Oh dear.'

Chapter Twenty-Four

The news of Daphne's illness reached George at the nursing home. He had been there for three months, going on four. Spring was almost over, he had missed Marina's birthday, and Italy had declared war on Britain. Now was his chance to leave and to swoop down to Hiraeth and save the day. It was quite serious, Marina had written in a note. Thank God Dr Dietrich opened their post or else the message might never have been passed on. With Daphne's illness playing out, there would be no time to dwell on Evangelina, and he could busy himself with getting her better.

It was easy to leave now that he had an excuse. Dr Dietrich said that he had suffered a nervous breakdown and that he ought to take it easy, to not go barging in. That people in his position are liable to break down at the first hurdle and that he should not get involved. How many doctor's bills could Marina afford? No, he must not add to her burden.

As he put on his hat and coat he thought about his stay and came to the conclusion that it had done him the world of good to get away. 'All people should get away, if they can,' he told the nurse who brought his discharge papers. It seemed Dr Dietrich was not taking any chances.

Off he went to the station, on his patriarchal mission to Hiraeth. He was going to send a wire to Marina to tell her to expect him, but he wanted to surprise her. To show up and prove how capable he was, as a husband and a father. But this was Marina he was talking about, and she loathed surprises.

*

'Oh,' Marina said as she opened the door. 'You came.'

'I've signed myself out.' He stepped inside. 'I'm home for good.'

'Don't let the War Office hear you say that, you'll be on the next ship back to Malta.'

His display of gallantry did not sit well with her. His coming and going, disappearing for long stretches, and now this. Why couldn't he have pulled himself together before?

'Anyhow,' she said, 'Dr Glendinning should be here shortly.'

'You telephoned Glendinning?'

'Yes. Is there a problem?'

'No. No problem at all.'

He dreaded seeing Dr Glendinning, who would surely ask about the nursing home. Now that his mind was clear and he felt rested and strong, he did not want to dwell on the past. Let sleeping dogs lie. He put down his suitcase and walked to the foot of the stairs. The house was cold and the bright sunlight filtered through the stained glass window in the hallway, reflecting prisms on the wall and floor. Marina stood in its direct view, unaware that it shone through her clothes. He watched her mouth move, transfixed by this vision before him; she could have said that he had six weeks to live and he would not have cared. He loved her so much.

'Are you listening?' she snapped.

'Yes.' He focused on the situation at hand. 'Yes, I am.'

'Good.'

He followed Marina up the stairs and along the landing. The house had begun to represent an empty shell to him, he had succeeded in separating the past from the present. He fully expected Daphne to have the cold or 'flu, as she was prone to at school, and was taken aback when Marina opened the bedroom door. She lay in bed, her thin body covered with a blanket, she turned her pale face towards the door and winced from the light. She was too exhausted to greet her father.

'Anyway,' Marina said as she closed the door. 'How are you?'

'Fine,' George offhandedly said. He was concerned about Daphne and felt his histrionics paled in comparison. 'When did this happen?'

'The sickness?' Marina thought for a moment before answering. 'Well, she went to stay with Mrs Hartley and came back two days ago. At first I thought it was a bug, but she's not getting any better and is awfully weak.'

'Poor darling.'

*

When Doctor Glendinning arrived, Marina led him to Daphne's bedroom. Instead of opening the curtains, she turned on the light. George loomed in the background, not wanting to get in the way. Pulling the blanket back, Dr Glendinning observed Daphne's thinness, and Marina rattled off a few facts about her health. She told him about Celia's death and how Daphne had not been herself, and of the incident in the snow. Upon hearing this, George was beside himself and he felt guilty that he had taken Marina's time, and had monopolised his own well-being over Daphne's.

They went out to the landing to discuss Daphne's health. They spoke in hushed tones, as though it were a grave secret and Daphne could not know. He diagnosed her as suffering from malnutrition.

'Did you not recognise the signs, Lady Greenwood?'

George pretended not to listen when the doctor spoke of the missed monthlies, his preferred euphemism. Then, he realised he was fighting a losing battle, for he took one look at Marina and thought her to be a bag of bones.

'It's not my fault,' she shrieked. 'She went off her food. I couldn't very well force-feed her.'

Why had everything suddenly become her fault? She did her best. Sensing this, George placed a caring hand on her shoulder, but she leaned forward, dismissing his gesture.

'To make matters worse, she also has a chest infection which could very well turn into pneumonia, if you're not careful. I take it she has not been at school?'

'No, we withdrew her back in September.'

'Ah, I see.'

Yes, he did see: he thought the child had been running amok in Marina's care and that she was a neglectful mother who was not fit to look after anything or anyone. She jumped to that conclusion, but what else could she think?

'My fault entirely,' George said. 'We... I... ran into some financial trouble. So you do see, don't you?'

Marina listened to Doctor Glendinning's orders about building up Daphne's bodyweight as well as her immune system. She was pleased when he suggested they go back to High Greenwood, if they could. The country air would do her good, and it was safer all round. George knew this was impossible but he remained silent, thinking it best if he said nothing at all.

*

The hollow rattle of Daphne's coughs filled the silent rooms of Hiraeth that evening. George and Marina lay awake in the bedroom, listening to her struggle for a breath and wheezing each time she inhaled. Unable to bear the sound of her suffering any longer, Marina got up from the bed.

'Where are you going?' George asked.

She turned on the light and began to rummage around in her dressing table. She found a bottle of Vicks and held it up to George, without answering him.

'What's that?'

'Cyanide pills.'

'That's not funny, Marina.'

She went to Daphne's bedroom and found her awake, writhing around on the bed, coughing and catching her breath. 'Sit up,' Marina said as she unscrewed the lid of the Vicks.

Daphne tried to sit up, but it induced in her a coughing fit and she fell back. Her ribs wracked back and forth, and Marina watched her shoulder blades jutting up and down as she coughed.

'When did you become ill?' she asked as she rubbed the Vicks onto Daphne's back.

'Don't... know...,'

'How do you feel now?'

'Wretched.' Her blue eyes had a haunting look about them, and her lips were pale and cracked. 'I felt sick two nights ago but thought it was down to Mrs Hartley's cooking.' Her dark hair was drenched in sweat and her nightgown clung to her body.

'Let's get you out of these damp things before you catch your death.' The latter part of the sentence, by Marina's own admission, was unfortunate. She retrieved a clean nightgown from the chest of drawers. 'Come on, arms up,' she ordered. 'I won't look.'

It made her think of Sybil, when her disease was manageable. Sybil was bed-bounded, too weak and dizzy to get up, and there was not enough air in her decaying lungs to fill her body. She coughed and spluttered, and Marina held a cloth underneath her chin as the blood spilled from her mouth, or from her nose because of the pressure building up inside of her body. When it dripped onto the pillow and blanket, Marina cleaned it with cold water. She knew Sybil would have rather died than let her maid see the mess, and Marina empathised with this feeling of pride and self-respect, even though there was no pride in depending on another person. Perhaps even once Sybil managed a grateful smile. No, Marina remembered, it was something else: she touched Marina's hand with her own freezing, bloodless limb and squeezed it, though her grip was weak.

'Don't worry,' Marina told Daphne. 'Your father's here now and when the time is right we'll go back to High Greenwood.'

Maybe she should not have said that. But she was sick of going along with George and trusting him, even though her instincts told her not to. She knew he would not refuse Daphne, and so she shamelessly used her to sway George's decision, or reveal the truth. Whichever came first.

Chapter Twenty-Five

Now that he was well again, sleeping next to him had become a chore. It was beyond the pale for Marina when she accidentally nudged him as she turned over to sleep on her stomach, as she was apt to do. Sometimes he crashed into her as he struggled to get comfortable, but she sensed it was a deliberate ploy to disturb her, or to prompt her to acknowledge him. 'Sorry,' they were forever saying. She could hear the low, drawn out creaking of the springs beneath the mattress as he edged closer to her, and she pretended to be asleep. But when he touched her she flinched, and that gave the game away.

Over the years she had become an expert at fobbing him off, and so she'd say, with a degree of embarrassment and through stilted euphemisms, that it was not the right time. The right time for what, he'd ask, knowing that she was, perhaps, lying and that he could make her feel obligated.

'It happens every month,' she said in a low voice, rapid like a hiss.

'It happens all the time,' he replied. His voice was less kind.

And so an air of hostility lingered between them. She would feel wretched but not sorry, and he would wonder if he was too forceful and less understanding. That he was forcing her to do something unsavoury, making it all seem wrong and sordid.

All those years ago, he told her it would get better. He waited a month until after they had married, and he only approached her because Sybil told him to. She thought it pathetic that her son's new wife would barricade herself in her room and keep him from her bed. It was grounds for divorce – there she'd go again with her rules and regulations for wedlock – or, if there was any proof that the new Lady Greenwood was untouched, an annulment. Less shameful and more tidy, but a blow to his masculinity.

Sybil had a word, and in a gentle yet assertive voice she asked if anything unpleasant had ever happened. 'Were you inferred with?' she barked, when Marina failed to catch her drift. She began to cry unexpectedly, and Sybil mistook her tears and sobbing as a confirmation that her suspicions had been correct. Marina did not bother to correct her, to tell her that nothing unseemly had taken place, and she knew Sybil thought her an idiot. Worse than that: spoiled goods.

That's when she knew he had taken up with Venetia Spry, the older woman. When they did reconcile, and his ego was quite bruised from the Venetia experience, he was insecure and less confident than before. It was a pleasant respite for Marina, and she liked it when he was humble. Perhaps he thought her maternal, for he started to speak of children and how they ought to have some soon. Sybil swooped in and stole Marina for another of their 'little chats', she was always there, always appearing like a spectre as though she were watching and listening from an invisible plane or portal.

'You know,' Sybil said as she eyed Marina, 'if you could give him a child or two. Boys. You could do whatever you want. It's *that* simple, really.'

Marina looked down at the grass beneath their feet and then up at the clouds closing in around High Greenwood. She let out a sigh. 'Do what I want? How could I do what I want with a baby?'

'Well, there'll be a nanny and we could hire a girl to do the feeding, if you catch my drift. I know just the woman, but I suppose she'd be a bit long in the tooth by now,' she was rambling, talking to herself more so than Marina. 'My friend, Lady Merivale, went on a tour of Cairo when her son was six weeks old. Think of the possibilities, my dear.'

'One doesn't feed their own babies?' Marina asked, somewhat astonished and intrigued.

'My God, what do you think we are? Animals?' She took a deep breath, quite put out by her question, and after a moment she mellowed. 'The point is, then he'd be free to take a mistress, and you could do... well whatever it is you do with your days. It's the perfect recipe for happiness, my dear.'

But they could never achieve the happiness they both sought. Every day, George was aware of the secret he kept from her and this created a barrier between himself and Marina. When he thought he might be happy or have good fortune, the secret presented itself and tore everything apart. And when Marina looked at Daphne she saw that brief moment with Gerald, and how she was deceiving George. He had once remarked that he was happy that Daphne belonged to him; he was a good father and she could not take that away from him. She'd rather be consumed by a lie, than ruin their lives. George wanted them to connect, and there were fleeting moments when they often did, but she always resisted.

When Marina got out of bed, she sat at her dressing table and brushed her hair. 'Would this have happened to Daphne if we'd stayed at High Greenwood?' she asked.

Wincing at the sound of the brush ripping through her thick hair, George had no defence. 'She would have been at school, surely,' he gently replied.

She slammed down the brush to punctuate her irritability.

'You don't bear me any grudge, do you?' he asked.

Of course she bore him a grudge. Instead of saying so, she said, 'I'd like to take Daphne to High Greenwood.'

Without a moment's hesitation, he looked her in the eye and said in an authoritative voice, 'Okay. I shall see what I can do.'

'And what about you?' her voice remained cold and distant. 'What will you do?'

'I'm feeling quite well again,' he replied in a matter of fact way. 'I suppose I'll go back.'

No, she thought: not go back, run away.

*

If put on the spot he would not have thought himself a calculating person. Not at all. That was Marina's area. Those who had known both of them, or had observed them as a couple and as individuals, would have said Marina was the cold one. An ice queen. She was difficult to know, difficult to love, and she only cared about herself. He never argued with that assessment, though he knew better. He was, to those who knew him: polite, slightly bumbling, well-meaning, not someone who would get on the wrong side of the law. But in his lucid moments he had begun to think like a criminal: how to dodge his responsibilities, how to cover his tracks. Not lucid, he soon realised, but scared. He was scared of being found out, scared of losing Marina and Daphne. The child had such a hold over him, he had not given it much thought before Louisa started to make trouble, before they came to Hiraeth. Ah, Louisa. He did not want to call at Morrow Place and stir things up. After all, she thought he was overseas. Had she been to High Greenwood after they had met, just before he left for the camp? Had she visited the house to ensure he was not lying? She was clever, and nothing would have escaped her.

'Right oh, I'm off out,' he called to Marina.

'Wait.' She walked to the top of the stairs. Daphne's faint coughs filled the house but she was getting better each day. 'Where are you going?'

'I have to go to the nursing home. Yes... I forgot to say, Dr Dietrich asked to see me for a follow-up. Sorry, I should have said.'

Marina stared at him for a moment, he was certain she could see through his lies. Daphne called her from the bedroom and she glanced over her shoulder.

'All right. Can you fetch some Bovril on the way back?' The coughing continued. 'Look, it's all right. I'll get some. God knows when you'll be home.'

*

He went to High Greenwood to see if he had any letters, from Louisa in particular. A taxi drove him from the station to the house and while it was waiting he went round to the servants' entrance and slipped through the kitchen without being noticed. He bumped into a flustered young woman as he made his way through the hallway. She failed to notice that he was a strange face, or perhaps she did not care, and muttered something about cooking for twenty. He stopped a familiar face, a middle-aged woman whom he had met before, when he gave the house to the evacuees.

'Mrs Bagshawe,' he greeted her. 'How nice to see you.' He placed his hand on her upper-arm, a confiding gesture that pleased her. 'I can't stop, taxi is running outside. I just wanted to ask if any letters have arrived for me?'

'Oh yes,' she told him. 'A great big mountain of them.' She had been saving them in a box in the library, out of bounds to the children and staff.

'Smashing,' he said. 'Odd request, I am sure, but if anyone should ring here or show up unexpectedly you might say that I'm out of town. Better still, pretend you don't know me.'

She agreed to the ruse and told him that a young woman had telephoned, ages ago, and the same woman had shown up. 'It happened months ago... at the end of last year,' she said. 'I haven't seen her since.'

'You didn't say where I was?'

'No sir, it's not my place to give out private information.'

He took the box and carried it out the front door and got into the taxi. Thank goodness it had a lid, and aware of how silly he looked carting a box around, he thought of stopping at a grocer's on the way to the station to buy some brown paper and string to disguise the box as a parcel. In a rush to catch his train, and feeling relieved at getting the letters and convincing Mrs Bagshawe to lie for him, George abandoned his idea and headed straight for the station.

There was only space in a third class carriage and lucky for him nobody sat in his compartment. The whistle blew and the doors were shut, and as soon as the train started to chug out of the station he took the box and removed the lid. He thought about pouring the letters over the seat but realised it would be just his luck for a person to get on at the next stop and sit beside him. He parted the letters with his hands, pushing them to either side, looking for familiar handwriting or a repetition of stationary.

There, he saw it. Louisa's letters were spiteful in their tone, short and threatening. She demanded more money, she said the allowance had run out and that she had been trying to contact him. The letters, similar in their style, stopped around last October. It made sense to him, he realised it was a lucky escape for them all. He had already left for Malta, and Marina and Daphne had decamped to Hiraeth. Despite their civilised meeting beforehand, she must have written to him to make sure he had left and that nobody was living there. The silence bothered him; he knew from experience that Louisa was not the type to lie dormant.

He got off two stops before Marigold Square and walked to Morrow Place. A strip of Italian-owned businesses had been ransacked and there were empty terraced houses with boarded up windows and doors. He followed a boy and a girl inside the front door.

'Do you know Miss Greenwood, the tutor?' he asked them.

They looked straight through him and continued to talk and climb the stairs. He followed them, and realising he might be dangerous, they let out a small squeal and ran up the next flight.

He banged on the door, hoping Joan or whomever she had taken a current fancy to, would answer. Joan answered. 'Yes,' she peered at him. Her hair was tied up in rollers and she wore a shabby robe, its pocket was hanging off. 'Who are you?'

Good, she did not recognise him. Taking a second glance, he could see that she was blind in one eye. 'I'm looking for Louisa Greenwood.'

She felt for her glasses dangling around her neck on a beaded string. Now she could see him out of her good eye. 'George. George Greenwood,' she said.

'I'm looking for Louisa. Where is she?'

Joan stared at him. He felt uncomfortable and wondered if she was angry at him. Finally, she answered. 'Is this your idea of a sick joke?'

The rubble, the bombed buildings. A sickening feeling formed in his stomach, he realised what had happened to her.

'She's dead,' Joan replied. 'Killed a few months ago.'

'Killed, you say?' he managed to ask. He could not believe it.

'Killed,' she repeated. 'Look, are you all right? You look as though you might topple over.' She reached for him, touching the sleeve of his coat. He pulled away. 'Steady on,' she said.

George began to walk away, slowly as though he had dreamt it all. Killed. She was dead.

'It happened on this very street, across the road,' Joan called after him. He did not turn around. 'Did you not read about it in the papers? Did you not hear the news on the wireless? It was an IRA bomb, in case you're interested. Not the Gerries.' She walked out to the landing. 'Look here,' she shouted. 'Don't think you can shirk your responsibilities. I also know what you did! Look here, I am talking to you.'

When he got outside he looked up at the evening sky and walked along the river, stopping at the bridge. Looking down at the water he told himself once more that Louisa was dead. Part of him felt sad, a sorrowful feeling that accompanies an unpleasant shock, and he felt guilty that, aside from his momentary grief, he was glad to be free of the financial burden of paying her to keep quiet. He poured the box of letters into the river, to the disapproval of those standing close by, smoking a fag and taking in the view. 'Oi!' an elderly man shouted. 'Pleased with yourself, are you? Bloody hooligan.'

He walked away and found a telephone box at the end of Morrow Place, and called Marina. The lie came naturally to him: he said his train was delayed because of the blackout and that he would take a room at a cheap hotel and come home in the morning.

She detected a change in his voice, he seemed distant and far away. 'Are you quite all right?'

'I've had some bad news.'

It was about High Greenwood, she knew it. She should have known he would fail and that it had all been an act. 'Oh, I see,' she said.

'I've had quite a shock. I'll... I'll talk to you tomorrow.'

Chapter Twenty-Six

Marina opened the door to find George standing on the doorstep, looking dishevelled and as though he had been drinking and had not slept. 'Forgot your key?' she asked.

'I don't have a key,' he said.

Lies, she wanted to scream at him. She knew he had gone into town, she felt the same air of instability she had felt at High Greenwood, when he would go away and not come back. The whispering over the telephone, the frequent requests for money. 'Who is she?' Marina demanded.

'Who?'

'The one you've spent the night with. The one you were messing around with before the war. The one you've been sending *my* money to.'

'I don't go around fucking random women, you know.'

The word startled her. It was a cold and crass word. He had meant to wound her, she knew by the sheepish look on his face after he had said it. She had heard him swear before, silly little nuances, the same words she used herself. But never that word.

She went into the kitchen and reached for the kettle and filled it with water. He stood by the window, looking out at the small, concrete square. He never did plant that kitchen garden. The news of Louisa's death, and the lie she had been keeping for him, consumed him and he felt as though he were drowning.

'My sister died,' he blurted out.

The words shocked her. 'Sadie? Clara? What on earth happened?'

He shook his head. 'No. Not them.'

And then it dawned on her: Louisa. She searched for the right thing to say but her words were inadequate. 'I'm sorry, George. I know you both... you both had that falling out years ago. But I am sorry.'

'What's that you're making?' He did not mean to ignore her condolences, but he wanted to forget about Louisa, and most especially Joan. If only for a moment.

She was surprised by the sudden change in conversation. 'It's Daphne's Bovril. Doctor Glendinning said to fatten her up.'

'May I?' He took the cup from Marina's hands, he never did like beef tea.

He went to Daphne's bedroom, like he had done at High Greenwood whenever she was in bed with the cold, and he sat down next to her. He passed the Bovril to her and she pulled a disgusted face before gulping it down. It was still boiling hot and her lips were flushed after drinking it. Cook used to call it her magic medicine: the more she could drink, the stronger she would be.

'You look sad,' she said to George. Her voice was hoarse from the chest infection and she had a slight cough, but was looking and feeling better. She was still pale and thin, but not as skeletal, and George could detect a relentlessness inside of her.

'Do I?' He smiled, but his eyes betrayed him. She nodded, still holding onto the cup. He took it from her and placed his hand over hers. 'I'm not sad at all, I'm just tired. Anyway, how are you?'

She turned and looked out the window, trying to see if it was still raining. 'I went to stay with Mrs Hartley, did mother tell you?'

'She mentioned it.'

'I must get back to her, but I don't think I could manage the walk to her house.'

'Well, I'm sure she understands that you're not well.'

'Yes,' she sighed. She felt the tears stinging her eyes and she clenched her teeth together to stop herself from crying. The more she tried to resist, the more the tears built up.

'You miss her, don't you?' George said in a low voice. 'It's all right, you can tell me.'

She nodded, the tears rolled down her cheeks.

'And you know why you feel the way you do? Because you loved Celia. That's why you're sad.'

'No,' Daphne said. 'You don't understand. Nobody understands. It was all my fault.' Now she was sobbing and trying to speak through the convulsions. 'If I hadn't have told you about her sneaking off. If I hadn't have said anything at all, she might still be alive.' She fell back, her head hitting the pillow. The tears ran down the sides of her face, spilling into her hair.

'Nonsense. I don't believe that for a moment.'

'You drove her home!'

There it was: out of nowhere, an accusation that he had played a part in ending a life. He felt overwhelmed with anger; it was a false accusation and she was jumping to conclusions. Making something out of nothing. When he drove Celia home he had been acting as a father, he had been looking out for her interests and safety. Surely the boy whom she'd met would have led her to no good? It was not going to happen on his watch.

'No,' he repeated. 'You are wrong. You're quite, quite wrong.' And then it struck him that Daphne was blaming herself for Celia's death: that she had, in some way, been instrumental in deciding her fate. He knew how that felt, but he could not tell her. 'No, darling,' his approach was kinder. 'It doesn't work that way. Celia would have gone home that night, anyway.'

'She would have?' Daphne sat up.

'Yes,' he lied. 'Yes. She told me that she wanted to go home. That she knew she had upset you and it was best to leave you alone.' If this tiny lie could ease Daphne's guilt, then how could it be bad?

He was silent for a moment, thinking about that night. Celia had sat up front in the car with him, they had driven in silence for most of the journey. Her face was pinched with anger, he could see her screwed up mouth as she tightened her lips in defiance. He knew she felt that Daphne had betrayed her. 'I didn't do anything bad,' she snapped. 'I didn't do anything wrong. Please don't tell my father that I was bad.'

'I'll leave the explanations up to you.' He did not want to converse about what she did or did not do with the boy. It made him uneasy, it was a dangerous topic.

'You will say that I had a row with Daphne, though? He won't be too cross about that.'

'Yes, fine.'

When he dropped Celia off she got out of the car and raced to the front door. Her mother opened the door to let her in. Mrs Hartley saw George and went to the car. He opened the window and spoke to her from the driver's seat. Yes, he told her about the boyfriend and Daphne's reaction. He tried to turn it into a joke and said that he was only telling her because Daphne had taken the news badly and perhaps felt jealous, and maybe she could speak to Celia and ask her to be kinder. And then he drove home, thinking he had put everything right between Daphne and her friend. He hated to see her suffer.

Daphne appeared calmer than before, and George touched her damp cheek. 'And so you see, she would have gone home anyway.'

She nodded and offered an understanding smile.

'Now, do you feel better?'

She nodded once more.

How he wished someone would have told him something similar, all those years ago. After he had confided in Louisa and used the alibi of being with her and Joan at the Tropical Ravine, he was cornered. Marina knew and, a while after her death, so did he: that Evangelina would have died anyway. She had cirrhosis of the liver, her insides were riddled with such badness. Through the years he had replayed that scene over in his mind, pausing, starting, trying to remember what had happened during the pivotal moment on the stairs. Had he pushed her? Had he fallen into her? A split second, the flash of light through the window, blinding him, the speed in which she fell.

'What are you two whispering about?' Marina hovered by the door.

'Nothing. We have no secrets, do we?' he smiled at Daphne.

He followed Marina down the landing and to the top of the stairs. He touched her shoulder, prompting her to turn around. He wanted to replay that scene. 'I love you,' he said.

Marina smiled at him, she did not say it back. She was about to step forward, to descend the staircase when he touched her wrist, hoping to take hold of her hand.

'I do mean it, you know.'

She looked over her shoulder and smiled once more, the words never came easily to her. She could not recall saying that she loved anyone. She loved things, of course, but people... Suddenly she felt aware of her footing, as though she was unsure of how to negotiate the staircase, her gaze was still fixed on George. His hand felt hot around her wrist and she slipped away from him, placing her hand on the bannister as she did so.

Letters spilled through the door as she reached the last step. George was watching from the top of the staircase, thinking that the day had been oddly rhythmic. Everything appeared to be happening as it should. For a fleeting moment he felt as if he had stepped outside of his body and was watching everything from another plane, as though life was going on without him and they would be all right, if he ever left. There was a letter from her publishing house, the coveted piece of paper inside.

'Anything interesting?'

'Yes. My next plot.'

'What is it this time?'

She read from the page: 'A sweeping love story set in the French countryside between a local woman who is hiding a German deserter in her château.'

'That ought to appeal to the Charabanc set.' He meant it as a joke but it sounded patronising and he coughed to disguise the fact she did not laugh.

'You know, Gerald called here while you were away.'

'He did? What did he want?' What nerve, he thought.

'It was an odd visit. Sorry, I meant to tell you about it. He came here unannounced, but that's not the point. The point is he offhandedly mentioned that he had syphilis, and asked if I would believe him if he did. Surely it can't be true.'

She did not mention the morphia or her taking it to him at the hotel, she felt that was betraying him in some way and it did not sit well with her, and George would feel smug and say, I told you so.

'Why wouldn't it be?'

She gave him a reproachful look. They had never discussed Gerald in great detail, not even when he came to High Greenwood for Sybil's funeral, and then to bring his wife and offer Marina the writing job. She always avoided the topic of Gerald Manners, and George was too besieged by jealousy to utter his name without it causing a petty row.

'Whores are his pastime, you know.' He lowered his voice, 'Did you know on the day we buried my mother he went to a whore, he told me that himself. That is low, don't you think? So, he was bound to end up with some unpleasant disease.'

The remark wounded her. She hoped it was not too obvious to George, but it was.

'Sorry,' he said. 'I shouldn't speak this way in front of you.'

'But his wife... does she know?'

'Yes. Yes, I'm sure she does.' He picked up Marina's letter from the publishing house and glanced over it. Keeping his eyes fixed on the piece of paper, he said, 'It's probably the reason they don't have any children.'

'What?' She was certain she sounded breathless. She was in shock. She wanted George to elaborate, to keep talking. Hurry up, finish what you were saying, she willed him.

'Oh, he didn't have it when they married. God, what a disaster that would've been for poor Amanda. I like her, don't you? He's had it for some time now, poor bugger will probably die from it eventually. She left him, years ago, but she won't divorce him because of the business. It's quite the saga.'

'How do you know this?'

'Sadie's great chums with Pamela. She gets all the family gossip from Pam.'

Her heart had stopped pounding and she felt light-headed, though rational once more. It had been an anti-climax; she had wanted George to say that Gerald was sterile, incapable of being a father. She wished he had said that. But what would that have meant for her? She was so ignorant about these things. *Syphilis*, she said it to herself, what an ugly word.

'It just goes to show.' Her heart was thumping again. 'That you never really know someone. Not completely.'

Chapter Twenty-Seven

George knew that he could not hide forever and that the War Office would be sending for him soon. This was his chance to put things right. The evacuees who had come to High Greenwood were paying guests from good families who could afford their children's upkeep. Of course this included their bed and board, and a fee went to Mrs Bagshawe for managing the house. The other staff, young women who were not exempt from being called up, were drafted in by the government. And the rest of the money, a small profit, went back into the trust for the house. It was agreed beforehand that the children and staff would sleep in the old servants' quarters in the attic and in a few small rooms which were down a narrow hallway, just off the kitchen. He was not sure how many children were there now; he said the house could take in twenty, perhaps twenty-five at a stretch, but owing to the influx of evacuees from the Channel Islands he knew he was no longer in a position to cite such stipulations. Somehow he could not envision Marina running a home for children, but she did seem adamant that Daphne ought to go back. He heard the drone of aeroplanes, a low humming noise that had been ringing in his ears for days. Each time he looked up he saw nothing and wondered if he was imagining it. This time he looked out the window but the sky was clear.

Marina was outside hanging up the bedclothes, which she said could do with an airing, when another blast of noise swooped overhead. 'George!' she called out as a fleet of aeroplanes flew past, quite low. She had never seen anything like it; she'd been on a seaplane once, and that was enough.

'They're not ours.' He shielded his eyes as he watched the planes. 'It's the Germans.'

'Good grief,' she said. 'How can you tell?'

'The engine. Our engines are far superior. Listen.'

She heard a clip, clip, clip noise. 'Sounds like it's stalling.'

'Exactly.'

*

Later that night they listened to the news on the wireless. The Luftwaffe bombing of Wales, Scotland and Northern Ireland made up George's mind for him: he would make arrangements to return to High Greenwood.

'Do you think we're safe?' Marina asked.

'Probably not,' he said.

She looked away, withdrawing herself from their exchange. It had been such a long time since she had slipped the gas mask over her head at High Greenwood, thinking it suffocating and unnecessary. It had been such a long time since she had taken the threat of war seriously.

There was something hanging over his head, weighing heavily on his heart, that prevented him from taking measures for their leaving Hiraeth. What if he were to be killed? What would happen to Marina and Daphne? Daphne could not inherit the house, and even if she could there was no money to give to her. It was a false promise, his taking them back to High Greenwood. If he were to die, the house would go to his father's cousin, and they would be no better off than they were at the moment.

'You're worried about something,' she said from across the room.

'Yes, but let's not dwell on it now. Let's go to bed.'

*

Daphne was feeling better and was up on her feet again. She had begun to gain weight but still remained thin, this was emphasized by her height which was now the same as Marina's. There was a distant look of ill-health across her face, a gauntness which Marina said looked becoming.

George asked if they ought to go up to High Greenwood and check it over. He said it would give Marina a chance to suss the place out, to see if she could live amongst many children and a household staff whom she did not know. She sensed this was a ploy to make her abandon her idea of returning.

'Perhaps we could even send Daphne back to school,' he remarked.

The thought of her alone at the house, while he was off at war, and looking after the children, was enough to make her relent. But she did not play into his hands.

'Yes, what a splendid idea.'

Daphne tired easily and Marina said it would be best if she stayed at home, preferably in bed. She did not put up a fight and Marina thought she was up to something.

'If you're going to see Mrs Hartley, you make sure you're back before dinnertime. I don't know . . . but I sense something is afoot.' She listened for aeroplane engines. 'We shouldn't be very long, should we George?'

'No. We'll go first thing tomorrow and be home for your curfew of dinnertime,' he teased her. 'The blackout isn't nearly as bad now the nights are on the stretch.'

*

The next morning Marina and George rose at seven o'clock and were dressed and out the door by half-past-eight. She said they, meaning he, could eat breakfast in the teashop at the station.

'Swell. Burnt toast and margarine, delicious.'

'Oh, I am sorry. I forgot the army served you pheasant under glass and French champagne.'

He liked the banter between them, it reminded him of the old days when her acid remarks kept him guessing whether she meant it or not. It was familiar and he welcomed it.

It was warm outside and the street was quiet except for a lone bus lumbering down the road. The air was heavy with a tinge of damp and a melody of birdsong jollied them along. He offered her his arm and she took it.

When they got to the station there were two waiting trains on their side of the platform with swarms of young children standing together, their names written on card and tied with string around their necks. Some mothers and various elderly relations and siblings were there, crying into handkerchiefs and saying goodbye. Marina glanced at the children as she and George approached the teashop; some had their hair shaved off and had runny noses and dirty knees, and others looked like Shirley Temple with their ringlets and smart clothes. The eclectic mix reminded her that everyone wanted the same for their children, regardless of their background and breeding. It no longer meant love, but, rather, ensuring their safety at all costs.

They found a table in the crowded teashop, filled with soldiers and more evacuee children having a last breakfast with their loved ones. She and George stood out from the others; they appeared as holidaymakers, two people who were embarking on a pleasure trip. It made her feel conspicuous and she tried to avert her gaze out the window, which hurt her neck because she had to turn slightly. So, she studied the smattering of children instead and it occurred to her how naturally sweet the little boys were, their ears tilted forward like curious puppies; the girls had a hardness about them, a spark of self-sufficiency. George came back with his tea and toast, interrupting her hare-brained observations.

'George,' Marina said in a low voice, 'that woman over there keeps staring at us.'

He glanced over his shoulder, there was nothing to cause him concern.

'Look, there she goes again,' Marina pointed to a woman who instinctively turned her head each time she caught her staring.

'I'm sure it's all quite innocent.'

She pulled a face to contradict him and slouched back in her seat. 'She's doing it again!'

'Perhaps she thinks you are Carole Lombard.'

'Ha-ha, very funny.'

The noise of the train irritated Marina, and the children were forever rushing through the carriages, yelling and playing silly games. George got up and drew the blinds; they were the only two in their compartment, except for an elderly man who ate sardines, causing Marina to wretch.

'Breath of fresh air?' he whispered to her.

They walked along the train and stopped where the carriages joined, leaning against the door to avoid being mowed down by the children. A conductor came along and blew a whistle to round them up, and they obediently followed him. Some of the girls cried and said they wanted to go home. Now it was quiet, Marina asked George who had told him that Louisa had died.

'What?' he offhandedly said. And then, 'Oh...,' there was a long pause. 'Oh, I heard from Clara, she wrote to me at the nursing home.'

'But I thought you said Dr Dietrich did not allow letters?'

'Hers slipped through the net.'

'Well, how is she?'

'Fine. She is in America, so that is all well and good for her. No rationing or bombs over there.'

The movement of the carriage jutted them back and forth. Marina held onto the flimsy wall for support, and George raised his arm and held it straight across, just above her shoulder, and pressed his hand to the wall. Her mind turned to America and she thought how lovely it would be to escape the war, even if American positivity did irk her.

Daphne got up and got dressed and left the house. It had been the first time she had been outside in weeks, the sunlight hurt her eyes and she wondered if Marigold Square always smelled the way it did that morning: a denseness to the air, a nothingness to stir the senses. High Greenwood always smelled of grass in summer and chimney smoke in winter. Marina had guessed she would run off to Mrs Hartley's the first chance she got, but she was wrong.

Instead, she walked up the hill, a slope really, and sat down on a bench positioned at the very top. She took a deep breath and imagined it was country air, and then exhaled as she looked around. The street was quiet except for a woman pushing a pram which squeaked, and a little boy held onto the handle as he chatted to his mother. Good morning, they said. The intrusive noise of aeroplanes flying overhead, prompted them to stop. Daphne looked up, her eyes watering as she did so.

The little boy raised his arm and pointed to the sky. 'Bombs!' he yelled at the top of his voice. 'Bombs!' His mother bent forward and twisted him around to beat his bare legs for having said that.

Daphne got up and walked away, glancing over her shoulder at the overwrought woman and the howling little boy.

'Now look what you've done,' the woman continued to scold him. 'You've chased that poor girl away.'

She went home and turned on the wireless. A siren wailed through the mesh speakers, with the voice of a gentleman warning, 'This is the sound of an air raid siren.' It wailed once more. 'This is a precautionary measure. When you hear this sound you must report to your nearest air raid shelter.' It was unbearable, nothing but bad news. She turned the wireless off and sat in silence.

*

The landscape of the countryside had changed since Marina's departure from High Greenwood. They watched from the window of their compartment as the train left town and edged towards the fields, which had been ploughed and transformed into vegetable patches. Hardly any cattle grazed, and George said something about livestock being slaughtered to grow food. They had seen photographs in the newspapers of beaches blanketed in barbedwire and lookout bunkers planted along the sand-dunes. There was little joy to be had.

'Why the long face?' George asked the station master as they stepped off the train.

He helped Marina down even though she didn't need it, but he liked to act the gentleman. Putting his hands around her waist, he picked her up and felt the bones beneath her flesh; she was as light as a feather.

'Haven't you heard?'

'Heard what?'

'The battle going on up there, in the skies. The Luftwaffe is at war with the RAF.'

'Hmm it has been a bit noisy up there,' Marina said as she looked up. 'Are we safe?'

'Safe enough. They've got their sights set on the Channel.'

Mrs Bagshawe arranged for the car to collect them from the station. It was odd to get into the car he had once driven, he was even more surprised to find it still worked. He sat in the front, next to a young woman who said she helped Mrs Bagshawe twice a week but was waiting to be called up. She hoped to join the Auxiliary Territorial Service, the ATS.

'And do what?' Marina asked from her place in the back.

'I hope to drive a lorry.'

'A lorry? How advanced,' said George.

Marina despaired at the young woman's sense of patriotism; she herself did not feel the need to volunteer her services, and George felt slightly ashamed that he was shirking his responsibilities.

The long and winding lane leading to High Greenwood came into view, and Marina sat forward in her seat, like a child who was excited to go home.

'Those trees could do with a pruning,' George pointed to the bowing lime trees. The roses were as decrepit as ever and the lawn was not as neat as he would have liked it to be. It made him feel agitated.

'I'm sorry if you think the grounds are a bit of a mess,' said the young woman, as though she could read his mind. 'But the girl they sent over was hopeless, so we're all trying to pitch in and keep everything tidy.'

'It's not your fault,' Marina interrupted. Yes George, it is your fault, her thoughts conveyed to him.

His churlishness spoiled the mood and she wanted to go back to Hiraeth. She had no enthusiasm to continue their day out. He folded his arms and quietly sulked, thinking he was justified in his remarks.

At the end of the dark and cavernous lime tree drive was High Greenwood, its stone facade overgrown with ivy and looking like a wreck. Marina knew what George was thinking, and she was thinking it too, but they both remained silent and united in their disappointment.

'Where are the children?' Marina asked as they got out of the car. The gravel beneath her shoes annoyed her, as it often did in summer, the stones slipping through the gaps.

'Oh, they'll be off somewhere for the day.'

Marina imagined them running amok through the woods or climbing around the graves at the back of the house. She held a dim view of children.

'So you don't keep them cooped up indoors?' George asked.

'No, sir. Two dozen children can be a handful, so we let them out whenever we can.' Her statement prompted Marina to think of them as a pack of hounds being exercised.

Today they were visitors at their home and it conjured up the feelings she had felt when she first came to High Greenwood, and how she tiptoed around Sybil, the staff, and every potentially volatile situation. Was this how the deposed aristocracy felt after a revolution? All of those vacant castles and châteaus, visited by the inquisitive public. Would Daphne bring her own descendants here one day and say, 'Look, this is where I used to live.' And, with the country so torn apart by war and violence, High Greenwood would appear to them as a fairy castle from a bygone age.

'Ah, Sir George, we meet again,' said Mrs Bagshawe as she walked towards them.

We meet *again*, Marina thought to herself. Why did Mrs Bagshawe say we meet *again*?

'I hope you're not too put out by our visit,' George shook Mrs Bagshawe's hand. 'I'm sorry I telephoned at such short notice.'

'Quite all right.'

'This is my wife.' George placed his hand on Marina's back and gave her a little push.

'Lady Greenwood,' Mrs Bagshawe shook her hand.

214

How Marina loathed touching people, more so strangers. She did not mean to automatically wipe her hand on her skirt, but she did and they saw.

'We'll take our tea in the drawing room,' George said.

He forgot the good rooms had been locked up, and Mrs Bagshawe felt in her skirt pocket for the keys and was embarrassed to have forgotten them. A cardinal sin for a housekeeper, but she was not a housekeeper by trade, rather a well-spoken woman who had previously worked two days a week at the library.

'Fetch my keys, will you Polly?' Mrs Bagshawe asked.

'So that's what our lorry driver is called,' Marina whispered to George.

They stood in silence, like actors waiting for their cue to enter a scene. 'Do you know Mrs Bagshawe?' George asked Marina.

'No, should I?'

'I help out at the library,' Mrs Bagshawe offered.

'Oh yes,' Marina lied. 'I thought I recognised your face.' That must be how George knew her, she thought.

The jingling of the keys met their ears. 'Ah Polly,' Mrs Bagshawe sang. 'You've saved the day.'

*

The boredom of Hiraeth was stifling, more so now that Marina and George had left for the day. After listening to the news of doom and gloom on the wireless, Daphne fell asleep. She had not meant to waste her day of freedom, but a tiredness came over her and she could not fight it. She was awoken by a knock on the door, three rapid bangs, and she thought Marina had fallen out with George and returned home. She was used to her parents snapping at one another, and Marina was never patient when she forgot her key to open the front door.

'All right, all right,' Daphne groaned. She was already shouting, 'Did you forget your key?' before she had opened the door. But the caller was not Marina and she felt silly for losing her temper. 'Oh,' she said to a middle-aged woman dressed in an ARP uniform. She wondered if Miss Fag had ever fulfilled her ambition of becoming an Air Raid Precaution warden.

'Good afternoon,' said the stranger on the doorstep. 'Does a Sir George Greenwood reside here? Or, failing that, Lady Greenwood, otherwise known as Marina?'

Had George bought something on the never-never, the way Mrs Hartley had when their wireless broke, and Celia had to explain to Daphne who the man collecting money on their doorstep was?

'I'm sorry, they've gone away for the day.' She was bleary eyed and quite drowsy and wanted nothing more than to go back to sleep.

'Do you know when they'll be back?'

'What did you say your name was?'

The woman extended her hand and said in an efficient manner, 'I'm Joan Rogan, pleased to meet you.'

'How do you do,' Daphne shook her hand and then withdrew hers, keeping it by her side.

'Anyhow,' she said, 'you tell your father that Joan Rogan called. He'll know whom you're referring to.'

'Yes, all right.' Daphne took a step back, almost retreating behind the door.

'You tell him that I called,' she repeated as she made for the gate.

'I said I would.'

Daphne remained behind the closed door, watching through the clear part of the stained glass window, off to the side. The mirage of Joan moved away and she paused when another woman of a similar age, but tall and thin, approached her. Daphne could hear the other woman's voice, it was more refined.

'Well? Did she buy it?'

'They weren't in,' said Joan. 'So I left a message.'

'Who answered?' asked the other woman.

'A girl. I suspect it's the daughter.'

'You didn't tell her, did you? You wouldn't stoop so low?'

'Shut up.'

Yes, that must be it, Daphne thought. The shame and embarrassment of buying something on the never-never. She remembered Mrs Hartley blushing when Celia explained how it worked, and she said she'd never done it before, they were just waiting for money to be sent from India. She was rather cross and flustered. Poor George, he'll be in for it when Marina finds out. She went back to the drawing room and flopped down on the sofa to resume her nap.

*

216

The drawing room was as they had left it, but it did not strike Marina as familiar. The sunlight beaming through the window burned her skin and she felt unbearably hot, a discomfort had set in; the slip beneath her flimsy cotton dress had twisted, its hem askew, and her bra pinched. She looked out the window at the endless stretch of lawn. The same place where she had sat when the news of the war broke, when she saw Gladys rush to tell George. A scattering of children ran towards the house, yelling. But as they got closer, Marina could see that they were crying.

'Look,' she said to George, who had been sitting in silence. 'Look, they're upset about something.'

The voice of Mrs Bagshawe could be heard, and the children's painful cries drowned out her words.

'What is it?' George went to the hallway.

'They say a plane's come down.'

'Luftwaffe!' the shrill voice of a young boy yelled. 'It was a German!'

'What happened to him?' George asked.

'He crawled out. He chased us through the woods.'

Marina felt frightened; she knew planes might fall from the sky but she never imagined it could happen so close to home. She got up, and as she moved to the door she heard the children break into laughter.

'Ha-ha!' the shrill boy yelled. 'We tricked you! We tricked you!'

She reached the door just as George got the boy by his shirt, his hands tightening around the collar, his fingers feeling for his neck.

'You think it's funny to joke about war!' he yelled into the boy's face. 'You think it's funny to scare people!' The children began to cry and Mrs Bagshawe was on the verge of tears herself.

'For God's sake.' Marina pulled at George. 'You're frightening him!'

It was as though it suddenly dawned on George that his victim was a child, about seven at the most, and that he was scaring him. He let go and the boy fell to the floor, he stepped back and looked at Marina. 'He...,' he tried to speak but was breathless and disorientated.

She put her arm around him and walked him back to the drawing room. There was no time to explain about the ship sinking and George almost dying. The children were too upset and would not understand. Mrs Bagshawe already thought he was a madman and offered Marina a pitiful look, as though she were a battered wife.

'I'll find Polly,' she said. 'I'll ask her to drive us to the station.'

'I'm sorry, Marina,' his breathing was rapid. 'I'm so sorry. For everything.'

*

It was still light outside when they got home, the trains had been delayed and they managed to catch one at seven o'clock. They sat in silence until the train began to pull out of the station, then he moved his hand closer to hers and held onto it. She did not remove it, instead she looked at his pained expression.

'Perhaps you left the nursing home too soon,' she whispered.

He shook his head. 'No, it's not that.'

'You know whatever it is you can tell me.'

'I know I can, but I'm a coward.'

She rested her head against the window and closed her eyes, pretending to sleep. The scene at High Greenwood played on her mind and she could not forget the look of terror on the little boy's face; the look of fright in Mrs Bagshawe's eyes. And then the collapse of George's anger. She felt the current of tension leave him when she pulled him away. She knew he was ashamed, and so was she.

*

Daphne woke up when she heard the front door close, she had been sleeping in the drawing room the entire time. She got up and walked to the hallway, watching as George climbed the stairs without saying a word.

'How was your day? Did you go out?' Marina asked as she took off her jacket. She looked worn out, and disinterested in Daphne's response.

Daphne yawned and, ignoring her mother's question, she said, 'Somebody called here looking for father. They told me to give him a message.'

'Well, let's not bother him now,' she dismissed Daphne. She was not listening to her and the words escaped her attention as she began to climb the stairs. 'I'm sure whatever it is, it can wait.'

Chapter Twenty-Eight

The bright rays of the morning sun, shining through the window, woke George up. When they returned from High Greenwood and went to bed, Marina was too exhausted to care about drawing the curtains and he was too ashamed of his outburst to talk to her about it, and so he withdrew into himself like he always did when he was wrong. The little boy was miles away at the house, and there was no second chance to redeem himself; he was certain they all thought him a monster. He could not argue with their assessment, for he could not control the monster inside of himself: the unexpected rages, the violence. He looked at Marina as she slept soundly on her side, her face close to his; he listened to her gentle breathing and felt her breath against him when she exhaled. Then he placed his hand on her cheek and felt her warm skin against his palm.

Opening her eyes, she looked up at him as she did little feline stretches. 'What time is it?' she asked.

'Early,' he guessed. The dawn chorus rang through the opened window and the house was silent. 'I am sorry. You know that, don't you?'

She nodded and offered him a kind smile, touching his face as though he were a stranger and she sought a semblance of familiarity. 'I've been thinking,' she self-consciously whispered as he moved closer to her. 'That perhaps if you tell me... tell me what's been troubling you... that you might not have those outbursts.'

He kissed her with the intent to make her stop talking.

Daphne crept down the landing, careful not to make too much noise. She was going to knock on the door and remind Marina about the visitor before she left for the day. The door was ajar and the strip of movement from inside the room caught her eye and she froze, her heart pounding in her ears. She felt cross and, as her blood pumped faster, jealous and resentful. It was as though the whole world had gone on living while she was miserable. And then she felt angry at George because he was supposed to be sick and she had felt sorry for him, had defended him when Marina became impatient about his illness and bitter about his homecoming. They can go to hell, she thought as she thumped down the stairs, loud enough to make her presence known.

'Daphne said that a woman called, looking for you,' Marina said after she pulled away, interrupting his kiss. She spoke to fend him off.

'Who?'

'I don't know.'

'Probably one of those religious quacks. They've been doing the rounds.'

'I wonder if it was Sadie. Would Daphne know her, do you think?'

He put his hands behind his head and lay back, contemplating who this caller could have been. Something dawned on him and his expression changed. 'I've been lying here long enough.'

Marina watched him get out of bed and go to the wardrobe and take his clothes. She sat up and pretended to look at her nails, examining them for any chips in the red polish. 'You might want to close the curtains before you get undressed,' she said.

'You think of everything.' He kissed her on the head before leaving the room.

Inside the bathroom, he pressed his hands against the edge of the sink and took a deep breath. He thought of Joan and how she would stop at nothing to destroy his life, to tear everything apart. The sound of Marina moving around the bedroom disturbed his thoughts and he began to fill the sink and splash water onto his face. He needed to shave, but there was no time.

'Do you think I ought to telephone Mrs Bagshawe?' she called from the other side of the door.

He was brushing his teeth and made a production out of it. Go away, go away, he silently wished. 'What for?'

'To, I don't know, explain. Try to make sense of what happened.'

'If you want.' He opened the door and stood in front of her. 'I don't think it'll do any good.' He moved past her and went to the bedroom and began to dress.

She waited outside and looked down the landing, thinking the future had been decided for her and she would have to stay at Hiraeth and, if so, she might as well paint the place. The door opened and he returned to the landing, fully dressed. He was distracted, a little agitated, and she picked up on this.

'I'm off out,' he said as he walked away, hoping she would not stop him. 'I have some errands to do.'

She watched him leave, wondering how he balanced this dual personality. How he could switch between being loving and attentive, to being a madman. All this time she thought the problem lay with her; she was certain it did, and now she was not so sure.

*

It took a while before Mrs Hartley answered the door, and Daphne was about to walk away when it opened. It was nine o'clock in the morning but the early hour escaped her and she banged on the front door, regardless. Wearing her dressing gown and with sleep etched across her face, Mrs Hartley yawned. 'Daphne...,' she yawned once more. 'What are you doing here? Is something wrong?' She leaned forward and scanned the street, her blood shot eyes watering from the daylight.

'I'm sorry,' Daphne meekly said. 'I didn't realise it was so early.'

'That's quite all right.'

'May I... May I come in?'

'Of course.'

The house was a mess: there were trunks stacked in the hallway, and paintings and pieces of furniture were either covered in sheets or set off to the side. A sinking feeling overwhelmed Daphne and she looked around, taking in the scene.

'Are you...,' she searched for the right words, not wanting to say it out loud because then it would be true. 'Are you leaving?'

Mrs Hartley let out a heavy sigh as she sank into the chair. She sat in contemplative silence before looking at Daphne. She had a pitiful look in her eyes and she held out her hand, willing Daphne to walk to her. She did so, taking Mrs Hartley's cold hand.

'I *was* going to tell you. I *was*.'

Daphne's hand began to tremble and she felt hot tears forming in her eyes. She blinked and they fell, rolling down her cheeks. They were silent for a moment and Mrs Hartley reached up and wiped the tears away.

'I didn't expect you to cry,' she said.

Daphne sniffed and tried to steady her composure, she did not have a handkerchief and she didn't want her nose to run. She was light-headed and her leg shook as she stood on the spot. Pulling her hand from Mrs Hartley's tight grip, Daphne sat down on the sofa and Mrs Hartley got up and sat next to her. She convulsed a few times as she steadied her breathing and a few sobs escaped.

'I don't know why I'm crying. I'm sorry.'

'I've wanted to tell you something for a long time. I never thought I *would* have to tell you. No...' She paused, a little hesitant before beginning. 'No, I *should* tell you this.' She stopped once more, to ask Daphne if she would like a drink and she said no, and wiped her tears away with her knuckles, the bones pressing into her eyes and causing the tears to sting. 'You must understand something.' She held onto Daphne's hand, her knuckles were wet. 'You must understand that I did what I did because it was for the best. Or so I thought.'

This is it, Daphne thought, she's going to talk about Celia's death. She looked at Mrs Hartley and nodded, taking a deep breath as she did so.

'Celia was always trouble. Whatever she did was always too much and in excess. Too boisterous, too defiant, too promiscuous. In the end, anyway. She was always trying to shock us,' Mrs Hartley said. 'Always going too far, never stopping to think of others.'

Daphne held her breath, she expected the worst. She sensed Mrs Hartley would speak of that night, the night Celia had died and, in a roundabout way, how it was all her fault.

'It's because my father brought her home, isn't it?' she blurted it out before Mrs Hartley could say it.

'What?'

'It's because my father drove her home. It all happened because she'd misbehaved at my house.'

Mrs Hartley fell silent, Daphne had expected her to deny it, but she did not. It was only part of the problem, a tiny part with a significant outcome. It could have been prevented.

'They had a row,' she wistfully said. 'They had a row and she stormed out of the house.'

And that's how it happened, Daphne thought. But it wasn't.

Celia had walked into the kitchen, after George had driven her home, to find her father sitting at the table, quietly drinking. She said sorry and quickly left the room. She hated being alone with him. When Mrs Hartley came in she called for Celia, and she came downstairs and followed her mother into the kitchen. She felt sick and frightened, and she knew what her father's reaction would be. Mrs Hartley had told him that George had to drive her home from High Greenwood because she sneaked off with a boy and they were concerned about what she had got up to.

'He never said that!' Celia wailed. She was frustrated with her mother and how she always misheard things and got it all wrong.

'First thing tomorrow, I'm taking you to the doctor,' Mrs Hartley shouted, turning sideways as she did so, steadying herself against the kitchen counter. 'He'll know what you've been up to. He'll tell me if you've been lying or not.'

Her father continued to sit in silence, his presence far more menacing than her mother's hysterics.

'I haven't done anything,' Celia pleaded. 'Please believe me. I haven't done anything wrong. I haven't been bad.'

Mr Hartley rose and edged towards Celia. Celia walked backwards with her hands behind her, feeling for any obstacles in her path. 'We had to leave India because of you.'

Celia shook her head, crying. 'No.'

'Stop it!' Mrs Hartley screamed. She could not bear to hear it again, to listen to the truth. Uncle Christopher was their closest friend, he was Celia's godfather, they trusted him.

'Slut.' Mr Hartley slapped her across the face.

Celia tried to plead her innocence, to explain that nothing untoward had happened but she did not know how to speak that way in front of her parents, or why they would think that of her. Especially her father, whose lips had turned white. Determined to prove that she was right, she ran out of the house, hoping to catch up with George's car. He had driven so slow, unsure of the area, and she hoped he would be as apprehensive when leaving the street.

'Come back here!' Mr Hartley roared from the steps leading to the front door.

It was almost dark and Celia ran down the path, her footsteps beating against the concrete, its impact pounding in her ears. She heard her father's footsteps coming after her, almost catching up with her. Glancing over her shoulder, she saw his red face and heard him gasping for air.

Mrs Hartley stepped outside and walked slowly to the middle of the pavement. She yelled for her husband to come back, to stop making a scene. 'You're going to have a heart attack,' she shouted.

Celia was becoming short of breath; she knew she must stop or she would have an asthma attack. The familiar tightness gripped her, but she was too afraid to stop. She knew her father would catch up with her.

'Celia,' Mrs Hartley began to slow down, eventually stopping. 'Ce –'

'Help me, mummy,' she gasped. She leaned forward and held onto her knees, her nose ran as she took rapid breaths.

'Oh come on,' Mrs Hartley looked at her, bemused. 'Stop faking.' She looked over her shoulder at her husband, who came towards them. 'Stop faking, I said!' She reached out, attempting to grab Celia. 'Stop it!' Celia could see her mother standing before her, a hazy vision whose mouth moved frantically but no sound could be heard. She saw her father running towards her, and a fear gripped her. It would have been easy to fall to the ground, to allow him to drag her home and then suffer the punishment. Without stopping to look for traffic, she darted onto the road. The screeching of the brakes sounded through the narrow street and the thumping footsteps of Mr Hartley stopped.

It was silent once more, and then a medley of unwarranted noise rang out. A dog barked and a middle-aged woman came out of her house, alarmed by the commotion. Celia lay in the middle of the road, the car had barely touched her. Mrs Hartley squealed, prompting the dog to bark again. The driver paced next to the car, stepping forward to Celia, then back again, and the middle-aged woman ran into the house to telephone an ambulance. There was no blood, no cuts or bruises, just a small, still body lying in the middle of the road.

*

George banged on the door, his fists beating off the flimsy wood until the skin on his knuckles bled. 'Answer the door, you bitch,' he shouted, his voice echoing down the landing.

When it opened he jumped back, startled to see Louisa in the doorway. She was in her nightgown and her hair was tied up in a net; her face looked different, fatigued and so much older. Her blue eyes widened at the sight of him, they appeared larger beneath her pale, sparse eyebrows.

Without a word he shoved her to one side and stumbled into the flat. It was quiet and the curtains were drawn, last night's dinner dishes were still on the table behind the sofa. He was disorientated and tried to comprehend the flashes of Louisa standing before him.

'What the hell is wrong with you?' she said as she walked to the curtains. She pulled them open, roughly, to show him how irritated she was.

'I thought you were dead.'

'What?'

Joan walked into view, tightening the belt of her dressing gown as she did so. She rummaged in her pocket for a cigarette and placed it to her lips, taking in George's frantic appearance. 'Oh that?' She struck the match, lighting her cigarette and exhaling. 'You fell for that?'

'What's he going on about, Joan?'

'It was only a joke.' She waved the match to extinguish the flame, its smoke swirling before her.

She did not expect George to lunge at her. He grabbed her by the throat, tightening his grip around her neck.

'Stop it, George!' Louisa pulled at his clothes, trying to pull him off her. 'You're going to choke her!'

Joan hissed, spit escaped from her mouth as she begged George to let her go. She tried to kick out, to claw at his face but he did not feel the pain and he continued to strangle her, his eyes scrambling around the room. He dragged her to the window and pushed it open, breaking the flimsy latch as he did so. The street below was quiet and he stood behind Joan as he slammed her body against the windowsill.

'See that down there,' he said as he pushed her closer to the edge. 'See it?' he repeated.

Joan tried to splutter a response but his grip was too tight and she pushed her head to attempt a nod.

Louisa jumped on his back, pulling him off Joan. He fell backwards and knocked Louisa to the floor, but she was unhurt and quickly stumbled to her feet.

'Get out,' she screamed. 'Get out before I call the police.'

Joan was on her hands and knees, coughing and struggling to catch her breath. She looked at George, who stood in the middle of the room, staring at her.

'No,' she said to Louisa. 'Make him pay.'

'Pay? Pay with what?' George shouted.

Louisa looked to Joan for an answer but she gave none. She went to the window and pulled it shut, picking up the cigarette Joan had dropped in the process.

'We'll get the police,' Joan called after him. 'Don't think you're off the hook.'

Louisa chased after him, following him down the landing. 'George, wait up,' she called. He stopped and turned to face her. 'I won't let her ring the police.'

He shrugged, he no longer cared.

'Just fix this.' Her eyes narrowed and she nodded, as though she were doing him a favour. 'For your own sake...,'

'It's as easy as that?' he asked, moving away from her.

'It always was.'

*

When Daphne reached Hiraeth, Marina was standing at the drawing room window. She smoked and looked out at the street, as though she were waiting for someone or something. 'Have you seen your father?' she called to Daphne.

'No,' she said as she came into the drawing room. She was exhausted and confused, and she burst into tears without warning. Marina asked what was wrong and Daphne shook her head, the rapid sobbing prevented her from speaking. She went to Daphne and guided her to the sofa, where they sat down.

'I went...,' she took a deep breath. 'I went to see Mrs Hartley.' Her voice became shrill, and she felt faint and looked down at the floor, the tears dripping from her eyes. She looked up at Marina, whose face had softened, and her eyes were kinder than before. 'And now I know.'

Marina put her arm around Daphne, feeling her bony shoulders jutting up and down. She pulled her close and placed her hand on her head, holding it against her chest. The tears soaked through her blouse, touching her skin.

Daphne was still sobbing when George came into the room, wearing his hat and coat, quite bewildered himself. Marina mistook his reaction for the scene playing out before him, and she looked up at him and gently shook her head, a silent warning not to ask what was wrong.

'Bad timing?'

*

226

'That was certainly a surprise,' George said as he settled down to a nightcap. He was hoping the brandy would steady his nerves and give him the courage to speak freely with Marina.

'A surprise?' her mouth moved, though her body and expression remained composed.

'Not a surprise. A shock.'

'Poor Celia,' Marina mumbled. 'Still, it must be a relief for Daphne to know. Poor little thing.'

'Do you think he blames himself? The father, I mean.'

'I'm sure he does. Yes, I think so. Wouldn't you?'

Her words made his blood run cold and he became more reserved, the mood in the room changed, and she picked up on this.

'I don't know. I suppose they were doing the best they could.'

She was tired of talking; she always felt self-conscious when he was in such a mood, and when she revealed too much about her thoughts and feelings. It always made her feel the way she did after she'd gone to bed with him, that somehow the next day she would look different and be someone quite unlike her true self.

'You said you were going back,' she said.

'Going back?' his voice was quiet. He was becoming withdrawn and, she sensed, moody. 'Oh yes,' he said in an enlightened tone. 'Yes I am, if they'll have me.' She leaned back in the chair, exhausted and disinterested in having a conversation. He observed this and quickly added, 'But before I go I want to talk to you. To tell you something.'

'Oh yes?'

'Yes. But let's not talk about it now. I'm tired, are you tired?'

'Yes I am.'

They went upstairs and George checked on Daphne, looking in at her sleeping body while Marina went into the bathroom to wash her face and prepare for bed. He saw the restlessness across Daphne's pinched face, the red stripes down her cheeks from crying.

Marina's mind was racing with the information Daphne had told her; her own sense of wretchedness was provoked by her treatment of the girl. She felt at a loss, unsure of herself, and entirely vulnerable. When she opened the bedroom door, George was sitting up in bed, as though he had been waiting for her and this eased the pain, momentarily. She did not notice the look of dread on his face, his eyes staring at her with a pleading expression. Perhaps she did, and it mirrored her own self-pity. Or their mutual need to be forgiven, by each other and themselves. He detected a quick sniffle, a tear falling from her eye.

He held out his hand and she took it. They looked at one another for a brief moment, as if they were trying to read one another's minds, to telepathically communicate. Silly really, since they were never that close. She did not resist when he pulled her towards him, putting her arm around his neck to steady herself. She did not object when he kissed her, her balance giving way as he leaned back.

She broke away and stood up, catching her breath. It was dark, and he could see her silhouette as she walked around the bed, going to the window. She drew the curtains, creating an extra layer of blackness, and he assumed that was it: her offering of affection had ceased. It was so unlike Marina that he thought he had imagined it all, in the pitch black of the bedroom, and he did not build up his expectations. She pulled back the blankets and got into bed, the sensation of being on the verge of tears had not left her, and she tried to steady her breathing. She did not speak loudly but there was a quiver in her voice when she said his name, prompting him to begin. He felt her cold hand touching his arm and she heard the familiar creaking of the springs beneath the mattress as he moved closer. This is what he had always wanted, for her to love him. To show him that she cared. She flinched when he touched her, and he thought that she would seize up the way she always did. She stopped for a moment and he did too, leading him to believe it was all over. She took a deep breath, as though for courage, before anything happened. And then it did, and she closed her eyes. She felt wretched again and her chest heaved as the tears built up in her eyes, an aching feeling in her throat, and he was oblivious that she was crying. He was too far gone, encouraged by her going through the motions of reciprocating his movements, lost in the cavernous surroundings.

'You're trembling,' he said, afterwards.

The house was quiet, and the silence of the street below slipped through the opened window, muffled by the blackout curtains. A buzzing sound, a nothingness, filled the room.

Marina ignored him, and keeping her back to him she buried her face in the crook of her arm to suppress the tears. He edged closer to her as she lay on her side and put his arm around her, resting it on the hollow crook of her waist. All he wanted was to love her.

Chapter Twenty-Nine

The next morning Marina pretended to be asleep. She had not slept much the night before, thinking how foolish she had been and how she had practically thrown herself at him, and so her groggy voice and bleary eyes fooled George when he leaned across, to kiss her good morning. This connection he thought they shared, an intimacy that had somehow been restored or formed, filled her with unease and she wondered if she had led him on. She squeezed her legs together, thinking him too familiar; his hand on her waist as he lay, draped across her.

'Where's Daphne?' she asked, stifling him.

He stopped, his hand suspended somewhere between her midriff and a place she did not wish it to be. He felt her stomach tense, and he pulled away and rolled on to his back, yawning loudly as he did so. After a moment he got up.

'I'll make us some tea, shall I?'

'Yes please,' she said, though she didn't want any. 'Without milk,' she added.

'Of course,' he kissed her on the forehead.

She waited until she heard the kettle whistling, and then she got out of bed. It was cold and she shivered as she went to the wardrobe, selecting her clothes. The door was ajar, and she wondered if he did that on purpose. She was more observant than usual, little things piqued her curiosity. Her body was heavy with fatigue and she had a dull ache in her stomach. She felt light-headed as she leaned over to rummage in the drawer for underwear. Ideally she would have preferred to bathe first, but she was too lazy. Such thoughts ran through her head as she dressed. Then, fastening her skirt, she heard an explosion, far enough away for their own safety but close enough to gauge the area which had been blown up. She rushed to Daphne's bedroom and saw her sitting up in bed, the noise having woken her.

'It's all right,' Marina said as she tucked in her blouse. 'Go down to the kitchen.'

They climbed under the kitchen table, a small circle which forced them to sit close to one another. Marina's elbow dug into George's side but he did not complain. He thought of the times he had wanted to confess to her, and how some eventuality prevented him from doing so. The small space at the back of the house was too small for an Anderson shelter, and George had already spoken of the false security a corrugated iron roof would provide. One hit from the Germans and it'll be on top of you, he had said.

'Next time we'll go to the air raid shelter,' Marina remarked as they climbed out from beneath the table. She stood up, dusted down her knees and fixed her hair, which hung lifeless around her shoulders.

'Or you could go to High Greenwood,' he said without looking at her.

'But you said it'll be no good if you...,'

'Die,' he finished her sentence.

Daphne looked at her parents. George stood in front of the kitchen window, looking at the stretch of concrete outside. Marina hovered next to the table, knowing that she was listening.

'Don't worry about me,' he said. 'I can make provisions for you both. It's the least I can do.'

She nodded. 'Okay, then.'

Later that evening, after Daphne had gone to bed, Marina and George listened to the wireless. The bombing had begun in earnest, said the newsreader's voice. They learned that the Agincourt Hotel had taken a direct hit, its entire top floor blown to pieces. She could not tell George that she had been there, or that Gerald was staying there, and she was not sure if he had ever left.

'You look like you've seen a ghost,' he said from across the room.

'Do I?'

The next morning, when all seemed quiet, Marina walked in the direction of the hotel. A row of houses, close to where the Hartleys had lived, had been blown up and smoke and dust continued to rise from the ruins, up to the sky. ARPs were rummaging around, pulling people from the rubble; some dead, some alive. They laid the bodies along the path, covered in grey ash, like the lost souls of Vesuvius.

'You can't come down here,' said an ARP.

She looked past the ARP's shoulder and saw what had once been a kitchen exposed on the pavement, surrounded by the gables of the former house, its roof and everything else gone. The bodies were being transported to a warehouse, which had offered its floor, since no funeral parlour could have managed. She could not fathom that it had taken place, two streets away from Hiraeth, in the early hours of the morning.

'If I were you,' said the ARP, 'I'd go home.'

'Where else has been hit?' Marina asked.

The ARP looked exasperated, she took a deep breath and sighed. 'Morrow Place, for one,' she said off the top of her head.

'That's by the river, isn't it?'

The ARP ignored her and continued with the task at hand.

When she got home George was waiting for her. He asked where she had been. She lied and said she had gone to the shop for cigarettes.

'You've got something on your mind,' he looked at Marina. 'I do too.'

She got up and walked to the window. 'The air raid shelter is just around the corner, isn't it?'

'Yes. I can show you, if you like?'

'I'm worried it'll happen tonight, the siren didn't go off last time.'

'No, it was a surprise attack.' He stuttered a little, his voice vibrating at the beginning. 'Th-th-this is how such things usually happen. So... so close to home.'

'Yes,' she said.

*

Mrs Hartley had left for India before the bombs were dropped. The anniversary of Celia's death had come round and Daphne expected some sort of shift to take place. She had thought of little else all year, and so on the actual day her thoughts were as before, if not more poignant. Marina said the mind was a powerful thing and that it stored trauma, the brain scarred by such things. And so it was no good trying to pretend. Daphne pondered the advice, it was so unlike Marina to speak this way. Never complain, never explain. That was her motto.

When Daphne had said goodbye to Mrs Hartley, after she learned about what had happened on the night of Celia's death, they did not offer to keep in touch by letter, and Daphne sensed Mrs Hartley wanted a clean break. She did not bear her any grudge at the time.

But as the days passed she thought of the hare-brained confession and of Uncle Christopher. There had been no mention of him except for the time Daphne had referred to his name, and Mrs Hartley's expression verified what Celia had said. There was a time when she thought Celia might have made it all up. The bangles were still in her bedroom, in the jewellery box Marina had given her, and she did not know what to do with them. Celia had always said they were a secret, but it was not a secret Daphne wished to keep.

'I never returned the bangles,' Daphne said to Marina.

'Well,' she shrugged, 'they're no good to her now that she's dead. People are no good to you when they're dead.'

Marina knew about Uncle Christopher, she had guessed enough to paint a sordid picture. There it was, the old feeling of shame and how after her encounter with Gerald she wanted to be somebody quite different from her true self. She could not put into words why she had undertaken this transformation except that Gerald must have been attracted to her old self, and if she could alter her appearance then what had happened would remain in the past, as though it had happened to somebody else. 'You look like a tart,' George had said after she dyed her hair blonde. He said it in jest but it wounded her all the same. Her mascara dissolved and ran down her cheeks. That is why tarts wore make-up, she told herself, their hearts were too hard to cry.

*

There were no air raids that night and George said it might have been a one off. She thought no, this isn't how bad things happen; it begins with something unexpected and then escalates. They went to bed, but Marina could not sleep, thinking a bomb would drop on the house when they least expected it.

'I want to tell you something,' George said from his side of the bed.

'Yes?'

'I've wanted to tell you this for such a long time.'

'Shall I turn on the light?'

'No, I'm afraid I couldn't look at you. I'm brave, here, in the dark.'

She thought he was being melodramatic and simpering; the two things which served to irritate her. His skulking around doorways, tiptoeing into rooms.

'The reason we have no money is because I had been paying Louisa off.' His heart was thumping and he was certain she could feel it vibrating off the mattress as he sat up in bed, concealed by the darkness. 'It's been going on for years. It happened just after your mother died.'

'I don't understand, why did you have to pay her off?' She reached over and turned on the lamp.

233

The sudden flash of light gave him a jolt, as though it had been shone on him to expose his wrongdoings. Panic gripped him and he thought of telling her another lie, but he could not bear to keep it going.

'The woman who called here while we were at High Greenwood was Joan, her friend.'

'I think she's more than her friend, George.'

'Yes, but that's not the point. She threatened to tell you what I had done.'

'So you're telling me this because you're scared of Joan? And if Joan hadn't come here you might never have told me?' Now she was becoming angry, and had forgotten that Louisa was dead, supposedly, and he never told her otherwise because that would confuse her more.

'No, it's not like that at all.'

'Then what is it like? You'd been paying Louisa money for years and years, we can't live in our home because you squandered the money, and now Joan is somehow blackmailing you. Is that right?'

'Yes.'

'Why? What sort of skulduggery did you get up to?'

The dismissive tone of her voice told him that she was not taking him seriously. 'I am responsible for your mother's death. It was all my fault.' There, he had said it. Just like that. It was easier than he thought.

He had wanted to tell her for years, and he wanted her to know that. It happened by accident. It was a nasty accident. That was how George began when Marina had moved from the bed to the chair at the other side of the room. She was not afraid of him, but she wanted to be away from him, so she could look him in the eye and create a formal atmosphere that was otherwise lacking by remaining next to him in bed.

Now he was standing up and pacing back and forth along a small strip of the room. 'It wasn't sinister, nothing like that,' he said. He was desperate for her to believe him.

'My mother fell down the stairs,' she said. Her body was trembling and she tried to control it, but she could not prevent her voice from quivering. 'Did you push her?'

'No,' the pleading in his voice continued. 'I never laid a hand on her.'

'Then how did you kill her?' She could not believe that he had killed her or that he was capable of such a thing.

'I... I.' He fought to control his stutter. 'I was coming from the bedroom.'

'Why?'

Her asking him why he had come from the bedroom threw him off and he could not decipher the words into a sentence; he could not soften the blow.

'My God,' Marina said, suddenly enlightened. 'You were sleeping with her, too.'

He saw the wretched look on her face, the pallor of sickness threatening to expel itself from her body. He could not do this to her.

'You know what... what sort of w-w-woman she was.'

She nodded, her brow creased, she looked ashamed. 'And so you had an affair with her. Is that right?'

'No,' he said, his voice construed in a way which made it seem as though he was interrupting her. 'No. Christ, nothing like that.' He saw the relief in her eyes, the settling of her stomach. 'I'm not that depraved, to sleep with a woman then marry her daughter.' How well he lied, but he reasoned that it was done out of love and to protect her. 'I went upstairs... b-b-because she asked me to look at something.' He had to stop, the stutter was coming back, a sure sign that he was frightened, or lying, or both.

'And then what?'

'She was d-d-drunk, you do know that?'

Marina turned and looked away, it was a cruel thing to say but he needed her to see that Evangelina had fallen because she was drunk, not because he had lifted his hand to her, or had tried to frighten her. That was not him, that was not the man he was today. She mumbled something about not being surprised.

'And I put my arm out to grab her, before she stumbled.'

She had tears in her eyes and was nodding, faster than he could speak. She wanted to believe everything he said.

'And she... she r-r-reached out and... and... and pulled at me.' He sat down on the edge of the bed, a distraction from the words he was trying to form. 'And... I f-f-fell f-f-forward and kn-kn-knocked her down.'

'Why didn't you tell the policemen that?' She thought back to that day and remembered him saying that he had found her. 'Why didn't you tell the truth?'

'My m-m-mother told me not to.'

Marina sighed and cast a pitiful look in his direction, which was etched with sympathy. She knew a thing or two about overbearing mothers. 'And Joan,' her voice was harsher, more authoritative. 'What has she got to do with it?'

'She and Louisa g-g-gave me my alibi.'

Marina nodded, taking in everything he said and trying to process it. It was too complicated, too much of a tangled web. First there was Celia and her secret, and now George and his. She had an anxious feeling in the pit of her stomach, a feeling that something was wrong and she could not settle until she had fixed it. She had not felt that way for such a long time.

'I don't know what to say.' She looked up at George as he sat on the bed, his body slumped over. 'Except, I wish you had told me sooner.' Her eyes glazed over, she was in deep thought. 'Though,' she spoke quietly, and to herself, 'God knows what I would've done with the information.'

'I'm so sorry, Marina.'

But she could not bear him a grudge, whether she believed his story or not. She had never been honest about Gerald, or had told him what she had done. At first she thought it must be her fault, that she had tempted him in some way and now she must pay the price. And as she grew older, she realised that he was the one who took advantage, that he was to blame. But how could he shoulder the burden when she was the one who had to look at the physical reminder of what he had done? George could not tell her that he had loved Evangelina, so he skirted around that part and told her half-formed truths. She could not tell him that Daphne was almost certainly Gerald's, and so she formed a barrier between herself and her child, to allow George the satisfaction of loving her and feeling superior when he rose to the role of father. And now they were lying to each other and secretly telling themselves that it was for their own good.

'When I come back we can decide what to do,' he said.

She looked in his direction and nodded. 'I think that's for the best.'

'Whatever I did,' his voice was more assertive. 'I did it because I love you. You must believe me, because it is true.'

'Yes,' she said. 'I believe you.'

Chapter Thirty

Marina had once said that people were no good to you when they're dead. But that's not true. The bombing on that night had taken with it not only Gerald, who lay in a state of delirium in his room at the Agincourt Hotel, but Louisa and Joan, who had slept in their beds at Morrow Place. The latter casualties struck George as poignant: even though he had confessed the truth, Louisa and Joan were destined to die. In a way he was glad of their meddling, for the lie had hung around his neck like an albatross, and now he felt free.

Knowing that he had struggled with a lie that had once been a misunderstanding, and then warped into something much bigger, inspired empathy from Marina. She could not tell him about Gerald, and so, in a way, she respected his courage.

'I forgive you,' she said.

They had four days together before he left for Malta. Their time spent in one another's company was not deemed precious and George was content to carry on as before. It was difficult to break their routine of coexisting under the same roof. On their last night together he told her that he loved her and, for the first time, he asked if she loved him. He had always wanted to know, always looked for a sign that she might feel the same as he, and he was always too hesitant to ask, too afraid to hear the answer.

'No,' she truthfully answered. 'I am... fond of you,' she added after a bout of silence. 'But I don't love you.'

No more secrets; no more lies. That is what he had said after telling her about Evangelina and she felt compelled to uphold the standard he had set.

'I see,' he replied. 'But do you think... that you... you could love me? That we c-c-could try again? When I come home, I mean.'

She gave a feeble shrug, an ominous gesture to prevent herself from committing to a straight answer. Behind the flippancy she felt assured that, although she could not answer his question, the slate had been wiped clean and they could begin anew.

'Yes, maybe,' she said.

On the day George left, he kissed Marina and Daphne goodbye and promised to return home safe. 'Don't make promises you can't keep,' Marina was tempted to say, but she did not. They stood on the doorstep watching him leave, his khaki army clothes carrying with him a mark of respect: that he was useful, that he was fighting evil. An awkward air lingered between them, a reminder of how things always were, but his mind was at ease knowing that Marina knew he had a part in Evangelina's death, even if he did not confess all that he had done. He offered to spend his leave, if any should arise, at High Greenwood.

'We can decide what to do when the war is over,' he said.

'Yes,' she agreed.

*

Now that George was gone and Gerald was dead, Marina felt confident about the near future. His wife had taken over the publishing house and this sat well with Marina, and she continued with her books, the money from which was ample in keeping herself and Daphne. She had learned how to be self-sufficient in the interim of George's coming and going.

'What will happen to us now?' Daphne asked.

For once, Marina had no answer.

*

George was sitting at his desk at the Ministry of Information. He put down his pen and passed a note to his secretary, a pretty English woman who reminded him, in looks, of Marina when young. In spite of the war and his duty, he felt content and, for the first time in years, his mind was clear and he could make sense of everything. They were having an exchange, doing ordinary things. He was looking at the tiny twin frames, each containing a photograph of Daphne and Marina. The thought of Marina changing her mind, of her growing to love him, spurred him on. He was quite sure that, when he returned home, she would be waiting. The droning of aeroplanes came closer, shaking the building overhead, and then blackness engulfed him.

SOME TIME LATER

There was a bright sky, a flock of birds in migration. The lawn was damp beneath him, his body stretched out in the sweltering heat. High Greenwood glistened in the sun, its oriel windows shining like new pennies. The motor was parked out front, a rickety wreck but useful. A metaphor for poor old George, now that he was back from the war. It would soon be over, peacetime was upon them.

They were so far away, Marina and Daphne, across the lawn. Their lithe bodies, moving around the car, fetching and carrying.

'Darling,' Marina called out, shielding her eyes from the sun.

Her voice, the only noise, was punctuated by the squeaking of wheels. Daphne pushed a wheelchair, her hands pressed to its tall, wicker back. It mowed towards him, a menacing foe crushing blades of grass in its wake. They had gone into town for it, he should not grumble. He thought it too extravagant. After all, Doctor Glendinning had said his legs would work again.

They stopped, hovering before him, two mirages out of reach.

'Now what?' he asked.

It was a question with a thousand answers. He had done everything she said: the exercises at home, the physiotherapy at the hospital. His face had healed nicely and all he had been left with was a scar carved across his cheek. A similar marking to Daphne's, whose wound was the result of Hiraeth succumbing to an air raid. They were lucky to be alive.

Marina helped him to his feet. She passed the walking stick to Daphne. He staggered to the chair, his arms slung across her shoulders for support.

'Don't worry,' Marina said. 'I'll take care of you.'

Acknowledgements

Special thanks to my friends and family for their support and, more than anything, their inspiration.

About the Author

LYNDSY SPENCE is the author of *The Mitford Girls' Guide to Life*, *Mrs Guinness*: *The Rise and Fall of Diana Mitford*, *Margaret Lockwood*: *Queen of the Silver Screen*, and *The Mistress of Mayfair*: *Men, Money and the Marriage of Doris Delevingne*. She has written for *BBC News Magazine*, *Daily Express*, *The Lady*, *Silhouette*, *JACQUO*, *Social & Personal*, and *Vintage Life*. She co-wrote *The Flower Girl*, a short film directed by Emmy Award winner Nick Nanton. Her books have been mentioned in *The Independent*, *The Spectator*, *Daily Mail*, *The Times Diary*, *The Financial Times*, *Vanity Fair*, Italian *Elle*, and on *Classic FM*. This is her first fiction novel.

37178539R00146

Printed in Poland
by Amazon Fulfillment
Poland Sp. z o.o., Wrocław